Rachel's Guard

Book 2
The O-Line Series

Jillian Jacobs

Published by Green Moose Productions
Copyright 2015 by Jillian Jacobs

ISBN: 978-1-942313-07-6

DEDICATION

To: Bill V.

ACKNOWLEDGMENTS

To the sensational six! My beta-girls: Tia, Lisa, Cheri, Sherry, Mom, and Jennifer.

Also thanks to Linda Carroll-Bradd. Best editor ever.

Any mistakes are my own.

CHAPTER 1

Warren "Bronco" Murray squinted against the early morning glare as he headed across Oak Meadows Assisted Living and Memory Care's parking lot. Frowning at the flowering trees, he held back a sneeze and swallowed two allergy pills before tossing his empty Gatorade bottle into the trash. He reached the entrance, and Doris buzzed him into the secured building. He flicked her a quick wave, and for a moment, he considered asking her if they carried some miracle hangover medicine in this high-dollar facility.

Probably not.

Spending last night consuming copious amounts of alcohol, stuffing his face with pizza, and hollering his throat raw during the pro-football draft seemed ill-considered in the light of day. Especially since he had a flight to Bora Bora scheduled to leave in a few hours.

"Hey, Bronco." Nurse Tash scuttled her large frame over. "I finished that suspense book you recommended."

In a place that oozed sadness and carried that constant acrid tang, Bronco found his favorite caregiver's bright smile exuded the sweetness of maple syrup on a stack of pancakes. "I missed you last time. You must've been on night shift." He wrapped one arm around her and gave her a squeeze. "So, did you like the book?"

"Sure did. That ending, though." She stepped back and braced both hands on her ample hips. "What in the world was that?"

"Don't know, Tash." Shrugging, Bronco sank his hands into the pockets of his designer jeans. "Up for interpretation, I suppose."

Tash tapped his arm. "Let me see that bling again." She tugged his arm free of his pants and pawed at his championship ring. "My, my, my…look at that sparkle." His hand still in hers, she looked him up and down. "Where are you headed looking so fine?"

"It's off-season, so I'm vacationing on a tiny, tropical island with a beautiful woman." Bronco glanced at his phone and skimmed said woman, Heather's, text that suggested her concern over his unscheduled pit-stop. Their friendship started when they were children, and had developed into more as a matter of convenience rather than true love.

"A beach vacation? I sure could use a break after our God-awful Ohio winter." Tash bumped his hip and then started grooving in the hallway. "Don't you want to take this fine woman with you?"

"Sorry, Tash, I've already got someone…a friend. But next time"—he waved a finger between them—"you and me."

"I'll hold you to that, son." Tash met his gaze and then poked his chest. "Now, go do what you came here for. She's having a bad day, so you'll likely not stay long."

Bronco headed down the hall, his heart heavy over his grandmother's Alzheimer's. The disease had steadily debilitated the family's matriarch over the past few years, leaving a confused shell in the place of a woman who'd once ruled in the boardroom, her home, and her social sphere.

Still disturbed after watching the living nightmare his best friend Owen had suffered last fall, he needed this vacation more than ever. Needed an escape to sandy beaches and bright blue skies. Needed time to reflect on the future in order to decide what really mattered.

After massaging his pounding temples, Bronco raked his fingers through his blond hair. During this trip, he planned to steer his relationship with Heather back to just friends. Continuing the way they had been wasn't fair when he went rock solid every time he considered the fire-breathing pixie, Rachel Harris.

Lost in deliberations, he bumped into a laundry cart abandoned in the narrow hallway—narrow at least for his six-foot six and two hundred ninety-nine pound frame. A body custom built for the Manchester Marauders' offensive line.

After rolling the cart closer to the wall, he tapped on his grandmother's open door and then stilled just inside the doorway.

Gloria Astor sat perched on her bed, watching a group of chattering women on a morning television talk show. Her white-blonde hair was shades lighter than his own dirty blond, but her pale blue eyes, identical to his, widened as he entered.

"Thomas? Wh-what are you doing here?" She raised a shaky hand to her chest. "H-How?"

Saddened by her distress, Bronco remained in the doorway and lowered his voice to barely above a whisper. "Hello, little G, I'm going out of town...and I wanted to—"

"No." Shaking her head, she scurried into the corner of her bed, slammed her back against the wall, and drew up her knees. "You can't have me."

"It's okay, G." Bronco sidestepped into the room, hands raised, palms out. "I'm not going to hurt you." His stomach sank as he watched the debilitating illness overcome her reason.

Tears trickled down her cheeks, and she clutched her blanket against her chest. "I told you to leave my daughter alone, Thomas. I warned you."

What is she talking about?

"You're dead. Dead." Eyes now steely blue, she jabbed a bony finger in his direction.

"Who's dead?" He eased closer to the bed. "And who is Thomas?"

Lost to her muddled memories, she leaned forward and slapped him across the face. "I warned you not to cross me, but you and that stupid girl got pregnant, anyway. I had no choice. But we fixed it, he and I."

"Fixed what?" Head still throbbing from last night's festivities, he winced from the sting, and then mentally shifted through all he'd read on calming those in the throes of this disease.

Hands clenched in her short, white-blonde curls, she bellowed, "Get it out of her. Get it out!" Eyes wild, she sobbed and wrapped her arms around her thin frame, rocking back and forth. "No, no, no."

Chills shot down his spine at the obvious disdain in her voice. But, for whom? Thomas? Though Bronco's mouth was drier than a desert, he choked down the sorrow over seeing her in such a state, grasping for a change of subject. "Grandmother, did you see how nice the weather is today? Those yellow flowers you like are blooming. I know the winter was—"

"How dare you speak to me?" She shot to her knees, one arm still wrapped around her trembling body.

Here was the true Gloria Astor. Strong and confident. Sure of her world, and of her place in it.

"You are dead, Thomas. I made sure of it. I killed you." Her face paled and she visibly swallowed again and again before bending over the side of the bed and retching.

Ignoring the tears threatening to slip down his cheek, Bronco smoothed and patted her back, confusion streaming through his thoughts over her words. What did they mean? She seemed so sure he was this Thomas. Had she killed this man? How much was delusion? And how much reality?

Stop! Focus.

Her body lay sideways on the bed, her head resting on the

edge as she wailed incoherently, still murmuring about death and Thomas.

Holding his breath against the stench of her sickness, Bronco stumbled into the hall, grasping the door frame for support. Was his stomach churning from her odd confession, or from the smell?

"Tash! Tash!" Hollering for help, he stepped further down the hall, wishing he could take a moment to digest the meaning of his grandmother's words, because…hadn't he always felt different? In his family, he was a sturdy oak in a forest of thin aspens. Was this why? Had his grandmother killed his real father? Or was she simply lost to the decline of her disease?

William Murray, his extraordinary father, looked nothing like him having a thin frame and distinguished bearing, while Bronco resembled a lumberjack, ready to take down an entire forest. As long-held inconsistencies clouded his mind, he plastered a hand against the blue-painted brick wall, breathing deeply, trying to stem the rising panic in his mind and heart.

Tash's shoes appeared in his line of vision. "What's wrong, sweet thing?"

"I'm not sure." He met Tash's calming gaze. "Grandmother's unwell." Shaking his head, he focused on what he could control. *Head in the game, Bronc.* "Do you have a mop? She experienced an…upset, and became ill."

"Sure, Sugar, just give us a minute." Tash patted his arm. "Why don't you sit?"

"I can clean it up. It's my fault." Just how true were those words? Was his father's death his fault? Had his grandmother killed his real father because his mother was pregnant—with him?

He studied the building's walls, but all he saw were tumbling bricks. Words crashing over and over in his head. Maybe he'd read too many true-crime dramas lately, spent too many late nights watching Investigation Discovery, and now his overactive imagination allowed his grandmother's recollections to create drama where none existed.

"Warren...are you all right?"

Zoned out for a minute, he refocused on Tash. "I'm sorry. Where's the janitor's closet? I made the mess. I'll clean it up."

"No, you go on and sit. You look like you're ready to toss your cookies, too."

"I upset her." Turning, he leaned against the wall and rubbed his eyes, trying to block out the cries still coming from his grandmother's room.

"No, the disease upset her, son. Some days the disease takes over. You know that. Now, come on." Tash took his arm and led him down the hall. "Sit in the lounge, and Tash will do right by your grandma and come get you when we're through."

Bronco nodded. "Sure. Yeah, thanks." Though he placed one foot in front of the other, he couldn't fight how his mind stayed in that room. He halted in the hall, struggling with the urge to return and question his grandmother until she gave him answers. Was she crisscrossing daytime dramas with real life, or had she really killed someone? She'd said something about "him" helping. What man had she meant?

Though his face didn't hurt from her slap, he had to admit her words stung and now buzzed a thousand thoughts in his mind. If her ramblings carried any truth, what lies had he been fed in his twenty-seven years?

And most importantly, who was Thomas?

CHAPTER 2

Red pen flying over the final pages of her new mystery novel's first draft, Rachel Harris jumped when her phone buzzed in her Jeep's cup holder. Life as a best-selling author required grabbing any downtime in her investigative job to bang out a few grammar edits on her next book. Interruptions while in the zone were not welcome. Glancing at the screen, she rolled her eyes.

Warren Murray—aka Bronco, aka overbearing pain-in-the-ass.

She rubbed her itchy eyes and glared at the decorative trees spewing pollen through the air with their tiny white flowers. Still, these budding trees did provide a small amount of shade for her surveillance point in the strip mall's parking lot.

After a few neck stretches, she lifted the camera binoculars and snapped a few more pictures of the unfaithful wife. Her client's hunches were correct: his wife *was* having an affair—with two people. Seemed his dear spouse enjoyed *ménage à trois*. But hey, no judgments. The recent surge in BDSM and wild-sex play was good biz for private investigators. Not that people weren't already playing unfaithful games, but now 'vanillas' were going all 'rocky road'.

She set the binoculars on the seat beside her and flipped open Bronco's text.

Where are you?

Rachel huffed out a laugh. Even through a simple text, the

man acted like he had every right to know her precise whereabouts. She already had a boyfriend—or, boy-something. Cultivating relationships was not her usual M.O. And why the hell was she delving into love lives of the eternally damaged, anyway?

Him. All. His. Fault.

Last fall, the oversized O-liner had barreled into her life, manhandled her, and butted his nose into her investigation for his friend and teammate, Owen Killion. Although, that specific job for her company, Harris Investigations *had* led her tiny butt into fuck-tastic Manchester Marauders' seats beside Owen's woman, Ember—her new BFF. Observing their sickeningly sweet exchanges caused an alarming amount of eye rolling and mock gagging. *Who loved like that?* Apparently Owen and Ember. Was she jealous sometimes? Hell no. Honestly though, maybe a little. Still, sugary relationships weren't her thing.

Wrenching open her backpack, she blindly fumbled around until she found a single piece of bubble gum hiding at the bottom, unwrapped it, and then popped the pink goodness into her mouth. Snapping bubbles, she considered ignoring Bronco's officious text. But, why not have some fun in Mr. Murray's candy-coated world, where the little women obeyed, and the big men fought the battles?

She texted back: *I am where I always am.* Chuckling, she shifted in her Jeep's leather seat and awaited his reply to that ridiculously vague statement.

Seconds later, his reply popped on screen: *Meet me at Starbucks on 116th Street in an hour.*

Audacious much? Rachel refrained from typing what was really running through her head, which was: *Oh sure, I'll just forget all about my paycheck and drop everything to have coffee with you.* But, that would require more typing than her fingers could handle. She thumbed through her emoticons until she found her favorite yellow hand flipping the bird and hit Send.

"Take that, Murray." Biting her bottom lip, she sighed. What really pissed her off was she *did* have time. After this Lady Ménage photo shoot, she technically had enough to report back to the husband's lawyer. Why couldn't people just stay faithful? If you wanted to cheat, have the balls to exit first. This was why she rarely handled personal services cases, preferring to stay within the corporate world where lawyers typically served as a buffer between her and the client. Yet, these real-life dramas served as fuel for her suspense novels.

Her phone pinged with another text. *I'd appreciate a few moments of your time.*

Now he decided to be polite? In an odd mood, even for her, she messed with Bronco a bit more, typing a reply sure to irritate.

Bugger off.

She latched her seat belt and left the shopping mall, which sat directly across from the seedy hotel Lady Ménage frequented. Hearing her phone's text chime, she hesitated at the parking lot's exit to read the message.

I'm sacrificing a $15k vacation to Bora Bora for this, so be there.

Oh, well la-di-da. Didn't he realize some people made that in a year? *Rich bastard.* She wasn't his servant. Flicking on her turn signal, she punched on the radio and sang along to "Bent" by Matchbox Twenty.

Unfortunately, curiosity tick-tick-ticked against her brain. What could cause the man to forgo a tropical vacation? Crazed female with a baby-daddy story? Stolen identity? Stalker? Death threats? Okay, now her author-self had taken over.

"Oh, for shit's sake." Banging her hand against the steering wheel, she whipped the Jeep into a U-turn, ignored the blaring horns, and sped toward the coffee shop and the man who seemed destined to drive her crazy.

CHAPTER 3

As if being ordered around didn't infuriate her enough, spending ten minutes searching for a parking space pushed her need to maim a certain Marauder past the red zone.

Storming into the coffee shop, Rachel found her prey and jabbed a finger in his direction. "Huddle up, Murray. You better have a big cup of coffee and some chocolate situation pronto if you expect me to sit through whatever national emergency caused you to cancel your zillion dollar vacation."

After realigning a bag of coffee she'd accidently bumped on the display stand, she noted his vacant stare. Had he even heard her? Better have, after she'd planned that whole damn speech while circling the parking lot. Heaving a sigh, she stepped closer to the tiny round table and plopped into the chair beside him. Bronco jumped as if he really hadn't noted her presence.

"Rachel, I...thanks for coming. Can I get you anything?"

"Sure. Ember's been weaning me off coffee, with all her black teas and herbal-shmerbal brews, but based on that shell-shocked look in your eye, I think today requires a double vanilla latte."

Bronco nodded and headed for the counter, but he glanced back. "Anything else?"

At the question, she couldn't help the appreciative gaze that traveled up and down his husky, yet down-in-the-dirt honed body. "Uh…get me the big one." At that double entendre, she bit back a laugh. "I mean the venti or grandie, whatever the hell it's called, and a big chocolate cookie or muffin." She'd work off the calories later, not that anything ever stuck to her miniscule frame.

"Sure, sure." He simply nodded.

A slither of worry slid into her empty stomach. Something was seriously wrong. Curiosity now piqued, she studied Bronco as he stood in line. Gorgeous beast. Frame perfect for the physicality of his football team's offensive line, he exuded hardcore determination every time he hit the field. Blondish hair, with vibrant light-blue eyes like ice chips that floated along in the ocean. *Holy crackers!* What was this romantic nonsense? She shouldn't notice the curve of his ass in those jeans, the thickness of his arms, or his very large dress shoes. *What size are those things?* And what did that denote about other portions of his body? *Yum.*

Rachel quickly averted her gaze as he returned to the table and set down a ganache-topped brownie, her coffee, and his own steaming brew. She squirmed when her stomach growled.

"Have you eaten today?" Frowning, he settled back in his seat, and then glanced at his phone when it pinged.

"Yes, my mommy put out cereal and milk this morning."

Bronco grunted, and then scrubbed his hands over his face.

"So, what's the national emergency keeping you from your tropical vacation?"

He sighed and stretched his long legs out into the aisle. "These chairs are for tiny people."

"Suit me fine."

"Point made." He waved a hand in her direction.

"Oh, good one, I'm short. Wow. Never had anyone tease me about that." She bit into the brownie and moaned. "Oh my God, this is amazing. Orgasm by chocolate, the only way to die." A sparkle hit his ridiculously blue eyes.

After gazing at her mouth for a moment, Bronco shook his

head and licked his lips. "Not the only way to die. Especially if you're doing it right."

Pleased to see him emerging from his slump, she teased back, "Doing what right? Baking brownies?" She raised a brow while holding back a grin.

He laughed and rocked back in his chair, which lifted the spindly metal legs off the ground.

"Ooh, I get it. You meant sex. Like you're good at sex." She waved a hand at his crotch and rolled her eyes. "Kill me by orgasm. Too funny."

"Listen, little sass-mouth, I'd have no problem proving I'm much more decadent than that brownie. And honey, you'd beg for a double batch."

She sniffed and sipped a much-too-hot gulp of her coffee, telling herself the liquid's heat was the reason for the fire shooting through her blood.

Bronco simply smirked.

Taking another bite of her brownie, she groaned again, as if lost in the throes of bliss. *Two could play this flirtatious game.*

He narrowed his eyes and shifted in the chair.

"I never beg." Rachel shot him a cheeky wink, and then wiped her mouth with a napkin. "So, what do you need, OBC?"

"OBC?"

"Orgasm by chocolate."

"Cute." He cleared his throat and stared at his shoes before glancing at his cell phone, which kept pinging.

Rachel waved a hand at his phone. "Do you need to—"

"I've always known there was something different about me."

With this abrupt comment, her heart twisted a little. Though perfectly content to give him a hard time, she'd rather not sit and listen while he berated himself. "What do you mean? Different how?"

He raked his fingers through his short blond hair, the vibrant tattoo of a pirate ship flexing on his forearm. "I look different…you see, my parents are…I should probably start at the beginning."

Something was truly bothering him, and for some reason, that disturbed her more than it should. "The beginning's good." She rested her elbows on the table, and then tapped her coffee cup with a finger. "I've got caffeine and chocolate. I'm set for a while. Talk to me, Murray."

"Before I start, I think I want to hire you. You should be paid for this…investigation or whatever this turns out to be." Bronco thumped his cup on the table, as if with that motion what he declared became law.

On the verge of taking a sip, Rachel halted with the cup near her bottom lip. "I'm available. Tell me what you need."

# # #

What you need. As if Bronco knew that answer. After thinking about his grandmother's words for the past hour, he'd finally made a decision and reached out to the one person qualified to find answers—Rachel Harris.

Then, with his game plan laid out, he'd called Heather. Though his ear still rang from her anger, he'd sent her off to Bora Bora with one of her girlfriends in his place. He'd explained what happened and, like a coward, confessed his interest in another woman, something he should have done in person.

Heather had countered with, "You never promised me anything, anyway. No strings, remember?"

Comfort was never a reason to continue a relationship. Heat and passion, those strong pulses of the heart, mattered. And they erupted every time he glimpsed Rachel's brunette hair, brown eyes, and pixie nose. She brought him to life in a way he'd never felt before. "Thanks for coming today. I don't know what…"

Rachel waved him off. "As of five seconds ago, you're my client. I'm billing you, so go ahead and waste your time thanking me. Blather on about dragging me here until you get to the point. This girl"—she pointed a finger at her chest—"could use some new Jeep tires."

Using that sharp-witted mouth, she dug back into her brownie, her tongue coming out to swipe at a crumb. Oh…the things he'd like to do with that tongue. *Wait, stop. Focus!* "Right." Bronco cleared his throat and ignored another text alert. Heather's friend had seized control of her phone and continued to berate his entire existence via colorful text messages. He sighed heavily, knowing he deserved each admonishment.

Refocusing, he met Rachel's gaze. "This morning, I visited my grandmother. And, well…she said she killed someone." Taking a moment to digest the words actually leaving his mouth, he studied the everyday events occurring right outside the window. Cars whizzing up and down the road. People entering the coffee shop for an afternoon pick-me-up. The normalcy of everyone living his or her lives, working through each day, while Bronco's world teetered on the edge of something he hadn't yet grasped. After taking a deep breath, he continued. "I believe…though I'm hoping it's not true…I believe my grandmother may have killed my real father."

Rachel's brownie fell from her fingers and landed on her napkin. "Killed your real father? Give me a minute to process." Brow furrowed, she cocked her head and studied him for a moment before removing the lid and blowing a steady stream across the top of her coffee. After taking a large gulp, she stuck out her tongue. "Damn, that's hot. Water temp must be set at a hundred degrees past tongue-scald." This time, she took a mini-sip. "So, your grandmother…she actually said that…used those exact words?"

"No, not exactly, but…she's not well, so I don't even…" Bronco glanced around the crowded coffee shop. "I don't know why I picked this place. It's so busy in here." Cramped, unable to breathe, too many people were crowding his space. But what was *his* space? After years of standing on the offensive line, he had prepared for direct hits, but this one, he never saw coming. Yet, deep down, maybe he had.

"Bronco?" Rachel waved a hand in front of his face. "You still with me?"

"What?" He met her gaze. "Sorry."

"Let's start from the beginning." Rachel opened her backpack, pulling out a pen and ragged spiral notebook. "We'll work this out. Don't worry."

"Is that your signature private investigator move? Soothe the madman until he talks?"

"*Are* you a madman?" She leaned back and lifted a brow.

"Possibly."

"Spill, OBC."

With a slight smile, Bronco nodded and then relayed as much as he could remember about his grandmother's episode.

"So, she has Alzheimer's." Rachel drew boxes around her notes. "Has she said anything like this before?"

"No."

"Huh. And this is your maternal grandmother, correct?"

"Yes."

Quiet for a few moments, Rachel tapped her pen against her bottom lip, shifted in her chair, and then sighed deeply. "First off, you're assuming a lot without any real evidence. Your grandmother is ill, Warren. And, perhaps"—she patted his hand like a mother placating a child—"your mental state is oversensitive due to Owen's and Ember's troubles last fall." She sat back, stuffed her chocolate-stained napkins into her coffee cup, and then she met his gaze. "May I suggest…considering a frank discussion with your parents?"

"Right, that would go over well." Bronco tapped his empty cup on the tabletop, and then glanced at his phone when

Heather's text tone sounded again. Closing his eyes for a moment, he banged his knuckles against his forehead. Once. Twice. Then met Rachel's gaze. "What am I supposed to say? 'Hey, Mom while visiting Grandmother today, she told me she killed someone and mentioned some guy named Thomas. Oh, and by the way, is he my real dad?'"

"Who keeps texting you?" Tapping a finger on his phone's screen, Rachel tilted her head. "The most selfish ass—"

Jaw clenched, Bronco flipped over his phone. "I'm not worrying about the texts. Reading them during our meeting would be rude."

Rachel picked a stray crumb off the table and dropped it into her cup. "Hmm…let's see. You just canceled a vacation, right? A vacation with the blonde?" She arched a brow and crossed both arms over her chest. "She's pissed, and that's why you're not answering your texts."

Though sure his cheeks were bright red, he mirrored her stance and didn't utter a word.

Rolling her eyes, she ticked off options with her fingers. "Here are your choices, OBC. You either straight up ask your parents, or I dig. And when I dig, I find." She jabbed a finger in his direction. "You ready for that?"

"If I wasn't so different…I look nothing like either of my parents. The only similarity is my mother's blonde hair." He shook his head. "I don't know. I'd ask, but why would they tell me the truth now, and if…if my dad…" *No.* He refused to think his father could have helped his grandmother kill anyone. William Murray, CFO of National Trust Bank, may be a bear in the boardroom, but he wasn't a murderer.

Rachel dropped her notebook into her backpack, slid the pen behind her ear, and then squeezed his forearm. "Bronco, are you sure your love of suspense novels and crime shows hasn't ramped up your imagination?" She scooted her chair forward as a woman pushed by with her oversized twin stroller. After smiling at the gurgling babies, Rachel met his gaze again. "Another option is your grandmother saw something on TV and inserted the story into her own past. She has Alzheimer's. How reliable are her words?"

While all these considerations were true, Rachel hadn't seen his grandmother. Her very real fear—and hatred. Something had evoked those emotions…something very real. He scratched his chin. "She does watch a lot of TV, but still, I'd appreciate if you—"

Rachel gasped and sat up straighter, her gaze riveted on a man wrapped around a blonde ordering at the counter. Her knee bounced under the table, and she blew out a breath that sounded more like a growl.

Unclear on this sudden change in her demeanor, Bronco tapped her shoulder. "Is that Spencer West? The mixed martial arts fighter?"

As if he'd heard his name, West glanced over, fumbling and then dropping his coffee.

Rachel murmured something that sounded a lot like, "Cheater-head."

What is going on? "Rachel, do you know West?"

"Yeah, all too well." Whipping her backpack off the chair, she shoved away from the table, and walked up to the man.

Fascinated by the scene, Bronco held back a grin as Rachel jabbed a finger against West's chest. Seemed he wasn't the only one who brought forth her ire.

West waved a hand between him and the blonde, all while shaking his head.

Too late, buddy. You're busted.

Rachel didn't say a word, just shrugged, but then, in a move so quick Bronco hadn't seen it coming, she leg-swept the guy, dumping him on his ass before leaving the building.

Well, well. Perhaps he didn't have to travel to Bora Bora to find paradise. Based on that exchange, his little pixie was now

flying solo.
    But not for long.

CHAPTER 4

"She drove by the restaurant again." His associate dropped a yellow file on his desk.

The man folded his hands in his lap and glared. "I don't recall inviting you into my office."

"I do recall telling *you* she is trouble."

"Leave the file and get out." The man combed his fingers through his dark brown hair. "I don't suggest bringing up the subject again. I told you I'd handle her, and I will." He tapped a pen against his sturdy mahogany desk.

The fool remained standing before him.

"I'd like nothing more than to erase you from this earth, so go ahead and disrespect me by ignoring my request." The man rose to his feet. "I could kill you with seven objects in this room. My father trained me well."

With a slight glare, the associate nodded, turned on his heel, and left.

The man pulled his .45 out of the drawer and left the gun on top of his desk in case he was lucky enough to get interrupted again. He'd missed target practice yesterday, and a few men on his brigade needed attitude adjustments.

He smirked. Nothing like a bullet between the eyes to end a disobedient employee. The associate had gotten off easy. His father would have beaten the upstart bloody for entering his office without permission. Hell, he'd shot people for leaving a speck of dirt on his pristine carpet. All while making sure his "son" observed his display of ultimate power. And taking a life was proof of your dominion over another. He'd learned that lesson quite well.

Settling into his leather office chair, the man briefly closed his eyes, but could still see the figures embedded on the backs of his lids. All the dead. His legacy, now that he sat on the throne. A throne he hadn't asked for, but he accepted all the same.

Opening the file, he studied the brunette in the photo. Throughout his life, she'd haunted his dreams and evoked strange nightmares.

Even in daylight, visions of the past overshadowed his mind. In those moments, he remembered her grape jelly scent, her quick smile. Little things he shouldn't recall, but did. They plagued. Distracted.

As a young child, he'd asked his mother, "Where did the little girl go? Why did she never come to read him stories, anymore?"

His mother would rock him to sleep, their only time together without his father leering overhead. His mother's beautiful blue eyes would overflow with tears as she told him the story of how they'd become a family. Her holding him just as tight as he held her.

Five years ago, his mother had died. And he knew who'd pulled the trigger and why.

Three years ago, his father had died, forcing him to take the reins.

While standing over his mother's grave, he'd sworn a vow— a singular pledge while holding back a raw scream. Vengeance was the only emotion thriving within his dark, soulless heart.

But, until the day he destroyed the man responsible for taking away the only person he'd ever loved, he would follow his merciless plan—through blood, tears, and death.

And in the last five years, he'd come close. So very close. But the brunette in the photo could end everything. She was a wild card he'd deal with very soon, because all around, they watched for the slightest twitch. Any hesitation, and his false persona would crumble like loose rocks tumbling down a mountainside, unceasing and uncaring of who lay beneath. In his world, the dust never settled, just mingled in the air, choking, blocking his wish for one clear breath.

And so he watched and waited.

CHAPTER 5

After singing along with country songs about lying cheaters, Rachel settled into the puffy lounger next to Owen Killion's yet-to-be uncovered in-ground pool. She shook off the late-night chill—and heartbreak—with another big swig of her margarita.

"I think I'm more irritated with myself. I should have ended things with Spencer months ago." Rachel took care to enunciate each word, since she'd inhaled mixed drinks for the past two hours with Ember and Maude, Owen's sister. Owen and his crew were servicing her Jeep in his mega garage.

The empty, covered pool before her could serve as a metaphor for the state of her heart. "I couldn't give Spencer what he wanted. Emotions. Love. All those girly, frilly feelings." She shivered. "Blech."

Ember, fully covered except for her head sticking out from under her Marauders throw blanket, shrugged, which shook her red hair.

Maude sighed from her perch beside Ember. "Funny. Rachel, you don't want love, and you could have had it, and I want it and can't find it anywhere."

"Sex was good," Rachel admitted. "None of that earth-shattering fairytale hoopla you see in the movies, but we worked each other over pretty good, at times."

Ember hummed in consideration. "Don't knock earth-shattering."

"TMI." Maude covered her ears, fingers raking through her thick red-brown curls. "I do not need info on my brother's sexual activities." Snuggling back under the blanket, she tossed the chip bag onto the ground, and then wiggled her orange fingers. "Cheesy fingers."

Laughing, Ember straightened from her slump. "We need cheeseburgers. You're supposed to eat cheeseburgers with margaritas." From under her fabric cocoon, she freed a hand and took a small sip from her half-empty glass. "Like that song." She proceeded into an errant rendition of "Cheeseburger in Paradise", to which Maude joined in with equal abandon.

Oh, sweet jeez. They'd had one too many shots. Ignoring the duet, Rachel glanced at the potted purple and yellow flowers surrounding Owen's back patio. So domestic.

Her pad in downtown Manchester exhibited no homey attributes—or a mother's loving touch. Owen's mom, Nancy, lived here, along with his sister. Poor Owen, living with three females since Ember moved in. No wonder flowers surrounded him.

To Rachel, Owen's all-female crew represented a fantasy family unit. Something she hadn't had since she was eight. *Don't go there.* Losing a boyfriend was bad enough. To think about everything else she'd lost would push her over the edge, or in this case, into the pool. "What time is it, anyway?" Rachel twisted in her chair, trying to reach her phone resting on the concrete patio.

Unable to grasp her cell as it had worked its way under the chair somehow, Rachel stilled, her attention diverted when Owen slowly nudged open the patio door, his thick arms overloaded with beer bottles. Bronco trailed behind, holding two empty glasses and a bottle of Pappy Van Winkle.

"When did you get here? And how do you have a bottle of Pappy?" Rachel pointed at the bottle, toppling half her margarita onto her blanket. "Dang it." She shook off her hand and licked the liquid from her fingers. Pappy, a fine Kentucky bourbon, was something a person found at the end of the rainbow. Liquid gold. "I want a shot."

"And I want my pillow." Unwrapping from her blanket, Maude rose and then stopped next to Rachel's chair, leaned down, and wrapped her in a lung-busting hug. "You'll be fine. Don't let that cheater get you down."

"Thanks." Maude's protectiveness made Rachel smile, as her friend rarely had an unkind word for anyone. "I'm good. I just need a shot of Pappy, and I'll be set."

With a final squeeze, Maude let go, and then ruffled her brother's brown hair as she walked by. What a sweetheart. Out of anyone, Rachel believed Maude most deserving of true love.

"Geez, it's freaking chilly out here." Owen bent and kissed Ember's nose. "Is there enough room under those covers for me?"

"No." Shaking her head, Ember's smile turned sly. "Go get us some cheeseburgers."

"You must be feeling fine, Stems, 'cause you don't eat cheeseburgers." Owen scooted Maude's now-empty lounger across the pavement until the chair practically sat on top of Ember's.

She shrugged. "Tonight, I'm up for anything."

Owen's head snapped around at that comment.

Rachel waved her index finger back and forth. "Girl, do not say those kinds of things to a Marauder."

Owen, her friend's dude, was pretty sweet to look at, with his brown hair and brown eyes, though not as handsome as Bronco. She preferred blue-eyed blonds. *Oh, no.* Rachel shook her head and drew up her knees as her world suddenly went willy-wonkers.

"So, what do you mean by 'up for anything', Stems? And if you're hungry, I've got—"

"Oh, please, Mr. Innuendoes-are-us. Shut it!" Rachel rolled

her eyes. "You two make me ill with all your lovey-dovey shenanigans."

Bronco settled a lawn chair beside her and rudely propped his feet on the end of her lounger.

"I'm going to remember you said that, Rach." Ember laughed and linked her fingers with Owen's. "One day, you'll eat your words."

"Impossible to eat words." Rachel waved her off.

"I could make you eat words from one of your books."

"What books?" Bronco halted the pour of Pappy into his glass.

Oh shit! Her author identity was a trade secret. "My...ah...my collection of books at home, and stuff." Rachel attempted to kick Ember's chair but only succeeded in spilling her drink again. "Who made these frilly glasses for margaritas, anyway? They're not shaped pro...proportionally. They're like those Barbie dolls whose bodies couldn't exist in the real world."

"What the hell are you talking about?" Bronco shook his head and took a sip from his glass. "I think you've had enough, Ms. Slurs-a-lot."

"Oh, of course." She whipped a hand in the air. "Add men to the margarita mix, and the party's over."

# # #

After deciding that sitting on the patio during a chilly spring night in Northern Ohio wasn't the wisest move, the group ventured to a late-night burger joint's drive-thru and then crashed in Owen's basement man-cave. A few hours later, and after goodnights all around, Ember and Owen headed up to bed.

Bronco crumpled his burger wrapper and tossed the greasy mess into the wastebasket Owen kept alongside the chair. He glanced at Rachel. "What do you want to watch now?" He'd shed his shoes and sweatshirt, lounging in jeans and a faded Marauders T-shirt.

"Hmm…I don't care. Unless I'm watching Investigation Discovery, I'm not interested." Rachel glanced up from flipping through her phone, which, besides the TV, provided the only light in the cozy room they'd adjourned to after their cheeseburger run. She tossed her phone onto the coffee table and sighed. "Ember's going to regret eating that burger in the morning."

"She'll work it off."

Wrapped in a fluffy green and black Marauders blanket, Rachel laughed. "Yeah, based on the way she and Owen were canoodling on the loveseat, I'd say they're working off those artery-cloggers right now."

Bronco shrugged. "He loves her."

"Smothers her is more like it."

"He almost lost her. After all they went through, he's allowed to be a tad overprotective." He sniffed. If the woman he loved almost died after being tormented by a madman, he'd likely hire a bodyguard to stick around 24/7.

"Smothers."

Bronco grunted, and then grabbed a throw pillow. "No, *this* is smothering." He leapt out of the La-Z-Boy and straddled her, holding the pillow over her face.

Rachel kicked, though she was unable to cause any damage while wrapped in the blanket. "Get off me, you smother monster." She struggled to break free of her cover. "You're ten times worse than Owen." One hand now loose, she shoved against his chin. "Overbearing ass."

Laughing, he settled beside her on the couch. "So, did you love him?"

"What?" Rachel flipped the hair out of her eyes. "Love who?"

"Don't play dumb. You don't have a drink fest like you did tonight unless you're hurting. How long were you and Spencer together?"

Rachel sighed. "We trained in *jiu-jitsu* together. Then I don't know...things happened...we started dating and sort-of progressed from there. Stupid really, as we were great friends." She flicked a hand in the air. "Probably fucked that all up."

"I see." Good. Not heartbroken, just upset. "I understand that kind of relationship. Heather and I started as friends, too." He leaned in to tuck a stray hair behind Rachel's ear. "Sometimes, relationships become convenient, and you stay for the wrong reasons. Then someone else comes along, and you realize there could be more." After this morning, his world might be slightly tilted, but he believed this burn between them was like an unstoppable bullet that had already pierced his heart and left a bleeding, gaping hole only Rachel could stem. This strong, independent woman was an equal. An uncomfortable, challenging answer to the spark that had been missing with Heather.

"Do you believe in more, Harris?" As he spoke, he brushed his lips against hers. "Do you believe in someone who makes you crazy, makes your heart pound, and makes you ache to rock deep between their thighs?"

She shivered and bit her bottom lip.

Overcome with raw need, he kissed a trail along her cheek and nipped her earlobe. "I believe this moment was inevitable." He shifted and braced his body above hers, rocking his hips against her core. "In this moment, you'll understand what it means to be taken by a man who believes in giving you more." Having worked his way back to her mouth, he kissed her.

Rachel moaned and arched up against him, meeting him with equal vigor.

Their tongues dueled, and the spark that had always burned between them lit to full flame.

He held nothing back as his tongue stroked hers. Angling his head, he delved deeper, pushed harder, and showed her everything he'd promised with each brush of his lips.

"No." Rachel pulled away and braced a palm against his cheek. "We'd be making the same mistake. Friends into lovers." She trailed a finger across his wet lips. "Not a wise move, Murray."

He shook his head and kissed a path from her ear to her neck, then drew his tongue along the dent in her chin. "Not a mistake."

"I don't believe in more."

"I'll give it to you, anyway." Rising on his knees, Bronco unzipped his jeans, relieving the pressure.

"Is that what you'll do?" Rachel braced a hand against his thigh, and then trailed upward to massage his over-stimulated cock. "One night. Tomorrow, we'll just blame the alcohol and burger-coma for the whole thing. Or, maybe we should drink more Pappy until we pass out and forget this…moment ever happened."

Bronco worked a hand under her shirt, brushed aside her bra, and tugged her peaked nipple. "You won't forget."

"No? I'm pretty far gone." She squirmed beneath him.

He yanked off his shirt, then lifted her and did the same. He tossed both shirts on the floor before cupping her face. "You won't forget because you don't want to forget, and this won't be a one night thing."

"I'd be using you to get over another man."

He kissed her shoulder and then worked his way up to her ear. "Nice try, but a complete lie."

In response, she dragged her nails across his back. "You believe your grandmother is a murderer. You have no idea what's a lie and what isn't."

"Well then, let's see if I can figure it out." He nudged her back against the couch before kissing her again. Throw pillows tumbled to the floor as he tugged the blanket from around her lower body.

She arched against him and hummed low in her throat.

That sexy sound ignited his already rigid cock, and had him rocking against her as he worked deep in her mouth in a dance he'd soon take within her body.

Before he became too lost in each silky caress, he stood, grabbed a condom from his wallet, and then shoved down his jeans and boxer briefs all at once.

"Wh-what is that?" Eyes wide, Rachel shrank against the couch. "Cock-a-saurus Rex? Can you knock down buildings with that thing? Holy smokes." She gripped his cock in both her tiny hands. "I need to take a picture." She shot up and tried to grab her phone.

"Are you crazy?" Embarrassed, yet pleased, he swiped her phone and slid it back onto the table.

Single brow arched high, Rachel pointed at his cock. "That thing belongs in a museum."

"No." Bronco unzipped her pants and tugged them off. "This thing belongs in you." He brushed her hair out of her face. "Lay back, pixie."

"No. I want you in my mouth."

"Then take me."

With a small nod, she clasped his hips and got to work.

All thought and sense fled when she took him deep down her throat. Then he almost stopped breathing when he felt her tongue work the end of his cock, circling the slit with her tiny tongue and then nipping the head. After feeling her hard tug against his balls, he edged close to finishing before they'd even started. With a growl, Bronco cupped her cheek. "Enough."

The popping sound as she released his cock hardened him further. Settling her against the couch, Bronco placed both hands on her face and kissed her. This was intimacy: the hot meshing of tongues, the soft sighs, the slick gliding of lips.

Rachel stuttered out a whimper. "Too much. Just take me." Her eyes were hooded as she bit her lip and trailed her fingers down his sides.

"Not yet." He bent and took a pink nipple into his mouth, sucking and licking until she tugged hard against his hair. He paid the same homage to the other before kissing his way down her stomach. Burying a finger in her wet heat, he licked her sensitive center until she begged and softly cried his name before her entire body stiffened then quivered.

With a smirk, he rose above her and handed her the condom.

"I'd take an order of that, anytime," Rachel murmured.

"Would you?"

"Yes, you're pretty good at it."

"I'm better with this." He palmed his cock. "Slide on the condom."

She gripped him in her hand and tortured him for a bit before caressing his balls. "You're gonna fill me too full." Licking her plumped lips, she guided on the condom.

"That's the point." He shifted their positions, and then lifted her until her core hovered right above his aching cock. "Then you won't forget, and you'll crave what I can give you, again and again."

With a hand braced against his heaving chest, she guided him home and sank down.

"Take me, sweet pixie. Ride 'til you come again." Bracing his hands on her hips, he lifted her up and down until she took the reins.

Unencumbered. Body arched back, with her hair falling around her shoulders, she was more than the vision in his dreams. Her perfect breasts bounced as she impaled herself over and over.

Too much. Too fast.

Too close.

He'd given her the dominant position, because he wanted to make sure she took. But would she give, as well? Would she let this heat burn between them, and take more than just two bodies undulating, sweating, and finding comfort in the night?

"Open your eyes." He pinched her nipple then grasped the

back of her neck, bringing her close for a demanding kiss. Panting each breath, he fought to keep their mouths melded together. Then he lifted her chest to his lips, sucking and biting as he rocked up against her core, meeting her thrusts in perfect rhythm.

She rode each wave, wrapping both arms around his neck.

He'd break down her barriers. Mark her body with his sweat, with each dart of his tongue, with each plunge deep within her body. He bit down on her nipple and brushed two fingers against her clit.

She gasped and cursed. "I'm so close. Let me...let me..." She clutched her fingers in his hair.

"Who's beneath you?" He kept up the assault on her neck, her mouth, as he drove up into her body.

"I won't forget. I'm...so full." She arched back and moaned his name.

"That's right. Say my name." On the edge of orgasm, he gazed at the vision riding his cock. Body flushed with passion, she trapped her bottom lip between her teeth, eyes closed as she met him thrust for thrust.

"Do you believe I can give you more?"

"Yes...yes, I-I believe...I believe, I'm going to come." She rocked against him twice more and then dug her nails into his upper arms as her whole body shuddered. "Oh, fuck...yes."

The sight of her gasping and lost to pleasure had him holding her in place as she came.

He held back his own release as she pulsed against his cock. Then, unable to hold his fraying control, he bent his legs for leverage and continued rocking up and down.

Incoherent curses tore from her mouth as she held on for the ride.

His toes curled as he stiffened, and then pumped once, twice, before everything tightened then released in a flood of pleasure so intense he shouted her name loud enough to wake the neighbors. Again and again, his cock emptied into her heat, shielded only by the condom.

He heard her moan, then felt her clench around him again as she experienced another round of bliss. Coming down from the intense high, he slowly worked inside her until he softened.

She collapsed against his chest. Spent. Gone. Her entire body still shivering with pleasure.

He'd known making love to her would take him to a place he'd never been before. Not only was his cock happy, his heart was in full bloom. Content. As if he'd found the one place he could find, not only comfort, but also strength. An odd combination, but something a man like him needed. Craved. All that, found in this one moment with this tiny woman who had no idea she'd dented his heart.

After a few minutes...hours...who the hell knew, he heard Rachel humming the chorus to Journey's "Don't Stop Believing".

"Keep it up, Harris." Bronco pinched her ass. "Go to sleep, or I'll have you believing again and again."

But Rachel, being Rachel, kept pushing. "Just a small-town investigator, loving on a big green couch, she took the midnight mammoth goin' anywhere."

Shaking his head at her personalized rendition of such a classic song, he tickled her sides. "What kind of fucked-up lyrics are those? Midnight mammoth?"

She jabbed his chest and continued. "Just a cocky boy, born and raised in North Ohio—" Tears of laughter poured down Rachel's beard-scraped cheeks, and just like that he had to kiss her again, and then, once more, until he'd worked himself up enough to show her how to really believe. Again.

CHAPTER 6

After widening the screen image on his iPhone, Bronco submitted the order for the online paternity test. Finger-combing his hair, he tossed his cell phone onto the coffee table, covered with sports magazines. Two nights of back-to-back drinking, eating crappy food, little sleep, and waking up alone added to worries his father wasn't really his father left him feeling like he'd been steamrolled by the Bears defensive line.

Maybe he should have waited, and let Rachel handle the investigative details of paternity tests and who, if anyone, his grandmother had killed. Had he even hired her to investigate? They hadn't decided, had they? Yawning hard enough to crack his jaw, he sat up and rubbed his eyes.

Who knew what burrow that little fox had escaped to after the intimacies of last night? He'd give Rachel a few days before stepping back into the ring.

In the meantime, he needed to retrieve a hair sample from his father. The paternity test's turnaround time was three to five business days, according to the website. He sighed and punched the couch cushion. Three to five days to mentally prepare for his world to flip upside-down.

What have I done?

Rachel was likely right. He did read way too many suspense

novels, and this scenario with his grandmother was similar to a book he'd finished a few months ago. Perhaps he *was* reading into things, but…what if he wasn't?

Owen's text tone startled him out of his contemplations. Bronco flipped over his phone and read his buddy's text. *OK to come down?*

Bronco texted back. *All clear.*

Which pissed him off all over again. Rachel had sprung, disappeared into thin air like the sweet-assed pixie she was. How could she just leave after those heart-anchoring orgasms they'd shared? He'd give her time to get over Spencer West, but in the end, he figured they were a done deal. He'd known from the moment he met her last fall. She'd given him a hard time for borrowing a library book instead of buying it. A miniature-bulldog brunette standing tall against him, and damn if her attitude hadn't drummed just the right tune against his heart.

Enough of Rachel Harris, though. He had a mission this afternoon and needed to get to it. Bronco snapped on his boxer briefs and headed to the horseshoe-shaped bar in hunt of a ginger ale.

Owen thundered down the stairs and then hesitated on the bottom step, looking way too relaxed as he tossed his phone from hand to hand. "You alone?"

"Unfortunately, yes." Wrenching open the fridge, Bronco dug a cold soda out of the cardboard box.

"What happened last night?" Owen waggled his brows.

Bronco huffed out a laugh. "I sealed my fate. Wrote the words on a white piece of paper, folded that bitch, licked the envelope, and sealed it shut. I knew Rachel was trouble. *Is* trouble, but I'm in. All in."

"She's gonna fight it."

Bronco shrugged. "She'll lose."

"Are you…" Owen bumped his heel against the carpeted bottom step. "Nah, man, it's all good. I'm happy for you. Just…I don't know…you want to lift some weights or something?"

"Sweat out all that Pappy? Sure."

Instead of heading upstairs to his weight room, Owen hesitated, scratching his stubble-covered chin. "So…did you order the paternity test?"

"Yeah." Bronco popped open his drink and finished it in four deep chugs. He'd filled Owen in on the details while working on Rachel's Jeep last night.

"Let me know if you need anything."

Though his head pounded with each step, Bronco headed over and hooked his best pal in a one-armed hug. "I got you and the team, so I'm good. Right now…honestly, man…I just need to work out. Get the juices flowing, you know what I'm sayin'?"

"I'll get you some clothes." Owen spun and hit the first step.

Bronco grabbed his elbow. "Hey, O."

"Yeah?" Owen glanced over his shoulder.

Bronco released his pal before pacing back over to the bar. Stretching his arms over his head, he groaned out another loud yawn. "I don't know, Big O. Things are just jumbled in my head. You know how I hate that shit."

Owen nodded, picking up an empty fast food bag and tossing it in the trash.

After a moment of watching Owen maneuver around the room, picking up the remnants of their mini-party, Bronco sighed. "Remember back at Ohio State, my sophomore year? I had that tutor with the glasses and all that dark red hair."

"Absolutely. She was a redhead, after all." Owen smirked, bunched up the throw blanket, and tossed it by the stairs.

Stifling the slight awkwardness over why that blanket needed to be washed, Bronco continued. "I can't even remember that girl's name." He grabbed a bottle of aspirin off the marble counter, shook four into his hand, dug two Gatorades out of the fridge, and tossed one to Owen. "I should have liked *her*, chose *her*. Maybe if I'd dated her, I would have focused on my education, but I only cared about football." Searching the floor for his shirt, he avoided Owen's gaze. They both knew his IQ was barely over negative two. "I'm not good at anything else."

"Bronc', you're too hard on yourself. You're the most well-read guy I know. You don't see me studying anything but the Marauders play book, right?" Two empty beer bottles clinked between his fingers before he tossed them into the recycling bin. "You're letting this thing with your grandmother, an unverified story, by the way, mess you up." Owen bumped Bronco's shoulder with a fist. "Don't do regret."

Bronco grunted, plopped down on a barstool, and finished off his drink.

"So, you didn't excel in school." Owen leaned against the counter and shot his Gatorade cap at the trashcan. "Shit, I missed."

Bronco shot his cap. "Made it. Two points."

They bumped fists.

Owen shrugged. "You've worked hard at bettering yourself."

"Thanks, Big O." Though appreciative of Owen's pep talk, he still held doubts about his intelligence, due to poor grades throughout his formative years. Still, he had graduated with a degree in Sports Industry. Over the past few years, he'd developed an interest in forensic science, but just thinking about taking a chemistry class gave him cold chills. "Growing up, I breezed through everything. Lived on easy street. Cars, money, job, women…so why aren't I happy?" He crumpled the empty Gatorade bottle in his hand. "Why isn't all that enough?"

"Because happiness isn't about those things." Owen removed the plastic bottle from his grip. "We done with this girly talk? 'Cause I need to get some reps in." Smiling, he shot the crushed bottle into the recycling bin. "Nothing but net, baby."

CHAPTER 7

After a grueling sesh in Owen's gym, Bronco turned his Audi Q7 onto the familiar street, leading to his parents' home. Each perfectly landscaped, palatial house was lined with mature flowering trees. He stretched his neck back and forth before flicking on his turn signal and pulling into his parents' long driveway.

Not showering after his workout and wearing yesterday's clothes, he looked like the criminal he was about to become. Stomach churning, he considered the best way to slip into his father's bedroom to retrieve the hair sample without being seen.

"Idiot." Bronco shook his head. Before moving into his downtown apartment, he'd been a resident here his entire life. So why was his heart beating like he was about to commit some major felony?

His parents were aware of his visit. Nothing out of the ordinary. In a few hours, they'd have dinner together, all while the tiny hair sample would burn a hole in his pocket. What did the results matter anyway? He loved his father, respected him, and knew he could count on him no matter what. So why not just ask?

He huffed out a sigh. Because asking might hurt his father, and that was the last thing he wanted. Maybe his dad didn't know. Maybe Bronco was just adopted. Maybe he'd lost his damn mind.

Hell, this whole nightmare was likely just an ill woman's imaginings. But, somehow, he believed differently.

Downing the ginger ale he'd pilfered from Owen's, he prayed his stomach would settle as he entered his parents' home. He slid off his shoes in the mudroom before peeking into the kitchen, searching for Lada, the housekeeper.

Both his parents' vehicles were gone since they generally took off a half-day on Mondays to play golf at their club. Golf was one game he hadn't quite grasped; he tended to smack that little white ball way too hard.

Meandering through the kitchen, Bronco snagged an apple and whistled as he searched through the utility drawer for scotch tape. Circling the tape dispenser around his index finger, he strolled toward the stairs in the foyer. He skirted one of a matching set of over-priced tables, topped with crystal lamps and expensive vases—artfully chosen by some décor business his mother just *had* to use, based on all her club buddies' recommendations. His mother was nothing if not fully prepared to have the best of everything. Gloria Astor's daughter exuded high breeding and class at all times. Her home was no exception.

The familiar scent of cologne struck his nose as he eased open his father's bedroom door and peered at the cherrywood bedframe. A dark green bedspread and monstrous desk took up half the room, but both items still managed to fit, as the square footage of this single room was likely more than most apartments. Breathing deeply to calm his nerves, Bronco wiped away the narrow trail of sweat trickling down his brow.

With a shaky hand, he tugged a piece of tape from the dispenser, cursing when it folded on itself. "I hate when that happens. Stupid tape." Shoving the worthless tape piece into his pocket, he tried again, and then bumped aside the stack of decorative pillows to search his father's pillow for stray hairs.

His father still sported thick black hair sprinkled with gray, nothing like his own dirty blond.

A shout sounded downstairs.

Cursing his pounding heart and his startled schoolgirl shriek, Bronco quickly snagged a few stray hairs, hoping they still had the follicles attached, before straightening the stupid velvet pillows. Then he dashed into the bathroom and grabbed his father's toothbrush, bracing his hand against the sink when he almost tripped over the stupid throw rug.

How the hell Rachel snuck around for a living, he didn't know. Still, the fear of discovery was pretty exhilarating. Maybe, once he retired, he'd sign on as her partner.

Yeah, that'd go over well.

Discomfited by his devious dealings, he quietly stepped from his father's room and then leaned against the doorjamb, taking a few deep breaths to steady his racing heart. "Hey, Dad. I'll be down in a few. I just finished a work-out with Owen, so..."

His father appeared at the base of the stairs. "Hello, Son."

At those two words, Bronco almost lost the tight grip on his barely-hanging-on-by-his-fingertips control, overwhelmed by the desire to rush down the stairs like a child who'd scraped his knee and fall into his father's arms to beg for comfort.

Staring down at William Murray's handsome face, a man he'd always thought looked a tad like a full-haired Bruce Willis, he contemplated how this evening would go. Could he refrain from asking his parents, as Rachel had suggested? And was that wise, if his father had no notion of the truth?

Flashing a fake smile, Bronco tapped a fist against the banister and quickly shoved his evidence-filled hand behind his back. "I...uh...I'll be down in a few."

His father's brow furrowed. "Are you okay? You seem a little out of sorts." He put one foot on the bottom step.

Damn, his sly poker face hadn't worked against someone who'd raised him and knew all his moods. "I'm good. Everything's fine."

Overcompensate much? Real convincing, Murray.

"Gonna hit the showers." Bronco ignored his father's puzzled look, spun on his heel, and headed for his old room, which still held a small wardrobe. On his way, he passed his mother's room and caught a whiff of her fragrance—custom-made in a French perfumery. Only the best for Gina Astor-Murray.

For her, money had never been an issue.

Or for him. However, he had a sinking feeling that the seventy-five dollars he'd just spent ordering the online paternity test would carry the highest cost of any dollar he'd ever spent.

#

After stuffing his dirty clothes and the plastic baggie of evidence into an old high school gym bag, Bronco glanced around his room before heading down to dinner. His mother had yet to redecorate, so football posters still lined the walls. He kept all his high school and college memorabilia in a corner cabinet. A king-size bed filled most of the space. Being a bigger guy, he'd always needed more room. Lots of memories existed here—most good, a few bad. He slung the bag over his shoulder and stomped down the stairs. Rounding the corner, he located his father sitting at the kitchen counter, sipping iced tea.

His father winced and waved Bronco over. "Red-alert, Son. Your mother is very distraught."

Instantly on guard, though quite sure his mother didn't know what he thought he knew, Bronco shoved his hands in his pockets to hide his white-knuckled fists. "Why? What happened?"

"Aren't you supposed to be in Bora Bora?"

"Oh, shit."

His father mumbled something that sounded like, "That's an understatement."

His mother barreled into the room. "Well, well, William, look

41

who's come to visit."

Gina Astor-Murray was in a fine fury over something—likely his Heather abandonment.

"Do you know this man? Because I sure don't. No son of mine would leave a kind, decent young girl stranded at an airport." Her voice rose as she stormed closer and jabbed a finger against his chest. "No son of mine would, for weeks, get a certain girl's hopes set on a romantic holiday, only to break her innocent heart."

"Mother, Heather and I—"

"No. No!" She poked him in the arm this time. "How dare you do such a thing to Heather? Her mother is beside herself." Gina whipped her long blonde hair over her shoulder. "Do you have any idea how embarrassing this is? Why would you do such a thing? Heather's mother believed you planned to propose. We even checked the club's calendar for next spring."

"Our relationship wasn't like that." He gritted his teeth when his mother ignored him.

"Weddings take time to plan, you know." She flicked her hand in the air and paced in front of the marble-topped island. "I can just imagine the phone calls being made right at this moment, disparaging our family name."

Biting back a less-than-respectful comment due to the lies he believed his mother harbored and her incorrect assumptions of his relationship with Heather, he stilled at his father's side.

Gina Astor-Murray seemed fit for some daytime drama, wearing tan capris and a peach polo bearing National Trust's logo on the front breast pocket. She halted before him once more and punctuated her point by poking the top of the island, her manicured nail clicking the marble with each word. "You will fix this misunderstanding with Heather."

Jaw clenched, he took a moment to choose his response. "Mother, with all due respect, I'm not marrying Heather. I don't love her, and she does not love me, not in a forever kind of way."

"What does that matter?" His mother braced both hands on her hips. "You have a duty to this family."

"Gina, leave the boy be."

Just like always, his father became the voice of reason. The sturdy tree holding strong against the gale force winds of his mother's ridiculous concern over her place in Manchester society.

"This, from you?" His mother narrowed her eyes, primed to attack in her usual cutting manner. "Really? From someone who knows all about duty?"

His father straightened from the kitchen bar stool. "Careful," he replied in a calm, even tone.

"Why careful?" Already panicked about his life being a lie, Bronco glanced between his parents, wondering if this current that always flowed just beneath the surface had all along been the result of something more. One thing he refused to tolerate was people treating him like he was stupid. This talking in circles around him exacerbated his already foul mood.

His father cleared his throat, brushing at some coffee grounds on the counter. "I'm sure your mother refers to her duty as my wife." He met Bronco's gaze. "Son, you must be aware, we married for the connection our houses would offer. We've got on well and have grown to love one another. But if you want more, if you desire to choose your wife out of more than duty, then I say, have at it." William Murray, his father in every sense of the word, rounded the counter and placed a firm hand against Bronco's cheek. "You deserve happiness and love."

His mother huffed out a curse. "What he deserves is irrelevant. He will apologize to Heather, and do what is necessary to make amends."

"Mother, I *have* apologized...many times." Bronco dropped his gaze from his father's intense brown eyes. There wasn't much more sincerity he could take, not when a bag of betrayal sat waiting in the foyer. "Heather deserves love, as well." He rubbed a hand over his scruffy stubble. "I won't proceed with a false relationship, no matter my supposed duty."

"I don't know why I bother." His mother sniffed. "You've been ungrateful since the beginning."

"Gina, enough." His father's tone hardened.

"Dad, listen." Bronco clamped a hand on his father's shoulder. "She's right. I shouldn't have backed out on Heather. I'm sorry for any embarrassment I've caused."

"You should be. You have no idea what I'll suffer—"

"Gina. I said enough!" His father pounded a fist against the island.

Fruit practically tangoed out of the decorative bowl and a votive candle rattled around before tipping on its side.

"Those women you surround yourself with, whose opinions you hold so dear, have much darker indiscretions than anything our son has ever done. So remember that when you chastise him. I imagine you're quite capable of slaying any comments from your so-called 'friends' with your vicious tongue." He raised a brow. "I've no doubt our family's honor is safe in your capable hands."

As she left the kitchen, Gina shot her final volley over her shoulder. "I'm the only one who ever worries about such things."

"Yes, you are." His father sighed and rubbed the hand he'd punched against the marble. "The rest of us just live. Imagine that?"

For some reason Bronco couldn't explain, although he knew the truth was based in love and a lot of empathy for the man standing before him, he wrapped his dad in a bear hug. Fighting back tears, for all types of reasons, he held on tighter. "I'm sorry, Dad."

William patted his back and, though muffled, murmured, "There's no need, Son."

And that should have solved it, ended every worry Bronco had about the truth of his paternity. So, why couldn't he let go?

CHAPTER 8

Private investigator rule number one: Never sleep with a client.

Rubbing her eyes until she almost popped out a contact, Rachel sighed as she pulled into the downtown parking garage. The skies looked a little gray this spring morning in Manchester. If she went anywhere else today, she'd have to reconnect the hard top.

"Nothing to it now, Harris. You've done the deed." If anyone walked by, they'd likely think her crazy, sitting alone and talking to herself. Although, when writing, she typically acted out facial expressions and maneuvered her body in certain ways so she could properly describe the actions to the reader. She was weird. And an idiot for sleeping with a friend, and a friend of a friend. Her only excuse was temporary insanity and maybe shock from the extra-large cock that had sprung up right before her eyes. "I mean, who'd pass up that shit? Really? No one, that's who." She laughed and banged her head on the steering wheel. "Ahh! He's driving me crazy."

Still, insane or no, she'd chosen to bury within her memory banks what would henceforth be referred to as the "mammoth" event. Mammoth breakup. Mammoth margaritas. Mammoth man. Mammoth cock. Mammoth sex. Mammoth seemed the only word capable of encompassing all that...largesse hanging between Warren Murray's thighs.

As the past few days crept by, she'd held off Warren through text messages. Her schedule truly was busy, and just yesterday morning she and her lawyer uncle had discussed a new case.

Speaking of clients...she hopped out of her Jeep, tugged down her skirt, and then took the stairs to ground level. After dashing through the light mist, she opened the door to National Trust Bank.

She had a meeting with Joe Chogan, financial advisor and underling of Gina Astor-Murray. Why she'd made this appointment still made no sense to her usually rational mind. Following up on an elderly woman's secondhand ramblings would not be considered one of her wiser choices. Yet, Bronco had seemed so disturbed by his grandmother's words. Once she dug and found nothing, she'd wash her hands of the whole Murray family and move on with her life. Bronco was a good guy, after all, and deserved answers.

After speaking to a perky gal at one of the teller counters, Chogan shuffled over, greeted her, and then led her to his office. He was a handsome guy, but he tanned and obviously highlighted his hair. Too much grooming to ramp up her hot meter. Yet, for an older man with thick blond hair and blue eyes, he was decent enough.

Decent. One word she'd never attribute to herself, but certainly to Bronco. And what would she tell Ember? Her best bud had called twice this week. Rachel avoided both calls, which was totally rude, but when had she ever let anyone close? She only felt a kinship to Ember because they'd both suffered a severe trauma in their lives. Granted, Ember almost died, but still, a string of understanding flowed between them that no other person could grasp—how it felt to be helpless and alone. Not a nice connection, but a real one, all the same.

After being invited into a chair and offered coffee, Rachel

tuned in to Chogan's investment spiel. She wrapped her jacket tighter around her shoulders. Freakin' cold in this money dome. Perhaps they believed freezing money would keep it in place. Icy temps along with Oriental rugs and art-deco lights that emitted no glow, created a "don't touch" aura.

Internally sighing over Chogan's blather, she tried to keep her eyes from crossing. Daydreams of the Wild West, dusty roads, tumbleweeds, thick mustaches, and banks with steel bars in the windows filled her mind. In the Wild West, banks had none of this pretentious shit that made you feel like you were privileged to offer one dime from your pocket.

"This would be a good investment for your level of assets." Chogan pulled some papers off his office printer, tapped them on his desk, and then spun them for her to read.

Dying to tug down her pantyhose, Rachel cursed Bronco Murray and his overactive imagination for the thousandth time. This suit disguise tipped the scale of what she'd do for a friend. Next time she went to the shooting range she would pin these stupid hose to the target and shoot the shit out of 'em.

"Ms. Harris?"

"I'm sorry. Could you repeat that last bit?" Though she tried to avoid bank meetings by donating her book earnings to charity, she realized investing somewhere would be a smart step. Her uncle frequently encouraged, more like ordered, her to develop a financial portfolio. The majority of her funds were donated to the International Centre for Missing and Exploited Children. What little she had left supported her PI business and fun spy toys, like the lipstick stun gun and her video recording bag that was camouflaged to look like a purse.

Chogan suddenly stopped speaking.

Rachel followed the direction of his gaze. Now, this was who she'd come to see—Gina Astor-Murray.

When Rachel had called for an appointment with Gina, she'd been unable to maneuver around the snotty bank receptionist, so she'd settled on Chogan. Her hope was that once Chogan saw how much money she had to invest, she would move up the ladder and finalize her banking with Gina.

Bronco's mother had a corner office across the open room. A very attractive woman in a very slick suit, Mrs. Astor-Murray stepped beside her secretary's desk to greet and lead a finely dressed brute and known criminal into her office.

How very interesting. Why would Nestor Marat, a Russian mobster, bank at National Trust?

Suddenly, leaving her money in these crystalline halls didn't feel quite so safe. Nestor Marat had a gold star on her hit list. Men who trafficked children deserved to be taken down, and his predecessor, Victor Pavel, had left behind a hell of a legacy. In between cases and writing books, she'd devoted hours to discovering just what that legacy entailed, and which children were moved through that criminal system.

Capping her hatred for now, Rachel glanced at Chogan, who had a sudden blinking problem, and perhaps a whale stuck in his throat based on the way he kept clearing it. "She's quite beautiful."

Slightly jolting in his seat, Chogan blinked again before meeting her gaze. "I'm sorry. Where was I?" He shuffled papers across his desk. "Ah, yes, if you'll follow the line across—"

"That was Gina Astor-Murray, right?" Rachel studied Chogan's expression, curious about his startled reaction. Maybe, he, too, knew who and what Marat was. "I'm friends with her son, Warren."

"How wonderful." Chogan flashed a fake smile. "Mrs. Astor-Murray is Vice President of Wealth Management."

"I'd like to meet with her before I finalize my options."

Chogan sat back and tapped a finger on the edge of his desk. "Well, you see, she really—"

"That man. Do you know him?"

"No." Meeting her gaze, he swiped a hand over his mouth, and then scratched his nose. "Not at all. Why?"

Liar.

"That man is Nestor Marat. If I were you, I'd find a reason to knock on her door, and then nicely ask him to exit the building."

Chogan slightly narrowed his eyes before sniffing. "Mr. Marat has business with our bank."

Rachel rested her elbows on Chogan's desk, shuffled his business cards in their holder, and then went in for the kill. "Mr. Marat is a criminal. And if that man is associated with your bank, then I'll not do business here." She stood, ready to leave. The fact that monster was meeting with Bronco's mother set off major warning bells.

Chogan stood as well, tensing as his gaze caught something by the door.

Rachel glanced over her shoulder and then sighed.

Bronco.

She'd done everything to forget the rise and fall of that heavy body. That mammoth man offering sweet, sexual healing with way too many orgasms to count.

All done. All over. No more.

Still, images of his thick body beneath her, urging her to completion, squeezed past her mental do-not-enter signs. That night, Bronco had played her like a football, tossing her all over that couch, working his fingers deep into her skin, catching her when she fell way past the line. Was it any wonder his Marauders teammates were known in the media as the O-line? As in "O-yes" and "O-right there, please".

Irritated by her libido standing up and shouting, "I'm here. Take me, now", she realized she'd fallen and now stood at the bottom of a cliff. When in the hell had she jumped off? *Well, dig out the hiking boots, bitch, 'cause you ain't climbing that mountain again. Involve your heart and that's where you'll stay—the bottom.*

As if detecting her presence, Bronco stopped mid-stride, zeroed his gaze, and headed over.

Without a doubt, she knew that mammoth man had pushed her tiny ass over the edge. And, based on his unsmiling visage and determined stride, he meant to keep her there.

CHAPTER 9

Not.

How could one little word make such a difference? William Murray *is* your father. But throw in the results of the paternity test Bronco received in the mail then add that three-letter word to the sentence, and his whole world flipped.

Sick, starved, and so very tired, Bronco clutched the yellow folder closer to his chest. He'd arrived without an appointment to have lunch with his mother.

Now that he knew for a fact William Murray was not his biological father, he expected Gina Astor-Murray to provide answers. In his mind, this would be a business meeting—a simple transfer of information. He'd chosen a professional setting, because he wasn't ready to lose his shit in front of his father. Not until he knew the truth. And his mother owed him that.

On his way to his mother's office, he glanced over to wave at Joe, and as if one surprise wasn't enough, there stood Rachel Harris. Talk about professional meetings, Harris was the President and CEO of Avoiders-R-Us.

Patience frayed, he clenched his jaw and redirected his steps to Joe Chogan's office. Poor man had been a family friend ever since Bronco was a child, but unfortunately, he wasn't in the mood for social niceties. Although, he did tap a knuckle against Joe's open door.

"Nice to see you, Warren, but I'm with a client." He nodded at Rachel.

"I see that, Mr. Chogan." He shot his gaze to Rachel who had the audacity to glance at his dick and smile before meeting his gaze. *What the hell?* "I'm borrowing her for a minute. Excuse us." Giving Rachel no time to refute his claim, he tucked his hand under her elbow and yanked her out of Chogan's office.

"Murray." Her tone remained perfectly calm. "I suggest you let go of my arm."

"I suggest you shut up. I've dealt with your avoidance shit long enough, and now that we just happen to be together, we're talking." He tugged her into the employee lounge and slammed the door.

A bank employee stood by the counter, stirring cream into her coffee, but upon seeing his face, she quickly fled.

Bronco nudged Rachel against the counter and jabbed a finger against her chest. "What are you doing here? And why are you avoiding my calls?"

"First of all, back off." She crossed both arms over her chest. "Second, I'm doing my job."

"What job?"

"Your job." She rolled her eyes.

Her nonchalance pissed him off and turned him on at the same time. "Listen, I'm..." Bronco raked his fingers through his hair and stepped back. "I don't need you to investigate anymore. I have the paternity results. I'm moving forward as you initially suggested, and just asking my mother. I-I need the truth. That's why I'm here. I can't eat or sleep, and while some of that can be laid at your door, most has been the not knowing. But now I know."

"I'm sorry, Warren." Rachel ran a finger along his forearm's pirate ship tattoo, tracing the lines for a moment, and then she shook her head. "I don't believe I should stop the investigation. I think there might be something...I've got an itch."

"Is this itch something I should know about?" Bronco smirked.

She punched his stomach. "We already scratched *that* itch. Not likely to happen again."

"Yeah, it will." Though he wouldn't have thought it possible, he smiled and finally noticed what she was wearing. "Nice suit." He let his gaze skim down her body. "Nice legs." Wrapping a hand around the back of her neck, he drew her close and kissed her. Let loose all his inner turmoil against her mouth. Diving deep with his tongue, he lost himself to her inner heat, her tongue tangling with his. When he hiked her onto the counter, she gasped into his mouth, which fueled him to kiss her face and neck. This escape from reality was what he needed. To lose himself in the silky softness of her body. "Rachel, let me…" He moved a hand up her toned thigh.

She squirmed away, stopping his hand from reaching her apex. "No, I'm not doing this again." Scuttling under his arm, she jumped down and began pacing between the two tables set up in the break room.

Glancing over his shoulder, he watched her pace for a moment, and then banged his forehead against the cabinet, trying to catch his breath and mentally talk sense into his throbbing cock. He really needed to get her to a bed. And soon.

"Bronco, for reasons you don't need to know, this case became a whole lot more interesting today."

"If I'm paying you, I need to know."

"You're paying me to investigate your grandmother's claims. This is a separate aspect, yet might be related. If I feel this latest development is relevant to your case, I'll inform you. Otherwise, it's none of your business."

The secrets this girl kept. How much duplicity did she see every day? Though he'd believed his heart broken over his parents' deception, he felt the red organ pumping heavily for this woman. Sighing, he turned and met her gaze. "Fine. What have you learned about my case, Ms. Harris?"

"Nothing." She braced her hands along the back of a metal folding chair. "At this point, I need information. In order to learn if someone did kill your father, I need to discover who had means, opportunity, and motive. I'd like to interview some of your grandmothers' current and ex-associates. Dig a bit deeper into your mother's past." She started pacing again. "But, that might set off alarms so we'll have to go about this organically." She stopped and tapped a finger against her bottom lip. "Are you mentally ready for that deep of an investigation?"

"I don't know what I'm ready for, but I'm taking the hits, anyway. My father and I are not a match."

Rachel stepped closer and wrapped him in a hug. She tipped up her chin to meet his gaze. "Bronco, I—"

He pressed a thumb over her lips and then bent to kiss her.

"Warren, is everything all right?" Joe Chogan entered the lounge.

After placing a small kiss on Rachel's plumped lips, he kept her in his arms, absolutely sure he didn't want Chogan to see the effect Rachel had on his lower anatomy. Rachel had to be aware, since he held her so close. Hell, she could have sat on the damn thing. "Sorry to pull away Rachel, but she and I had business to discuss."

"Ms. Harris." Joe waved a hand in her direction. "I'd be happy to continue."

Bronco shook his head, and gave Rachel a squeeze, in case she thought to agree. "She can grab the info on her way out. I've invited her to lunch with Mother and me."

"Oh, I hadn't seen that on her calendar for today." A small line formed between Chogan's brows. "Well, of course, your mother won't mind. She's meeting with a client right now, but she should be done shortly."

"Thanks, Joe. We'll be out in a minute."

"Sure thing." Joe left, but he didn't shut the door.

With a glare, Rachel huffed out what sounded more like a growl than a sigh. "You know, Murray, it wouldn't hurt to ask sometimes, you overbearing ass." She stomped on his foot before heading into the hallway.

Following, he grasped her elbow and pressed her against the wall. "Listen, I'm sorry, but can't you give me a break for a little while?" He tucked a piece of shiny hair that had escaped from her clip back behind her ear.

"Damn it." She shook her head and broke into a wide smile. "Don't lay on the guilt. I actually think you're human, and I start to feel an odd sense of…hell, I don't even know what it is, so just stop it." Her arms were flailing all over and she looked everywhere but into his eyes. "Don't be nice…it's weird."

"Weird?" He bent closer, placed a hand on her hip, and whispered, "Or is my little pixie feeling compassion?"

Jaw clenched, Rachel rolled her eyes. "We doing lunch, or standing here discussing feelings?" She poked his belly. "Maybe you ought to check and make sure you're still packing the mammoth down there."

"Mammoth?" Furrowing his brow, he blinked. "Ah, I see." He was sure his grin spread way too wide across his face. He dug a hand into her hair and tilted back her head. "So, I made an impression."

"No." Rachel sniffed.

"Mammoth?"

She tried to turn away, but he kept her in place. "You know, you're a big guy."

"I'm glad you know that, too." He kissed the tip of her nose then worked his way across her cheek. "You couldn't have described what's between us any better. We are mammoth." He trailed his tongue along her jaw.

Rachel shivered and arched against his thigh.

"You're lucky we're in public, Harris, or I'd rock you against my leg until you came. Then I'd strip you down, pin you against this wall, and drive up into you until you didn't know where you end and I begin." Bronco bumped his hips against her once and then let her go.

Rachel glared. "Believe me, I know where this"—she waved a hand between them—"begins, and I sure the hell know when it ends."

Bronco just grunted. He wouldn't get anywhere arguing with her. He'd already pushed his luck. Lucky for her, he was a patient man. Still, he'd investigate why she was so reticent about relationships. "Rachel, how can you say we'll end? I'm about to introduce you to my mother." He chuckled at her gasp.

"From now on, you need to respect my personal space." She waved her arms in a circle around her body. "This is my inner sphere. Stay out of it." She huffed off toward his mother's office, straightening her thoroughly mussed hair.

Bronco followed, walking right past his mother's secretary.

"Warren, wait." Mrs. Morris shot out of her chair and rounded her desk, blocking their entrance with her frail body.

The woman had been with the bank for far too long, had even been his grandmother's secretary for a time near the end of Gloria's career, and she took her job just a tad too seriously.

"You can't go in. Your mother is with a client."

Bronco shrugged. "Family first, Mrs. Morris." He tapped the folder against his open palm. "You can blame me if she gets upset." He knocked before opening his mother's door, but after taking in the horrific scene, quickly stepped back, bumping into Rachel. Stomach churning, he blinked against the vision of his mother in a heated embrace with Nestor Marat.

"What the fuck?" Bronco stomped across the room, glaring at his mother while she adjusted her clothing. "Not only do I find out William Murray is not my real father, but now I find you here doing this…being unfaithful, with him of all people. What the hell is the matter with you?"

"Real smooth, Warren," Rachel muttered, standing just inside the door.

Bronco slapped the DNA file down on his mother's desk. "I want the truth. Not that you have any idea what that is anymore."

"Keep your voice down." Tugging on her jacket, his mother shot Rachel a glare before redirecting her gaze. "How dare you come into my office making demands?"

"Right, and he's not making demands?" Bronco pointed at Marat and sneered. "Or was he just leaving a deposit?"

"Warren." Marat clutched his shoulder. "Be careful how you speak to your mother."

At that touch, Bronco closed his eyes and took a deep breath before he destroyed the entire room and everyone in it. Clenching his fists, he opened his eyes and met Marat's gaze. "Get your hands off me before I knock them off."

"Son, I'd be careful whom you threaten."

"Son? Is that supposed to be some kind of fucking joke?" Bronco shoved Marat's shoulder. "'Cause if you, of all people, have the right to call me that, I'll end my shit right here."

Rachel stepped between them and clutched his hand. "Enough, Warren. Please, you're upset."

"I'm a hell of a lot more than upset."

Rachel rose up on her tiptoes and jabbed a finger against his chest. "Calm down."

Sliding on his jacket, Marat pointed at Rachel. "I know you."

"Oh, of that I have no doubt. Believe me, I know you, too." Rachel wrinkled her nose, her upper lip curling with disgust. "I think you should leave. Leave this office. Leave this country. We'd all be better off."

"Careful, little girl."

Bronco instantly saw red. Fucking around with his mother was one thing, but a whole other thing to threaten his woman. "What the hell is this? Don't speak to her—"

"Warren, enough!" his mother shouted

"Get out of here, Marat, and if I ever—"

"Bronco, please..." Rachel clutched his arm and tugged. She shook her head only once, and somehow that conveyed a very serious warning.

He glanced at Marat again. All he saw was an asshole in an expensive suit. A man who'd betray a friend. A man who'd been a welcome guest in his parents' home many times throughout the years. A guest who had definitely overstayed his welcome. "I won't keep what I've seen from my father. He deserves to know when there's a snake in his grass."

Marat huffed out a laugh. "Warren, if you believe your father—"

That word coming out of that bastard's mouth was the last straw. Bronco couldn't control the right hook that soared through the air and landed against Marat's jaw. "Do not speak of my father. Ever. Now get out."

"Oh my God." Rachel stood beside him, hands plastered against her cheeks. "What have you done?"

What did Rachel know about Marat that he didn't? Why did she seem almost afraid? As if Marat was someone to be feared.

His mother rushed over and knelt beside Marat. "Nestor, I'm so sorry."

Fury fired through Bronco at her apology. This whole sickening scene was a nightmare he'd never forget.

Marat rose, shifted his jaw back and forth and then nodded to his mother before leaving.

"How dare you!" Gina spun and slapped Bronco's face.

He let her hit her mark. He needed to feel something. Anything that would ground him in reality, even if that something was pain. "No, Mother. How dare you? With Marat? Really?"

"My life is my own."

"Right," Bronco scoffed, his tone overly derisive. "Let's talk about your life, Mother. Let's start by you telling me who my real father is?"

"Wh-what?" She stumbled back, eyes wide. After a moment,

they narrowed. "Get. Out."

Rachel pressed the yellow folder into his hand.

"Thanks." He handed the folder to his mother. "Explain this."

She glared but grabbed her reading glasses from the desk and opened the folder.

Her expression gave nothing away, which was either due to her plastic surgery, or her cold heart.

After a moment, she closed the folder and waved a hand at Rachel. "Who is this person?"

"Rachel Harris, meet Gina Astor-Murray, my mother."

"Ms. Harris, I'd like you to leave."

Bronco grumbled out a laugh and braced his back against the far wall of the office. "Is that what you'd like? Well, I'd like to not walk in and see my mother wrapped around another man. I'd like answers as to who my real father is. I'd like you to start telling me the truth." He rubbed his sweaty palms against his jeans. "Shall I continue?"

"Your father is your father." She flicked her hair over her shoulder. "DNA means nothing in this case."

"DNA means everything." He gasped. Hurt, scared, and confused, like a child abandoned by his mother. No, not abandoned, but somehow changed forever. No longer would he see her as his mother, but as a woman he'd never really known. A woman built by lies, and once he peeled back the layers, all he saw was a grotesque representation of something he had no idea how to define. "Why lie? Why not just tell me?"

"Are you hurting?"

"Yes."

"Then you have your answer."

"Actually, I have no answers, but I will. Who was my father?"

"This is not the proper place or time to discuss this matter, Warren." Gina rounded her desk and sank into her black office chair. "Come by the house tonight." She nodded at Rachel. "Ms. Harris, you may go."

"Grandmother mentioned a man named Thomas. Is Thomas my father?"

With a sharp gasp, she shot out of her chair, eyes wide. "Sh-she said what?"

"We had an interesting chat. What I want to know is how much of what she said was real? She said she killed Thomas."

His mother's face turned ghost-white. She opened and shut her mouth a few times before sinking back into her seat.

Though he wished otherwise, he worried about her. He softened his tone. "Did you know?"

His mother shook her head. "What is it I'm supposed to know, Warren? You want to know if your grandmother killed Thomas?" She stood, ripped the folder in two, and threw the pieces in his face. "Take your file and your disgusting accusations and leave my office."

"Who is Thomas?" Bronco grasped her arm, desperate for the truth. "Is he my father? Did you have him killed?"

Again, she slapped his face. This time she didn't hold back.

He gritted his teeth and accepted her punishment.

She shoved past him, grabbing her bag and phone as she headed for the door. Hand on the knob, she stopped and, though she didn't turn, she finally gave him an answer. "Yes, Thomas was your father. And you're just like him."

CHAPTER 10

After listening to Marat's multiple voice mails, the man finally returned the call. "I have one question, Nestor. Why were you at the bank today? I believe Father warned you about continuing a relationship with that woman." He shifted against the car's plush leather seats, keeping his tone even as his driver delivered him to his evening meeting.

"You wanted back into the bank, I got back in. Chogan knows his place. I was just visiting an old friend."

"You must think I'm a fool." The man studied his perfectly manicured nails. "I won't ask again. Stay away from Gina Astor-Murray."

"What about the girl? She's digging into something a little too close to home."

"I know exactly what she's investigating, and it touches on you, not me. Perhaps I'll let her discover what you've done. She's a smart one, after all, only a matter of time before she finds out." The man couldn't help the wave of pride that swelled at her accomplishments over the years, especially given her background.

"Accidents happen."

"Touch one hair on her head, and you'll end. Not quickly, but slowly." Clenching his jaw, the man ended the call and considered painful ways to quell Marat's insolence. Nestor believed he was the one destined to fill Victor Pavel's shoes. But Marat wasn't his son—not that *he* was, either, but he *had* been adopted, in a way.

So, Rachel was working her way through the cobwebs of the Astor family's past. He knew exactly what she'd find.

He also knew, more than most, that finding answers about one's past didn't change the present. Didn't, and wouldn't offer any solace. Answers rarely put all the broken pieces back together again.

He'd been watching Rachel a long time, and why not? He knew exactly who she was. He even respected her dogged determination to find him.

And if not for his intervention, Rachel's life would have ended long ago.

But, one thing he'd never do was murder his own sister.

CHAPTER 11

As Rachel led Bronco through the parking garage, she could feel the anger emanating off his body. If she turned, she had no doubt she'd see steam pouring out his ears. What a nightmare. In her job, she frequently delivered bad news, but she had never stuck around to witness the fall out. Damn, that scene was ugly. Though, throughout the whole incident, she was scared to death Bronco might trigger that psychopath Marat. Push too many buttons on that Russian menace and he'd kill Bronco just because he'd interrupted what looked like a pretty heated bang-session with Gina Astor-Murray.

Arriving at her Jeep, she leaned against the driver's side door. "Bronco, you want to get some lunch or something? We could talk...if you needed to. I mean...after all that, you could vent...or whatever."

No answer. She couldn't even tell if he was listening...or breathing. He carried the folder scraps in his hand, and stared out the horizontal opening of the garage. Pigeons cooed nearby, and cars swished along the streets. Brick buildings blocked the skyline, and a slight mugginess remained in the air after the earlier rain.

"Bronco?"

He turned, his cheek bright pink.

She lifted a hand to soothe him.

Grabbing her wrist, he brought it to his nose, closed his eyes, and inhaled. "I feel dirty, and I can't catch my breath." He met her gaze. "What am I supposed to do with all this...filth and...disgust?"

"Use it to make you stronger."

He nodded. "I can do that, but I need more." After wrapping her hand around his neck, he lifted her onto the Jeep's hood.

"Bronco, I'm so sorry." She caressed the side of his face. "She got you good a few times. But listen...about Marat, don't push him."

"Why? How do you know him?"

"I work in the underbelly of this city all the time."

His jaw clenched and he shook his head. "What does that mean? I'm sorry, but I'm not firing on all cylinders right now. Explain, please."

She bit her lip and considered the best way to describe Marat. "You know Batman right?"

"Yes," he answered with a small smile.

"Well, Marat's the Joker. Doesn't care about anything. Just loves chaos. And he keeps winning, over and over. No one is willing to stop him, because in doing so, a person would pay too high a price."

"What price?" Bronco ran his hands up her thighs before wrapping them around her waist.

"He'd destroy everything you love and a few people you forgot you ever even knew. He's lethal, and he hides behind a fortress of cash."

"The fortress is Superman, Rach."

"Bronco." Rachel breathed deeply, praying for patience. "Take Nestor Marat very seriously. Your mother is insane to think she could carry on an affair with him and not suffer serious repercussions." She tipped his chin with a finger, capturing his gaze, because making him grasp the seriousness of the situation was vital. "He isn't your family friend. He's likely using your parents' banking connections for some nefarious scheme. He knows nothing else."

"I'll talk to my father."

"Don't." She grabbed a handful of Bronco's shirt. "Don't talk to anyone. Forget the whole thing. Please." The thought of what Marat would do to Bronco if he messed with the man's business affairs churned her stomach. "I'm worried enough about what he'll do to you for punching him. He doesn't forgive, or forget."

"How do you know all this?"

"I've been looking into the Russian mafia for a long time."

"Why?"

"They traffic kids...among other things."

"I don't know that I can let all this slide, though. You know? I love my dad, and when I see him next, I won't be able to hold all this in." He rubbed two fingers against his breastbone. "All these secrets are too much." He shook his head and studied the pavement for a moment. Then, in a voice barely above a whisper he spoke. "May I have one moment? Can I just hold you?" When he looked up, everything he was feeling was right there in his clear blue eyes. "I need to feel something real. I need you. Please."

Rachel held open her arms and released an "oompf" when he tightened his arms around her. *Great.* In opening her arms she'd done a hell of a lot more than just console him. Her heart creaked open, as well. A narrow opening, but more exposure than she had experienced in a long time, and it ached, or maybe winced a little, like being in a dark room for too long and then getting hit with a ray of light. And Bronco was certainly a bright beacon.

He sighed and tugged her hair free of its clip before burying his face in her neck and breathing deeply again.

She squirmed, more than ready to spread her legs farther and welcome him deep inside. Perhaps, in a small way, she could give him a momentary respite from the pain.

Funny how such a big man could draw comfort from someone like her. Someone who had nothing to give. She knew this. Understood why she avoided relationships. Hadn't her uncle paid enough therapists to tell her so? Until this moment, she'd done everything wrong, so this time, with this man who was so deeply hurt, just once, she'd do something right. As tears fell down her cheeks, she swore she wasn't crying, swore this big man couldn't really evoke deeper emotions.

Clutching the hair on the back of his head, she tugged, and then, after meeting his gaze, she kissed him, holding back nothing. Offered comfort in a way she understood.

And he took.

Diving deep, oblivious to the world around them, their kiss turned hot, wet, and overly primal. Each worry temporarily assuaged with a tangle of tongues.

He ran his hands through her hair and pressed harder, drove deeper. Taking them exactly where she wanted to be led. Out of control and fuck the consequences.

Bronco spread her thighs, ripped away her hose and shoes, and tore her panties. Breathing heavily, he halted and met her gaze. "If I'm going to stop, I need to hear it now."

"Take what you need."

He whipped out his wallet, pulled out a condom, and then stopped again. "Wait, we're in the middle of a parking garage."

"I don't care." Rachel grabbed the back of his neck and kissed him while scooting her lower body closer to the edge of the Jeep's hood. Though she was a little higher, she knew he'd hold her steady. "I want this, and you need it." She bit his chin. "Hurry."

After dropping his zipper and rolling on the condom, he wrapped her legs around his waist and lowered her onto his cock.

"Mmm...speaking of Superman. You've got a cock of steel, Murray."

"Do I?" He nudged deeper, rocking into her body slowly,

but with a steady beat. "It's all for you, baby."

Then, no words were necessary. Just gasps and cries. His lips against her neck, her lips. Her body pressed against her Jeep.

A frantic pace built pleasure as he plunged into her body over and over. Fast. Heavy. Deep. A single line of sweat dripped down the side of his face as he pistoned his hips, bringing them both closer to the edge.

With that thick cock, he brushed the perfect spot deep within her core, until she tightened and then released with her orgasm, incoherently murmuring his name against his neck and biting down hard on his shoulder.

A moment later, he shouted his own pleasure, and with a slow, sure glide, he kept her body thrumming until she slumped in his arms from an overabundance of bliss.

His breath tickled her ear as he nuzzled her neck. "So fucking hot."

At the same time, voices echoed through the lot.

Rachel erupted with nervous laughter and clutched him tighter.

"Stop." Bronco quickly slid from her core, and then dropped her to her feet. "I can't believe we just had parking lot sex." He slapped at her hands when she tried to help him zip up. Meeting her gaze, he shook his head and laughed, too.

"That was crazy hot. Damn, woman, the things you do to me." Twining his fingers in her hair, he bent and kissed her. A soft kiss. An appreciative kiss that carried on and on. "This is why you're good for me." He trailed a finger down her cheek as his words whispered against her wet lips. "You know what I need. Every time. You're here, and you know." Again, he drew her close.

No longer amused, but stunned by the emotional connection she felt, Rachel shivered. Aftershocks surely, because his touch and his words were too sweet, like an overload of sugar that seemed foreign on her tongue. She preferred the salty side of life.

She eased away, breathing steadily and evenly. "Listen, based on what just happened, I think we need to move."

"Move?" Bronco pulled back and met her gaze. "We could go to my place."

"No. Get out of the post-orgasm haze, Murray." Rachel slapped his arm. "I have a feeling your mother is on her way to visit your grandmother."

"My grandmother?"

Sighing, Rachel bent and picked up her shoes. "Are you feeling better?"

"Yes." He quirked a smile.

"Good, then let's go."

"All right." Without any argument, he rounded the Jeep's front to the passenger side. *Huh?* Seemed sex was the answer to men's compliance. *As if women didn't know that the world over.*

She hopped into her Jeep and headed out of the lot. "I know you're a little scrambled, but I need you to think."

"Not scrambled, sleepy." He settled against the headrest and closed his eyes.

"Stay awake." She shook his shoulder. "We had our leisure time, now we need to work."

He simply hummed.

"I have no idea what that meant, but anyway, think. I need you to find answers to these questions. What was your mother's life like when you were born? Who were the major players? Friends? Family? Coworkers? What about your grandmother's life? Your father's? What do you know about their lives from before you were born?"

"My mother was—"

"No, I want you to really think about this. I'll get you my notebook when we stop."

"Where are we going?" Bronco rumbled.

"To your grandmother's facility."

He released a single grunt that could have meant anything.

"You really haven't been sleeping, have you?"

"No." Bronco scrubbed a hand over his face. "And now I'll have nightmares of my mom with Marat." His whole body shuddered. "Vile." Then he stilled and paled a little. "Rachel…you don't think…that my mother…she won't hurt my grandmother, right?"

Since he looked like he was about to become violently ill, Rachel took his hand and squeezed. "Big man, you need to chill with that overactive imagination. Reading all those mysteries has warped your brain."

"I'll tell you who is warped, R.W. Hardcastle. Her books are full of this kind of stuff."

Rachel held back her grin and changed the subject slightly. "Are you still getting your books at the library?"

After a loud yawn, he yanked on the seat belt. "What is it with you and libraries?"

"I'm sure the author would rather you buy the book."

He rolled his eyes. "I did 'buy the book,' Little Miss Author Police."

"Good."

"What do you care? Besides, I'm sure Hardcastle makes enough."

"Excuse me?" Rachel scoffed. "This, coming from a man who bumps into people for a living?"

"I do more than bump into people," he mumbled, and then flashed a wicked grin. "You like it when I bump into you."

While true, this whole situation had spiraled so far out of her control, she was in super freakville with no exit in sight. She attempted to regain a modicum of control. "Just consider our furious little interludes more of an animalistic purging of our very basic needs."

"You can call it purging if you want. I think I'll call it fu—"

She punched his arm. "Zip it."

"Fucking."

"No! No, no, no." She shook her head. "Let's focus please."

When he chuckled, he almost experienced his first flying lesson, because it took everything in her not to slam on the brakes, both literally and figuratively. "What's the name of the other patient in your grandmother's room?"

"She's alone. Why does that matter?" Fun over, Bronco was back to resting his eyes.

"The name of her neighbors then?" Rachel pulled into the Oak Meadows lot. "I need a way in."

"Why?"

"To eavesdrop."

"Oh." With one eye open, he nodded. "But my mom will recognize you."

Rachel shot him a glance and raised her brow. "Do I have to remind you what I do for a living?"

"No, I know what you're capable of." More alert now, he let his gaze skim down her body.

"Are ya' through leering? 'Cause I need to get inside, perv boy."

"Boy?"

Rachel took a deep breath. "Bronco, the names, please."

He rattled off a few names. Rachel tried not to be overly impressed that he knew so much about the facility and the people inside, because that would make him even more of a stupid-ass superhero in her eyes and she needed no reminding. Especially when her lower body was still marching a parade celebrating his wonder-boy super-cock. "Got it." She opened her door. "Stay here."

Bronco grabbed her elbow. "Rachel."

Impatient to move, she snapped, "What?"

"Thank you."

"Yep. No problem. It's good." She nodded and all but leapt from the Jeep.

During the entire trek up the sidewalk, she mentally spouted various curses that had everything to do with how sweet the damn man was, and how she wanted to shove all that sugar straight up his ass, because she didn't know what to do with it all. Her heart wasn't some chocolate-coated cherry.

"I'm a fucking prune, bitches." She laughed, almost hysteric with the syrupy-sap circling her mind. Luckily, no one heard her talking to herself. Maybe she needed to stay in this facility until her mind switched back to normal. Besides, she was ninety-nine percent sure they had plenty of prunes.

CHAPTER 12

"What is that woman laughing about?" Bronco watched Rachel throw back her head and laugh as she made her way up the sidewalk. "I think we're both losing our minds." Had to be, because he'd just had the hottest sex of his life in the middle of a downtown parking garage. After losing sleep these past few nights, he could barely keep his eyes open, because that sexual session took the burn right out of him.

He jolted when his phone rang and glanced at the screen. "What's up, Jason?"

"Bronco, what the hell, man? Why aren't you here?" By here, Jason Stafford, his Marauder teammate and friend meant, Bora Bora. A couple of his offensive-line teammates had rented bungalows next to his. He could really use a tropical escape right about now.

"A family emergency came up." He pinched the bridge of his nose. Emergency didn't even begin to describe his predicament.

"Heather said you had some trouble with your grandmother, or something."

"Listen, just take care of her while she's there, will you? And by that, I don't mean you can sleep with her."

Jason chuckled. "So, where you at?"

"Well, I'm not in Bora Bora."

"I'm aware. Beaches here are clean, and the water's crystal clear. Thought you needed this trip?"

"I did." There was silence for a moment until Bronco heard a door creak shut.

"Listen, Owen filled me in on the situation with your father. You okay?"

"No. I'm not, but when you get back, you'll help me pound it out, right?"

"Too true, Bro."

"Thanks for calling, Jason."

"That's what we do when we're on the line."

"Yeah, when we're on the line."

"Later."

Bronco hung up. At least that hadn't changed. He had his teammates—his brothers. No matter what he went through they stood at his side. From what he knew of Jason's background, he really had no room to whine about anything.

Still, he took a moment to feel saddened, betrayed, and disturbed by what had just occurred in his mother's office. He had no illusions his parents had the perfect marriage, but was there ever any love between them? Or had deep secrets bound them together? Had his mother and father conspired to have his real father murdered? What would he and Rachel find down his family's rabbit hole? And, once beneath the surface, how much different would his world be?

Again, his iPhone chimed and he about hit the roof. He rubbed his chest where his heart beat like he'd run a marathon.

A text from Rachel. *I'm in.*

He hopped out of the Jeep and leaned against the side. His clothes were sticky after the sex and the humidity in the air. Small puddles remained from the morning rain. His stomach grumbled, and he realized he hadn't eaten since lunch the previous day.

Another text came across from Rachel. *Gina is here.*

The bubbles appeared as she wrote her next message.

Mom asking your grandma what she said.

Bronco rolled his eyes. As if his mother would get any sort of reliable information from an Alzheimer's patient. This whole thing was so unbelievable. He almost regretted starting this investigation at all.

But, the curtains were drawn back now, like that 'Clockwork Orange' film where eyes were pried open and the person made to watch violence and death for hours on end. Surely, this was a horror film, and he wanted a refund.

In his family play, he knew all the characters except Thomas Northman. He'd received his real father's name with the DNA results and was fascinated this unknown man could pull his workaholic mother from the office to come here and ask questions. Didn't that mean something? Surely, his mother's actions meant she had nothing to do with Thomas's murder, or else why would she be here?

Speaking of answers, Rachel hadn't texted for way too long.

He typed out: *What's going on?*

Better get in here.

"Great." Shoving his phone in his pocket, he lumbered up the sidewalk, buzzed into the building, and then headed to his grandmother's room. Screeching and what sounded like metal furniture being thrown erupted as he turned into the hallway.

Tash and another nurse hauled his mother from his grandmother's room.

He'd never seen her act so undignified. Based on the dire threats spilling forth, which promised retribution if his grandmother really had killed Thomas, perhaps his mother had cared. *Interesting.* At one time, Thomas Northman might actually have cracked his mother's stoic demeanor.

Rachel popped out of the room beside his grandmother's and skittered his way.

For a single moment, he zoned out and just concentrated on

her. Her silky brown hair, the way she smoothly moved, her fit body, and those deep brown eyes.

"Are you going to do something about this?" Rachel jerked her head in his mother's direction.

He shoved his hands in his pockets and rocked back on his heels. "Probably."

His mother started cursing Tash. Words like lawyers, battery, and assault spewing from her mouth. When he heard her threaten to have Tash fired, he intervened. "That's enough." He shifted between her and Tash before clutching his mother's upper arms. "You need to calm down before you upset the other patients."

"Wh-what are you doing here?" His mother's face was wet with tears, and she had a red scratch along the side of her neck.

"I could ask the same of you." He kept his voice barely above a whisper. "What did you expect from Grandmother? A confession?"

"Bronco, get her out of here." Tash's chest heaved, her gaze stern. "Go on now."

His mother leaned into his side, and together they walked down the hall. He stopped next to Rachel. She didn't say a word, so he tugged her along, too. Outside, Bronco walked over to a bench beneath an oak tree and plopped down his mother.

She sat quietly for a moment, smoothing her hair back from her face and wiping tears from her cheeks. "I want to know what she said, Warren." She pointed at the building. "Word for word. Right now."

He shook his head, unsure where to begin.

"Let me." Rachel rested a hand on his arm then turned to his mother. "Mrs. Murray, why don't you tell us what you hoped to achieve here?"

"Young lady, this is a family matter."

"Mother, don't—"

She waved him off. "This is no business of hers." She sniffed. "Do you have a tissue?"

"No." Rachel folded both arms across her chest. "Warren hired me to investigate Thomas' murder, and that's what I'll do. No matter how uncomfortable my questions make you."

This was certainly rock meets hard place. Bronco felt almost removed from the situation, which was good, because he had no idea what to do now. Any woman who stood tall against his imperious mother was certainly worth her salt. He shifted at the inappropriately solid hard-on pushing against his jeans. He glanced at the Jeep and sighed. No parking lot sex this time. Not only that, he owed Tash an explanation and an apology. "Mom, let me take you home. We'll brew that tea you like and talk this through."

"No, I have to get back to the bank. I've had enough interruptions in my day."

Bronco refrained from mentioning Marat hadn't seemed like much of an interruption.

His mother stood and smoothed her skirt down her thighs. "I'd like to know what your grandmother said about Thomas."

"You're not in a good mental state right now."

"I haven't been in a good mental state for years, Warren. Now, talk."

"What could possibly be wrong with your life?" Rachel interrupted. "You have a cushy job, great husband, criminal lover, successful kid." She ticked off each point with her fingers. "You're healthy, beautiful…what else do you need, lady?"

Eyes narrowed, Gina Astor-Murray lifted her chin. "You know nothing about my life, little girl."

"Seems all peaches and cream to me," Rachel scoffed. "Maybe you just like creating your own blend of madness."

"I don't have to answer to you." Gina shifted her gaze to Bronco. "Now, about Thomas. What did your grandmother say? What did she do?"

Overwhelmed by the day's events, Bronco pinched the bridge of his nose. "I was hoping you'd tell me."

"And why should I know anything?"
Bronco shook his head. "I have no idea."

CHAPTER 13

After leaving Bronco with his mother so they could discuss family matters in private, Rachel headed to Nestor Marat's best-known haunt. Switching off the Murray family drama, along with all the lingering feelings from her parking lot tryst with Bronco, was a welcome respite. Time to switch mental gears and get some work done on a case that had started when she was eight years old.

Marat's Bentley was parked in the lot for Khlebosolny, a restaurant known for its ties to the Russian mafia. The title meant hospitality and while this place might be known for offering bread and salt to their guests, the salt was likely more for preserving the corpses.

Among many other things—like human trafficking, gun smuggling, and cyber-crime—Marat's men were heavily involved in the heroin business, which originated in Afghanistan. Years ago, one of the Russian mafia brigades had branched off to America, but the group was still rumored to be overseen by a 12-person council back in the homeland.

Just thinking of Warren's high-class mother in a place like this boiled her blood. The woman was playing with fire. And if Gina Astor-Murray pissed off Marat, she might find she'd put her own son in danger.

Rumors floated around that Marat had bumped off his predecessor, Victor Pavel. Unfortunate, as Rachel would have loved the honor.

Her investigations into trafficked children had led her to Pavel, who she believed held the key to her missing brother. Now that Pavel was dead, she had no idea who'd open the lock, but she wouldn't give up until she knew the truth. Couldn't give up. After all, her brother's disappearance at age three had been her fault. They'd been at the park, and she'd run to the public restroom after asking a friend to watch him for a moment, but when she returned, she couldn't find him. Erik was nowhere. Gone. And she'd never forgiven herself...and neither had her parents, regardless of the fact that Rachel had only been eight-years old.

Answers to all her burning questions were within that building, in someone's memory, or maybe the depths of some intricate file system. The business conducted inside that restaurant should spoil every meal ever served. Evil cloyed to each bite. How many people became violently ill after eating in a place founded on death?

The money they made was obscene—the power even more so. If people knew how far their tentacles stretched, they'd shrink in fear.

Marat's interest in a woman married to the CFO of one of the country's premier banking institutions hadn't surprised her in the least. Not much could shock her, but fear of the men in that building's actions definitely sent a jolt or two down her spine.

If she had to disrupt Bronco's mother's affair to keep him safe, she would. Losing him when he was...important...maybe even more than a friend, seemed inconceivable now. She'd already lost one person she loved. Damned if that big beast got hurt on her watch, too. Not now, not ever.

After parking in a busy grocery store lot down the street from the restaurant, she settled against her seat. Her iPhone jingled with Ember's ring tone, "Girl on Fire" by Alicia Keys. Her friend epitomized that song, due to more than her red hair. Ember had earned her title after walking through flames her whole life. Then, last fall, everything hit a fever pitch, and she had almost died. Ember was more than her friend. She was one of the strongest women Rachel had ever known. One day she hoped to be as strong. She hit the green button on her phone. "Hey, girl."

"Want to meet for lunch?" Ember's cheery voice came over the line.

"I slept with Bronco."

"So, is that a yes or no for lunch?"

Rachel laughed. "This is why I love you. Nothing throws you."

"When you've lived on the edge your whole life, you learn to roll with things rather than tumble into oblivion."

"Oblivion." Rachel sighed and tapped a finger against the steering wheel. "If only."

"So, you slept with Bronco. Shall we discuss this over lunch?"

"No."

"Then why bring it up?"

"I've had enough psychoanalysis, Miss Brooks. Don't need it from you."

"I've had plenty myself."

Rachel didn't respond. Ember definitely won that round.

"Warren's a good guy, Rach."

"Yeah." She traced the Jeep logo on her steering wheel, forcing away the memory of those same fingers caressing Bronco's skin. "Yeah, so let's do lunch."

"Where?"

For a minute, Rachel considered asking Ember to meet her at Khlebosolny, but then remembered she liked her friend and would hate to see her poisoned by evil. Not only that, Marat had seen her earlier at the bank and would get suspicious. Plus, their security monitors had likely tagged her Jeep. Right now, her face was probably zipping through some kind of facial recognition software. These secretive bastards likely monitored and detected vehicles doing multiple drive-bys. They had to. Though she'd love a tour of all their high-tech surveillance equipment, she did value her life.

"Rachel?"

"Right…sorry…Let's do that healthy food stinkhole you're always raving about."

"Isn't that a lovely picture to paint before we eat?"

"You're the one always going on and on about healthy-smealthy foods and going green."

Ember chuckled. "Well, aren't we full of snark today? You okay?"

"No." One major disadvantage to friendships—friends always knew when something was up. "I'm a disaster. You know this."

Ember hummed on the other end of the line. "Is it Bronco?"

"Hell no." Rachel held the phone away from her ear and stuck out her tongue at the screen.

Ember laughed. "Hell yes."

"Whatever. Just meet me at the twig and berry place."

"The hell it isn't about Bronco, if you've got twigs and berries on your mind."

"You are a dirty-minded freak, which is why I love you. I'll meet you in thirty." With a chuckle, Rachel flipped off her phone, glared one last time at the Russian restaurant, and then headed to dine with her friend, intending to discuss something quite a bit more substantial than a twig.

CHAPTER 14

Spending the last few days with Owen at the Marauders Training Center made Bronco feel marginally better. Especially after picking up Rachel and taking her to his parents' to interview Lada, their housekeeper.

On this crisp spring morning, things were definitely good. Almost as good as Rachel in her skinny jeans and form-fitting purple T-shirt. "We're here." He nudged her knee.

"Thanks. I may need a nap after the long haul up your parents' driveway."

As he rounded the hood of his SUV, he chuckled over the truth of that statement. Opening her door, he smiled at her scowl. Seemed his pixie wasn't a morning person.

"Good morning, Ms. Harris." He kissed her cheek and wrapped his arms around her waist. After considering the current status of their relationship, he'd decided to use moments like these to gently woo her. Might as well let her figure out they were meant to be on her own time. She still needed convincing. Him, not so much.

"We're in a much better mood today, aren't we?"

"I've had a few days to decompress." He shrugged as he led her through the garage and into the kitchen. He hoped Lada would be here, since Rachel had requested he not alert her to today's visit. Knowing they were there for an interview might frighten Lada, and Rachel believed her questions were better answered without giving the housekeeper time to bend any recollections into a more positive light.

"So, how did the chat go with your mom?" Rachel hopped onto a bar stool.

"We've agreed to disagree." Bronco opened the fridge. "Drink?"

"Soda or water, whatever." She flicked her fingers in the air. "Disagree how?"

"I told her what I'd learned. The next morning she called and asked that I stop investigating. I told her I couldn't. She then expressed her displeasure with a few choice words, to which I didn't respond, since I've been disrespectful enough lately."

Rachel rocked side-to-side on her chair, as if listening to some beat only she could hear. "She called me this morning."

"What?" Bronco wobbled then dropped a ginger ale. "Damn it. What did she say?"

"Nothing I haven't heard before." She shrugged. "I'm a private investigator. I piss people off. Death threats. The usual."

"Death threats?"

"Well." She bit her bottom lip. "Okay, maybe the occasional death threat."

He wished he had a punching bag to destroy. The severe headache he thought he'd finally kicked to the curb threatened to make a comeback, especially when he considered his mother's influence in this town. "Rachel, my mother does know a lot of people."

"Pffttt." She slashed her hand through the air between them. "I'll be fine."

After tapping the can's top, Bronco opened his ginger and took a long sip then handed Rachel a water bottle. At this point in their relationship, he wouldn't push. His intention wasn't to change her, just to keep an eye on her. "My mother and

I…we…we've never been close, but still…" He sat beside her and ran a finger along the rim of the soda can. "Our relationship has changed. I don't know if I'll ever forgive her for what she's done, or the things she's said." He raked his fingers through his hair. "And my father…that's a whole other issue, because we *are* close, and I don't know how much he knows."

"That's nice."

Bronco raised a brow. "What's nice?"

"That you and your dad are close."

"What about you?"

"Me?"

"Yeah. I don't think I've ever asked about your family. Kind of rude, actually. I'm sorry." Here he was trying to win her over, and he hadn't even taken the time to find out about her family. *Real smooth, Murray.*

"Sorry is correct. We're a sorry family, indeed."

"How's that?"

"We're investigating your family, Bronco, not mine." She opened her water bottle, took a sip, and then stood. "We doing this interview or what? 'Cause I have other jobs today."

"So the Harris family saga is off limits?"

She clucked her tongue. "Yep."

"Then how about some breakfast? I don't think Lada gets here until around 10:30."

"As long as you're doing the cooking."

"Oh, I'm cooking, all right." Grinning, he ruffled her hair. "How about a mammoth omelet, Harris? Ever had one of those?"

She slapped his arm but laughed. "You're so not funny."

# # #

"How long have you lived in the U.S.?" Sitting at the kitchen table, Rachel studied the Murrays' housekeeper.

A tall, thin older woman who still had thick waves of dark brown hair, Lada had aged well, likely in her mid-fifties. If Bronco's mother had hired this woman from Pavel's crew years ago, then the odds were high she'd been brought over for prostitution.

"We come from Russia to work." Lada fiddled with a button on her plain blue button-down shirt. "Mr. Pavel got me job here many years ago."

Bronco placed a cup of peppermint tea before each woman.

They nodded their thanks.

He remained standing, leaning against the kitchen's bay window.

Rachel inhaled the soothing scent. "How old were you when you came to America?"

"Thirteen." Lada glanced at Bronco. "I work another...job until I become too old. Now I do clean work." She twisted her fingers together over and over on the tabletop. "Miss, please. I do not wish to speak of Mr. and Mrs. Murray. I just clean house. I need job."

"It's all right, Lada," Bronco interjected. "We need your help with one more thing. Does Nestor Marat visit Mother here? If so, how long has this been happening?"

Lada's lips drew into a straight line, and she leaned back in her chair. "Mr. Murray, I mustn't say."

Rachel patted her hand. "I understand why Marat scares you, ma'am, but I'm very worried about Warren's mother...and Warren. You and I both know how dangerous Marat can be."

"Yes." Lada nodded. "A few years ago, he came frequently. No more." Her cheeks turned bright red and her hands shook. "Though, lately...your mother, she...I-I notice she have more pretty things." She cleared her throat. "To wash. More things for under her clothes, you understand?"

Bronco grimaced. "I understand."

The visual of Bronco's mother in fancy lingerie was not

anything Rachel wanted imprinted in her brain.

"May I go home now?" Lada stood from her chair. "I come back tomorrow to finish."

Poor woman was scared half to death.

"Sure, Lada. Thank you." Bronco clutched her hand. "Please don't worry, neither Rachel nor I will tell anyone what was said here."

She nodded and headed for the foyer, but stopped and glanced over her shoulder. "Your father is good man. Deserve better than your mother." Eyes wide, she covered her mouth with her hand. "I'm sorry, I shouldn't have said."

"No, I appreciate your honesty." Bronco ambled closer and gave her a one-armed hug. "Anytime you need anything, let me know, and I'll try to help."

"Thank you, Warren. You good boy."

With a raised brow, Bronco returned and sat beside Rachel. "That went okay." He took a sip of her tea. "Huh, not bad."

"Who else on your list of contacts can we question?" She pulled her notebook from her backpack, making notes about Lada's comments. She never took notes during an interview, because she'd learned if she wrote while questioning, then the interviewee tended to get distracted and focus on what she was writing.

"Another person you might want to speak to is Eva Stone. Perhaps she knows more. She lived with us as my nanny, and then later as my tutor."

"You had a tutor?"

"Yes." He fiddled with the vase of tulips on the table and sneezed. "Man, my allergies are driving me crazy."

Rachel frowned at the blatant change of subject. "So, what about your tutor?"

Bronco sighed before standing and opening a cabinet with various medicine bottles. "School wasn't easy for me." He popped a couple allergy pills into his hand and grabbed a glass from another cabinet. "I had to pass my classes if I wanted to play ball, hence the need for a tutor. Although, Eva was really just someone who read me stories as a child, took me to museums, things like that..." After filling the glass with water, he dumped the pills into his mouth.

Rachel tried not to notice his throat working as he swallowed, or his strong jaw. She had no idea why she wanted to lick his throat, jaw, and everywhere in between. The man was a walking popsicle. "I bet you were a cute baby."

Bronco smirked. "I'm cute now." Rinsing out his glass, he left it next to the sink. "Know who else is cute?" He flicked a finger against the tip of her nose. "You." Pulling her from her chair, he drew her into the sunroom off the kitchen.

Floral cushions topped sturdy wicker furniture. Potted plants lined the corners, a small bar sat off to one corner, and two ceiling fans stirred the air.

"What are you doing?" Rachel shook loose from his grip. "Listen, Warren. The first two times, they were sort-of you comforting me, me comforting you, but this...this is different. We're friends, we have mutual friends, and I'm working for you." She shook her head, because the rest of her body was saying *yes*. "I don't know how we got off track."

Bronco kept walking until he backed her into a couch. "I figure what we got here is like a football game. I'm offense and you're defense." He tucked a stray hair over her ear. "I keep pushing forward, and you keep pushing back. Right now, we're in the second quarter of the game."

"Bronco, this isn't a game." She shoved away and stared out the long windows at the Murray's immaculate landscaping. "I don't want to hurt you, or give you ideas of what this can be between us, because it isn't wise. Nor would it ever work."

"As I said, offense"—he pointed to himself—"defense" he pointed to her and bent to whisper in her ear, "I've been playing this game a lot longer than you. I know every strategy, and I will win, make no mistake about that."

Rachel threw her hands in the air. "I'm not a prize or a trophy, Bronco. Not only that, you'll try to dominate my life. I've no doubt you'll come up with all these restrictions you think I need to live by, and I won't." Infuriated by his expectations, she paced by the window. "I'm not some complacent chick."

She had to make him understand, because he was right. He would win in the end, but he deserved better. She'd push him away because she was scared to let someone in, because, throughout her whole life, the people who were supposed to give a shit had left. She'd abandoned her brother, and her punishment was abandonment by everyone else.

With this man, her thick skin and cocky demeanor disappeared, and some silly girl who wanted to have candle-lit dinners and long mornings lolling in bed appeared. That wasn't her. Couldn't be, she didn't do intimacy. But this big jerk wouldn't let go. He *would* play out the whole game, but she knew she'd falter. And what then?

He'd leave.

But what if he didn't?

What if he could be the one person in her life who loved her enough to stay? Perhaps, for just a while, she could be something to him. Maybe he needed someone to see him through this mess. A friends-with-benefits endeavor.

"All right, Bronco, listen. This is how this thing"—she waved a hand between them—"will work. I understand this is a tough time for you, and as your friend, I'll be here."

"Rachel, I don't want just friendship." Shaking his head, he sank onto the floral cushions and scrubbed a hand over his chin.

"Well, I don't want to lose you as my friend, so how about we play by my rules for a while?" There was no denying she wanted him, but this relationship needed to be put on the same level as all her others—use sparingly. In his sweats and T-shirt, he looked ridiculous perched on the edge of the floral couch cushions.

Bronco rubbed his hands up and down his thighs before meeting her gaze. "All right. Come show me these rules." He held out his hand.

She scoffed. "Capitulation, Murray? I don't buy it for a minute."

"You've always been a smart woman."

As she walked over to stand before him, she suppressed an inner voice that declared she was the one capitulating—accepting the inevitable, for the moment. She locked her hand around the back of his neck, climbed onto his lap, and then whispered against his lips, "I won't deny I want this, but only this. Don't expect more." She rested her forehead against his. "I won't lose you as my friend."

He drew her closer, running his hands up and down her back. "My life has always been so perfect, Rachel. I don't know how to live like this. I'm...it's like I'm on a roller coaster, only on this one, I'm getting hit by bricks, and they just keep coming." He sighed and combed his fingers through her hair. "I just want it to stop."

And this was why he'd break her heart. Soft words whispered only to her. Opening his cares, his worries, in a deep, husky murmur against her ear. Then expecting her to soothe him, to offer solace. Her life had been anything but perfect, and she had every sympathy for a person whose life was normal one day and completely flipped the next.

Because she understood what he needed, she lifted her shirt over her head. Then did the same for him.

"Rachel, if you don't want this..." He held her at arm's length.

She leaned forward and kissed him. "You think you're on the offensive, Murray. I'm not so sure I agree." She wrapped her arms around his huge shoulders, and then brought her lips to his. This time, she would be the aggressor.

With her own game plan in mind, she kissed her way down his chest before sinking to her knees before him and tugging down his sweats. His mammoth cock was on full display, rising erect against his stomach and beading with pre-cum at the tip.

She worked him up and down with both hands, keeping her grip tight before swallowing him as far as she could go.

He arched against her, gripping her hair in his hand.

Minutes passed, hours, she had no idea as she serviced him, teasing, licking, using every skill she possessed to drive him mad, and by the grunts and deep groans coming from his throat, her efforts were appreciated.

"You'd let me do this anywhere, wouldn't you?" Rachel nipped the edge of his turgid cock. "I'd put you on display in the middle of a club, and everyone would watch, jealous that I was the one holding all of you. Wishing they were the ones taking you deep down their throats." She rose up on her knees and took him deep in her mouth, bearing down hard with suction. After releasing him with a pop, she said, "They'd watch you come down my throat, begging for a small taste, and I'd give it to them." She licked her lips, met his gaze, and then gasped.

The heavy-lidded heat burning from his eyes didn't scorch, but the look froze her in place. He pushed against her chest. "You wouldn't give them anything, because I wouldn't be finished with you." He shoved aside the coffee table, scattering candles and magazines. "I'd show everyone you were mine. And make sure you understood the same."

Rachel's heart beat heavy, with lust and with a small dose of fear. She'd roused the beast, and now she would pay.

Now on his knees before her, he unsnapped her bra before lifting her breast to his mouth, laving and biting at her nipple.

She tore at his hair, yanking and tugging, trying to draw him up to her mouth. Trying, and failing to take control once more.

Finally, after she'd completely lost her mind and was so ready she'd surely come the minute he touched her, he kissed her. Hard, demanding, as lost to lust as she.

She bit his lip. "Is this all part of the show? Because I don't need the preliminaries. I just want you to fuck me."

Bronco kissed her neck and bit her shoulder. "No, that's not what you want." He lowered her onto the Oriental rug and tugged down her pants. "What you want is slow and steady. What you crave is everything only I can give you." He worked two fingers over her slick folds.

She jerked and came so hard, yet felt so empty. Once she could breathe again, she growled, "What I need is for you to get that mammoth cock inside me."

But the man refused to take orders, just kissed her again, over and over until she swore she'd orgasm from that alone. His magic fingers worked over her body, touching just enough to drive her crazy, but not enough to offer release.

Sweaty, pissed, more turned-on than ever, she drove her tongue deep, tasting every nuance of him. A tinge of peppermint remained in his mouth, and she craved every drop.

Digging the nails of one hand into his shoulder, she set his length at her core with the other. "Take me."

For a moment, he sat back. "I'm clean. Get tested all the time through the team's doctor."

"Me, too. I mean, I'm clean, too." She wiggled. "And I'm on the pill. Now, shut up and slide in that cock, Murray."

He smiled, wrapped her thighs around him, and slammed into her waiting heat.

She closed her eyes and reveled in the onslaught, absorbed each slap of skin, heavy breath, and heated murmur from Bronco's body.

Using that mammoth cock, he hit just the right spot over and over.

Shivering with bliss, she came, biting her hand to stop the screams.

He gave her no quarter, just lifted her against him and

continued the ride.

Sweat slicked his skin, and she licked each drop along his jaw and shoulder, each drop of salt the perfect flavor on her tongue. Unsure of how much more she could take, too overwhelmed by the sensation of his body rising deep within hers, until she was sure he'd touch her very soul, she egged him on. "Would you ride me like this? Show them how deep you can go? They'd watch all those muscles flex in your back, and your ass clench as you drove deeper. Would you scream my name when you came, let them all know you were claiming me?"

He shut her up with a hot, wet kiss that scraped their teeth together, until he released a loud groan and jerked against her.

With each strong pulse, she felt the waves rise, grip hard, and then she came again. Pleasure poured from her core and shot through her entire body. She was so worked up she might've blacked out and visited the stars. Dear God, the neighbors likely heard them both, as loud as they screamed, encumbered, lost to orgasmic bliss.

No matter how much she might try to deny what was between them, she couldn't lie about how he made her feel when they were wrapped around each other. Sex like this could quickly become an addiction. *Great.* She was hooked on a mammoth cock.

She buried her face in his neck, unwilling to let him see her so weak and pliant. Her body was doing a good enough job of that on its own, he didn't need to see capitulation in her eyes, as well.

She felt Bronco's chuckle against her chest. "Hmm?"

"I've always known you've got a mouth on you, but when you use it for sex..." He kissed her temple. "You drive me insane."

Rachel raked her nails up and down his back. "I'm good at that."

Bronco stood, keeping her in his arms.

"Whoa, big man, what do you think you're doing?" Rachel

glanced around the room. They really needed to consider more private venues for their sexual encounters.

"I don't *think* I'm doing anything. I *know* I'm taking you to my bed." He kept on walking, through the kitchen, and up the stairs. "I believe we'll be more comfortable there."

She shook her head. "No. No more. Some of us have jobs to do."

Shifting her in his arms, he opened his bedroom door, and then kicked it shut behind him. After a few more steps, he dropped her on his king-size bed. "You're working for me, today. And I need reassurance you know what you're doing."

Rachel combed her fingers through her thoroughly ruffled hair. "Sorry, I don't sleep with clients."

"Good to know." Bronco lay down beside her and ran a finger down the center of her chest. "But, I'd like to think I'm more than your client."

"Listen, I just got out of a relationship." Rachel slapped away his hand. "I told you earlier, we're not...this whole idea of sex all day in your bed...I don't do snuggling and staying for more. I can't let this be more than sex, Bronco. I explained this to you earlier. Yeah, you get me all hot. Yeah, I like you, but this wouldn't work between us. So, don't put me in a position where I'm forced to walk away."

She sat up on the bed, angry for some reason, as if he'd trapped her and now she couldn't break free. "I can't be here. This bed is too soft. This room is all cozy and shit...I need to go." Panic had her hopping off the bed. Panic that rose from knowing she wanted to stay here all day, wrapped in his arms as he took her over and over again on those soft navy blue sheets, until she released everything. The things she wanted to do with this man could fill all the pages of every sex book ever written, and once she finished, she knew she'd want to do it all again. Damn man and his super sexy skills.

"Rachel...listen, just relax." He shifted to the side of the bed and reached for her. "Come here." He pulled her closer before clasping her chin in his hand.

"No." She jerked away. "Get your bear paw off my face."

He chuckled. "I thought it was a mammoth paw?"

"Damn it, Murray." She bit her lip to hold back a smile. "You don't do casual."

"I don't?" Bronco sighed and sank back, bracing himself on his elbows.

Rachel avoided looking at his still-rigid cock, displayed between his thighs like some sci-fi beacon created to draw her closer and closer into its beam. She shook her head. "No, you don't do casual." Rachel opened his dresser drawer, looking for clothes. "I mean look at that blonde you're dating. How long have you been seeing her?" She slammed shut his underwear drawer and opened another. "Ah-ha!"

"Heather and I grew up together."

"Exactly." She tugged a T-shirt over her head before reopening his underwear drawer. She pulled out a pair, knew there was no way in hell they'd fit, but shoved her legs into them anyway. "You stick. You need a conventional woman, like Heather. I'm not wired that way."

"Rachel, you don't even know Heather." He stood and grasped her shoulders. "I think you're frightened, and I can deal with that, as long as you accept what you're doing. Don't push off all *your* excuses onto me. I know what I want."

"You have no idea what you want." Pulse racing, Rachel headed for the door.

"Again, you're deflecting."

Knowing he was right, yet unwilling to let him win, she glanced over her shoulder and flipped him off. "Deflect this."

"Is that an invitation? If so, I accept." He chuckled and ran his hand up and down his cock.

"You are a serious pervert."

"Me? I wasn't the one doing all the dirty talk earlier. That was all you, baby."

When that smooth voice and that hand rocking up and down started to hypnotize her, Rachel opened the door and left. All the way down the stairs, she yelled every curse word in her vocabulary, because those words were a hell of a lot easier than allowing *his* words to sink deep.

Words that revealed the stupid man knew her well, and that he just might be capable of winning the game after all.

CHAPTER 15

"So, you believe a woman with an extensive case of Alzheimer's admitted to killing Bronco's father." Blue eyes wide, Clayton Kincaid, Manchester police detective extraordinaire, cocked a dark brown brow.

He always smelled like chlorine from his daily swims. The guy was seriously hot, but a bit too thin for her taste. Rachel liked her men beefier, like Bronco. Not that she would ever admit that fact to him, or anyone else. Yep. Denial worked, and had continued to work quite well for the past couple of days.

Clayton twisted back and forth in his creaky metal office chair. "Not only that, Gloria Astor had some unnamed accomplice who you believe ties back to the Russian mafia, somehow."

Thoughts of sexy men aside, Rachel propped her feet on the top of Clayton's metal desk and wrapped her fingers around a Styrofoam cup of fairly decent coffee for a police station. She leaned back and closed her eyes, for the hundredth time in days wondering what the hell she was doing. With this case. With Bronco.

Sighing, she opened her eyes and stared at the nicotine-stained ceiling. Must be remnants of a time long past as they no longer allowed smoking inside the building, which seemed anathema to the whole cop image. "My head's not on straight with this guy, or this case. You know Bronco's a steamroller. This admission by his grandmother…Bronco believes her. And he has proof that his father isn't his father. His mother is unfaithful, and she has ties with child traffickers, not to mention murderers for hire. Pavel's death-unit could be behind Bronco's father's demise. Killing one man is nothing in their vast array of criminal activities."

"This is a private matter, Rach." Clayton shook his head. "Not grounds for a full police investigation. Bronco understands that, right? You've filed for discovery, received the traffic crash report, death certificate, autopsy and toxicology reports, plus all these articles." He flicked a finger at her copies of newspaper articles covering Thomas Northman's car accident. "Everything in that pile indicates death due to drunk driving and tumbling down a deep ravine."

"Nah, something's off about all this. I need to talk to the cop and tow truck driver who were at the scene. See if anything seemed odd, because these reports indicate Northman swerved." She sniffed, taking in the stench of sweat and whatever other bodily fluids lined the police station's offices. "It really reeks in here. Light a friggin' candle, or something."

Clayton sighed. "Harris…listen, lots of deer live in Northern Ohio. And Northman's accident occurred in the fall, during rut. Likely just wrong place, wrong time. No mystery there."

Rachel barely refrained from kicking him. His rational mind wasn't what she needed today. For once, they were actually on the same side in an investigation, because usually she assisted her uncle with criminal defense cases. "While I don't relish the thought of sending Bronco's grandmother to jail, I would like to find answers for him. Luckily, Evidence still had a sample of Northman's blood. I sent it off to my toxicologist." She shrugged. "I'm betting another substance impaired Northman's driving."

Her stomach growled, since she'd skipped breakfast. Maybe she could talk Kincaid into taking her out for pancakes. "I wish we could still investigate Northman's car. The fire after the crash could have been intentional to mask other injuries or foul play."

"The coroner ruled accidental death due to the combined effects of traumatic and thermal injuries." After closing her file, Clayton crossed his all-too-toned biceps over his chest. "I wish Bronco the best, and I hope he finds peace with his family issues, but we all have family issues, Harris. Some of us live in that nightmare every day. You know that better than anyone."

"I know he's hurting." She ran a finger along her coffee cup's rim. "And for some girly-frilly-bags-of-fluffy-kitten-shit reason, I want to ease his pain."

"Better ways to ease a guy's pain." Clayton smirked.

Rachel rolled her eyes. "You have no idea." She held her hands more than a foot apart. "No one can handle that. He's a freak of nature down there. I don't know how he walks around with that thing all day."

"I know." Miming a gun with his forefinger and thumb, Clayton made a clicking sound out the side of his mouth, which made half his face scrunch. "It's a tough job, but guys like us have no problem carrying the extra weight."

"I'll have you know I'm refraining from rolling my eyes…again." Rachel closed her eyes instead. "Mental dick comparisons are the last visuals I need right now."

Clayton chuckled, and then smacked her upside the head. Hard.

"Ow!" Rachel jolted from her stupor. "What the hell?" She rubbed the sting just above her ear and hauled her legs off Clayton's desk, sitting up straight in her chair. "I almost spilled my coffee."

"You were seen driving by Khlebosolny the other day."

Just as she put her arm down, she flinched as he smacked her again. "What the hell, Kincaid? You can't get away with police brutality in the middle of the police station. Don't hit me again, or I'll sic my O-liner on you."

"Your O-liner? I'm sure he'd chain you to his bed, if he knew your shenanigans." He poked her forehead with his index finger. "And don't joke about police brutality. That isn't funny."

"Don't smack me, then."

"I'll smack you as many times as needed to knock some sense into that thick skull." Clayton jabbed a finger against his desk. "Stay away from that place. I've warned you before. Next time, I'll smack your ass."

"You'd love to smack my ass, Kincaid." Rachel batted her eyelashes and shot him a wink.

"Hardly, I'm more into blue-eyed blondes. Tall blondes, with nice sets of—"

"Shut. Up." This time, *she* smacked him.

After a tense moment watching an officer lead a sneering cuffed guy by, Rachel shook her head before hitting Clayton with her next words. "Gina Astor-Murray is having an affair with Nestor Marat."

Clayton cleared his throat and nodded. "I know."

Rachel held back a growl. His knowledge of her intel was no surprise, since lots of criminal activity tied back to that restaurant. Marat's crew had so many high-ranking officials in their pocket that the authorities could never get a conviction. Money talked and big-ass criminals walked. Same story since forever.

"Does Gina know who Marat is?"

"Absolutely. Years ago, Gina hired her maid through Pavel. She might be vain, but she isn't stupid." Rachel sipped her coffee, though, after discussing Pavel, the taste seemed bitter. "In my opinion, she's one of those privileged women who likes to play on the dark side, getting dirty, rolling around with some bad boy. And that's all well and good until he slits her throat, or gets her high and hooked enough to slit her own."

"I know why Marat's of interest to you, and I understand the need to find answers and closure, but you have to steer clear of Khlebosolny. If we saw you, then they saw you." Clayton leaned forward and braced his hands on her knees. "Back off, Harris."

Rachel bristled. Kincaid had no right to speak to the dangers of her job. Wasn't his job just as dangerous? Plus, after clocking plenty of hours at the gun range, she could hit the bullseye every time. Admittedly, she'd been in a few scrapes, but her *jiu-jitsu* training was suited to defensive maneuvers against bigger opponents. And, after training since she was ten, she was the only brown belt in a class full of men. So, Kincaid could shove his concerns where the sun didn't shine. "Listen, Kincaid—"

"No, you listen." Again, he jabbed a finger against his desk. "You want to find answers for Bronco? Then do your job. Ask questions. Investigate. Then, put a lid on it and walk away. He's got to do the same." Clayton leaned forward and ruffled her hair. "I admit the story adds up, in a way. Gloria Astor certainly had means, motive, and opportunity." He tapped his pen against the yellow notepad on his desk. "Girl gets pregnant, Mom finds out, disapproves completely, so she kills the guy and forces her daughter to marry the first eligible man. But, not just any man. One with financial and social standing. A man a few years older, who can rein in her daughter. Families have been arranging marriages for hundreds of years. Still are. Even here in the U.S."

"Killing someone for social standing is mental."

"After six years in the business, that surprises you? Greed, lust, hate, fear, jealousy, and sometimes just because, are all reasons humans kill one another. In essence, we are animals, walking around like we're civilized, but when put to the test, not all pass."

"That's where we come in." Rachel nodded, tipping her cup in salute.

"Yeah. Still, the senselessness of it all gets to me sometimes."

"Harden up, Kincaid."

"I...I'm almost too hard. Right now, with everything going on around the country, the media questioning each policeman's every move, and taking everything out of context, along with all the negativity..." He shook his head, short brown hair not moving one inch out of place. "We can't effectively do our jobs. Everyday citizens don't understand what we do. They don't see behind the smoke and mirrors, but we do. We pass through that smoke every day, and see that burned-out mess on the other side. And it hardens you, until you wonder why." Clayton shrugged and ran a finger along the edge of his desk. "Why bother?"

"I'm sorry. I understand." Rachel leaned forward and took his hand. "I know I give you a hard time, but I do love you, all right? I'm here, and I get it."

Clayton pinched the bridge of his nose with his free hand.

Felt good to know he was comfortable enough to talk about his troubles. "I know what it's like to lose everything and you just want to know why."

"Makes good fodder for mystery books, as well." Clayton tossed his pen at her.

"It does." Rachel studied him. He'd made similar comments about his job before. "Thinking of going private, Kincaid?"

"I'd just like to choose my own cases." Clayton shrugged again. "Say someone walks in with a case involving two DB's, little girl and boy." He tapped the yellow folder on his desk. "Father is an abusive asshole who's been brought in countless times, until this night, when he loses his mind and kills them both. Yeah, someone walks in with a case like that, I can say, nope, too much for me. Give it to the next guy."

"You interviewing for a job, Detective?"

Clenching his jaw, Clayton swept his gaze around the bustling station house. "I'm tired, Rach. After my brother Michael's death, things haven't been the same. I've lost something, more than just my sibling, but a desire to do this job."

"I understand, especially...based on..."—Rachel cleared her throat—"how Michael died." Clayton's brother had been at a local bar with his boyfriend. When a patron took offense and asked him to step outside, the big asshole knocked Michael against a brick wall. Michael hit his head against the building's corner and died instantly. Cops had been in the bar, watched the fight, and hadn't stopped it. Clayton had almost lost his badge when he went after the men for not protecting a citizen, his only brother, who had stood and lost against a much bigger opponent.

"What about your brother?" Clayton redirected the conversation. "How's your search going? Any closer?"

"I know Pavel took him. All evidence points to him. I've interviewed girls who worked for him at the time. From what they can recall, he gave a boy to his main lover around the same time Erik was abducted." Rachel thrummed her fingers against Clayton's desk. "And, based on their physical descriptions, I believe that boy was my brother."

"Child trafficking is an ugly business. Let the authorities handle it."

"Nestor Marat." She growled out his name. "I need one hour with him, and I could make him sing."

"You touch one hair on that man's head, and he'll kill everyone you love. And leave you alive long enough to suffer through all the deaths."

This argument was an old one. Clayton had trod down this road many times. One day, she would get her hands on Marat, because he held the answers. Held the key to unlocking all the pain and suffering. Someday, she'd fling open that door and unleash her primitive side on a man who'd destroyed her life and hadn't a care for the damage he'd left behind.

Capable of changing the subject as well, Rachel nudged Clayton's leg with her shoe. "So, let's talk about this disenchantment a bit more. Are you looking to hang up your private eye shingle, or you want to share some of mine? We'd be Harris and Kincaid."

"H&K." Clayton nodded.

"Yeah, like the gun company." Rachel straightened in the hard metal chair. "That'd be so boss. Heckler & Koch's motto is: No Compromises. That'd work for us, right?"

"No compromises." Clayton brushed a hand over his stubble-covered chin. "I'm willing to give it a go if you are."

Rachel opened her mouth to respond, but she couldn't think of anything to say. *Well, hell!* She hadn't expected to obtain a partner today. Hadn't she just two days ago walked away from a man who wanted the same thing, only on a more intimate level?

Connections. Why were so many men asking for more? And why did she feel the need to give them both a chance? Wasn't this her Achilles heel, saving people to make up for losing the one person she never should have lost? "Sure. Why not? H&K has a bad-ass ring to it." She tossed her empty cup into his garbage can. "Tell you what, come see me in a week. If you're still interested, then we'll talk, and I'll have Uncle Harris draw up paperwork. Yeah?" She stood and stuck out her hand.

"I'll see you in a week." He clutched her hand and shook it vigorously, ending with a little squeeze.

"I'll see you in a week, what?"

Clayton furrowed his brow. "What?"

"I believe you meant to say, I'll see you in a week, boss."

"Oh, no…"

Rachel laughed as Clayton wrapped her in a headlock and listed all the reasons why that wasn't happening.

Guys were such jerks.

CHAPTER 16

"After everything I've done for you, you dare to question my motives now?" The man, Erik Pavel, glared at the U.S. Marshal who'd lead him into Witness Protection years ago and now served as his contact for the FBI and other agencies. Everyone wanted a piece of him, but this cowboy hat-wearing son of a bitch, Leonard Moore, was the only one who shot straight.

In his lifetime, Erik had dealt with enough liars to know a man who spoke only truths. Moore's partner, on the other hand, could die, and Erik wouldn't shed a tear.

He glared at the blond marshal who tanned, gelled his hair, and went through women like old socks, even though he'd been married for five years. *Bastard.* Nothing Erik hated more than a man who disrespected women. After all those years watching his mother get treated like less than a servant, he fought back the bile each time he was in this man's presence.

Erik remained in the doorway of the shady hotel room, which served as their meeting place. Two guys against one. Never good odds. His father had made it clear: never trust anyone or give them your back. A lesson he'd learned quite thoroughly after suffering through his father's various traps.

Erik glared at the blond he'd dubbed Metro, due to his grooming habits. "You'd have nothing without me. Pavel would still be alive, and more girls would be dead. I've given as much as I can without drawing suspicion."

"So, you deny knowing anything about Marat's house on Fifth and Columbus?" Metro sneered. "Thought that sort of thing churned your stomach, *Pavel*?"

"I've already answered that question." Though furious over Marat's deceit, he answered in a bored tone and kept his gaze on the tips of his highly-polished shoes. "I don't have time to repeat myself. These meetings you demand are becoming too frequent. I can't keep slipping away at a moment's notice."

"You'll shut it down?"

"Again, don't make me repeat something I've already said I'd handle."

"He's growing more restless. More brave." Leonard fiddled with the coffee pot. He'd been trying to get the damn thing to work the entire time they'd been in this hovel.

"Then take care of him." Erik shrugged. "I told you, I won't kill anyone for you. Pavel was mine to take down, but any others are on you."

"What about this investigation your sister is conducting? Do we need to interfere?"

"Not yet."

"Are you aware she's purchased a black market Electromagnetic Pulse generator? Have any idea what she plans to do with that?" Metro propped both hands on his hips. "She continually drives by Khlebosolny, and she's been trailing Marat."

"I'm aware of everything, gentlemen. Including where you spent last night, Marshal." He tipped his head at Metro. "And you accuse me of unfaithfulness. Care to look in the mirror?"

Metro stormed across the room and started swinging.

Erik leaned into the punch and grabbed his hand, wrenching Metro's arm behind his back and knocking the asshole down before landing on his back.

Leonard just laughed.

"I've been hit in every way possible, by every possible weapon, so your love taps wouldn't mean shit." As the man squirmed, Erik tugged harder on his arm. "When my father died, I vowed no one would ever touch me again. I'd rather not unleash my Pavel side, so I suggest you take my comments like a man and own up to your infidelities."

"Fuck you, Junior."

That topped it. Erik lifted the Metro's face only an inch off the thinly-carpeted, thoroughly disgusting floor. "Apparently, you've forgotten how much I despise that nickname. But, since you brought it up, do you know what Pavel Junior, would do to you?" He leaned closer to the man's ear. "Ever hear of the "elephant"? After I cuffed your hands behind your back, I'd put a gas mask over your face. Then I'd close off your breathing tube." Visions of his father's men doing this very thing seared through Erik's mind, and he fought back the wave of nausea. "Once you were gasping for air, I'd reopen the tube, and you'd breathe deeply, only you'd be breathing in CS gas. Or, maybe I'd—"

"Erik, that's enough." Leonard stepped closer, but didn't touch him.

Smart man.

Shaken by the rage coursing through his body, he bashed the asshole's face against the carpet, and then stood and readjusted his shirt. "You need me more than I need you." He jabbed a finger at Leonard. "Remember that, because I'm tired of reminding you of who I really am."

"Believe me, I know who you are." Leonard slapped a package of Marlboro Lights against his palm, drew out a cigarette, and lit it with the lighter Erik had bought him last Christmas.

"Good. Don't call me for a while. I have work to do, and you're interrupting."

Leonard nodded, blowing a wave of smoke between them.

"When your partner wakes up, tell him if he calls me Junior again, I'll break every bone in his body." He nudged the blond's arm with his shoe. "Killing people is too easy. That's one thing my father never understood. Letting them live while you deliver pain over and over is the way to end a man's life. Believe me, I know." He opened the hotel door and then glanced over his shoulder. "I died a long time ago."

CHAPTER 17

Bronco watched his mother prepare his father's usual after-dinner coffee. A bottle of Baileys sat beside the steaming pot.

Though he usually enjoyed the aroma of his father's special blend, Bronco grimaced, his stomach souring at the odor tonight. After a tense day playing a horrible, even for him, round of golf with his father, he'd come home for Sunday dinner. The whole thing reeked of artifice and lies.

He'd yet to speak to his father about the test results, or his mother's affair.

Throughout the entire meal, she had glared daggers with her ice chip eyes.

His appetite was nil, since he'd felt like an imposter who didn't know the rules of the game he'd been dumped smack dab in the middle of. Lying and withholding all the turmoil within wasn't how he and his father operated. They were pals and shared every aspect of their lives. At least, they had, but now...now he joined in the deceit.

Unable to take the silence, he clutched his mother's arm. "Please, tell me about Thomas Northman. I deserve to know." If he learned about the past, maybe he could keep Rachel from looking into Marat. A few nights ago, he'd met Clayton for beers. As always, the detective had plenty to say about Rachel, but what really bugged Bronco was the man's warnings about her investigations into Marat. Something had to give. Information had to come from a source other than a Russian mobster.

He gently squeezed his mother's arm. "I've always known something was off about me. Proportionally, I'm the odd duck." He pulled a second coffee cup from the cabinet. "Not only that, I have some things I'd like to say about Marat."

"Marat is none of your business." His mother wiped coffee grounds off the counter, avoiding his gaze.

"Do you have any idea how much lying to that man out there tears my insides apart?" He took a deep breath to keep from crushing the coffee cup in his hand. "What happens in this family *is* my business."

"Fine." She yanked the cup from him. "Meet me upstairs after I deliver his coffee."

Bronco nodded. He passed family portraits as he headed up the stairs to her bedroom. A picture-perfect family existed behind those thin squares of glass. No cracks or chips, not even a hair out of place. But maybe he'd missed the real portrait, one like classic literature's tale of Dorian Gray, whose painting absorbed foul misdeeds and showed the horrid truth. Or, maybe that image was now in his head, and the sickness of that caused sleepless nights.

As he opened his mother's door, he realized his parents had occupied separate bedrooms for as long as he could remember, an oddity he should have noted. When he married, he'd never have separate beds. Was Rachel a right or left side sleeper? She had avoided him for way too long. Their last interlude was the hottest sexual encounter he'd ever had. Her dirty fantasies were now stuck on replay in his mind. Damn woman needed to stop fighting the inevitability of their connection. They had more names on his list to interview. He'd use that excuse to reel her in.

Thoughts of his wayward woman were interrupted when his mother entered the room. Even on Sunday, she'd gone to the bank, or said she had. She'd shed her blue jacket and just wore her skirt and a silky white shirt. Gina was still a stunning beauty. Her weight was always perfect, and her facial features had only needed a few small nips and tucks along the way.

Why did she need more? This room, this home, his father, why weren't they enough? Why did she have to entertain a dangerous man like Marat?

She disappeared into her custom-designed closet. The sound of items being slammed around and dropped came from behind the half-shut doors. After a few muffled curses, she returned with an old black leather purse, shaped almost like a briefcase. "You want to know about Thomas." She dumped the purse's contents on the maroon duvet. "Here you are."

Feeling like Godzilla was tearing down buildings in his stomach, Bronco took a deep breath and sank onto the bed. He brushed a finger across photographs, a class ring, newspaper clippings, and a small blue velvet box. Opening the box, he studied the diamond ring.

"Thomas wanted to get married." His mother stood beside the bed, her hands clasped together at the waist.

"And did you want to marry him?"

"Yes. We told my parents together." Sitting beside him, she took the box from his hand. After a moment, Gina handed it back and then stood, wiping her hand against her skirt. "Our plan didn't go over well."

"Grandmother is strong-willed. Obstinate. Very opinionated. But I never got a sense she was malicious."

"Mother suits her personality to the situation. She always said, be a chameleon, Gina. They can't take what they don't know."

Bronco paused for a second before glancing at his mother. "Maybe when I'm not so confused about everything else, I'll make sense of that statement." He closed the ring box and opened a small plastic photo album. A face so similar to his own stared back. A hulk of a man in a football uniform, with blond hair and a killer smile. Bronco closed his eyes to hold back the tears.

His father.

The photo had Thomas's name, number, and position in the corner. The picture was from one of those team photo shoot packages that provided fifty various-sized copies. Taking a few deep breaths, he opened his eyes and studied the man in the photo again. "Who was he?" He dug his teeth into his bottom lip, refusing to cry in front of his mother. They didn't do emotional moments. This situation was awkward enough.

"That was during his junior year at college." She sniffed, sinking into the intricately carved wooden chair that matched her vanity. With her back to him, she removed her earrings and bracelets. "I visited Mother again this morning to ask about Thomas, but she wasn't lucid." She paused a moment before turning in her chair. "Warren, you must not believe what she said. She's very ill. And I-I find I cannot fathom she would...that she engineered Thomas' death."

"This man"—he flicked the photo with his finger—"died in a very convenient car accident a few weeks after you told your parents you were pregnant. People kill for ridiculous reasons." He slipped his father's class ring on his finger. "While I don't like believing Grandmother arranged his death either, I saw real fear in her eyes that day. Real hatred. Honestly, she frightened me."

His mother joined him on the bed again and thumbed through the photo album of her in various poses with his father. She tugged a photo from behind the clear casing and ran her thumb over Thomas' face. "He lived for football. Just like you. I've always...one thing that never made sense, he never would have jeopardized his chances at going professional by drinking and driving."

In the photo, Thomas smiled at the camera, and Gina's head was turned toward him with an expression Bronco had rarely seen on her face—love. "Did he have a real chance at going pro?"

"Yes." His mother dug through the scattered papers for an

old newspaper article, headlined, "Local Boy Set to Go Pro". "He was heavily recruited, even in high school."

"Did you love him?"

"Love?" She shrugged. "Perhaps in a way. I believe I was more in awe of him. His freedom. His bravado." In her reverent tone, Bronco caught a glimpse of the starstruck girl she'd once been. "I know he wanted more from me, but...I-I'm not capable of deeper emotions." She sighed and squeezed his hand. "I'm sorry for that, Warren. Thomas was thrilling, larger than life. A whirlwind in my carefully plotted Astor world. I wanted him, so I maneuvered my way into having him. I suppose my mother did teach me how to lie, cheat, and steal for what I wanted. As an Astor, a person won. End of story."

"Thomas was a prize."

"Oh, yes, in so many ways."

Bronco breathed through the tightness in his chest. How unfair that this powerhouse, this handsome man, was snuffed before truly having a chance to shine. To live. And though he loved his father, in this moment he'd give anything for one second with the dynamic man staring back with his same eyes. Selfish maybe, but perhaps that trait ran in the family. Just how much had his mother done to win Thomas? Though he knew the question was rude and disrespectful, he asked, "Did you get pregnant on purpose?"

"No." Steel blue eyes flashed, and she released his hand. "I was still in college. Honestly, being pregnant does nothing for the figure."

"High priorities, Mother."

She flipped her hair over her shoulder, quiet for a moment before she met his gaze. "I don't regret having you, Warren. My past and present actions may not be laudable, but I am still your mother." She waved a hand between them.

As if pushing the words through the air and down his throat would make them easier to swallow. "What about Dad?"

"What about him?"

"Do you love him?"

"I care for William. We are a team, and that benefits me in many ways."

"Very cold."

"It's what I know."

"Do you know about Nestor Marat's ties to the Russian mafia?"

Frowning, his mother stood and paced before her window seat. "Forget what you think you know of Nestor Marat. Stay away from him."

Fury over her warning rising to the forefront, he bit back a sharp retort. "I'll say the same to you."

"He gets me in a way your father does not."

"You know what else he gets? Little girls, perhaps even little boys, for grown men. That's sick shit, Mother."

She scoffed, flicking a hand in the air. "You have no proof of this."

Bronco's blood pressure spiked, and he couldn't stand the flowery stench of his mother's indifference any longer. "Who are you?" He stood and started gathering his father's items. "I need to be away from you. And I'm keeping these things. I deserve to know more about my father." He shoved all the items back into the bag. "Let me be clear on one thing, if nothing else. I will find out if he was killed."

"You will leave it!" His mother shrieked, her eyes wide.

Though the feeling in the pit of his stomach burned, he stood tall against her arrogant manner. "I won't."

"You've always been stupid."

Well, well, didn't she play dirty? Slicing his heart with the one insult she knew would cut deep. "Quit while you're ahead, Mother. Continue, and our relationship will end here."

She stepped toward him. "Do not threaten me, Child."

"Threats?" William's voice shot like a brick wall between

them.

Bronco snapped shut the bag.

Just inside the doorway, his father leaned against the door frame. "What's going on in here?" His gaze traveled down to the bag in Bronco's hands.

Bronco bit back a sob. Fights with his mother. Pictures of his real father. A girl who pushed him away. Worries that he was truly stupid. All these thoughts swirled in his head. And this man...this man in the doorway who'd always loved him despite his flaws. This man didn't deserve such deceit.

The lies creating a barrier between them tore at his soul. Over-emotional, Bronco stomped over and wrapped his arms around his father, unable to contain one truth. "I love you. You are my father, but I need to learn more about Thomas Northman." He bit his lip again as tears escaped and wet his cheeks. "I'm so sorry."

"He knows?" William mumbled against his shoulder.

"He does." His mother remained by her window seat.

"I knew this day would come." His father pulled away, but clutched Bronco's upper arms. "I'm sorry we kept this from you, Son."

"I feel like a baby for crying." Bronco wiped at his cheeks. "Listen, Dad, I don't know what to think, yet...but this doesn't change how I feel about you. I just need some time."

His father headed for a side table, withdrew a few tissues from the box, and handed them over. "Who told you?"

"Yes, tell him, Warren. Tell your father who you're investigating."

"Warren?" His father braced both hands on his hips. "What's going on?"

"Fine." Bronco set the bag on a decorative chair by the door and told his father everything—from the initial visit with his grandmother to the current investigations into Thomas' death.

William sank onto the bed, pinching the bridge of his nose.

"Warren, I need a moment with your mother, and then we'll discuss how to proceed. Is that all right?"

"Yeah, sure. You two talk." He had no desire to be a part of their discussion, although, he was curious if his father had known Thomas personally. Plus, there was one more thing he wanted to make clear. Though his heart broke a little, he needed to speak. "Mother and I…I'm not sure how she and I will continue at this point."

His mother slammed a hand against her vanity's tabletop. Glass bottles danced and clinked together. "William, if you don't intervene, he'll get himself killed."

His father sniffed and flicked a speck of lint off his pants. "By whom? Nestor Marat?"

His mother opened her mouth, and then closed it.

"You think I don't know, Gina? Hell, I even knew about Joe Chogan."

"Joe?" Bronco stilled. He hadn't believed his mother's indiscretions could get any worse, but Joe Chogan? Another family friend? At this rate, he'd never forgive her. "Joe Chogan, Mother. Really? Hasn't he been married like, forever?" Bronco's stomach flipped at the thought of Joe's wife, Claire, and their two kids. "What kind of…who does that? He has children. He works with you every day. That is just…I can't even find the word to describe what that is."

"Warren." His father shook his head. "I will call you later."

"Yeah, sure, but just remember this: I need the truth. Don't call until you can give me that." He grabbed the bag off the chair and headed down the stairs, ignoring his mother's screams of fury and his father's low murmurs.

On his way to his SUV, he wiped the stupid tears off his cheeks. "Oversensitive idiot, crying like a little baby." He kicked his Audi's tires. "Fuck!" The only thing that could soothe him was hours against the training sled. Or Rachel. He dug out his phone to call her when it pinged and flashed with a text from Clayton.

FYI Last night during an investigation Rachel's vehicle was fired at by rubber bullets. Not injured. Still, get her tiny ass straight.

And, just like that, desolation turned to rage, which coursed through his veins like liquid fire. As his heart pounded, he wondered how much more the poor organ could take. He called Rachel. When she didn't pick up, he cursed her with every name in the book before calling Ember.

"Hey, big guy."

"Where is Rachel?"

"Bronco, I think——"

"No thinking. Where is she? Please, Ember."

Ember sighed.

In the background, Owen shouted. "She's at *jiu-jitsu.*"

Bronco ended the call, threw the bag filled with mementos of the father he'd never know into the passenger seat, and then ripped down his parents' drive. Flexing his fingers, he considered just how pink he'd turn Rachel's fairy ass.

In his time of need, his first thought had turned to her.

Obviously, she hadn't done the same.

CHAPTER 18

"Rachel!"

In the middle of a sparring match at the end of her *jiu-jitsu* class, Rachel froze at the sound of her name and the front door slamming against the outer wall.

Bronco stood in the doorway, surveying the area until his gaze met hers.

She scrambled to her feet, cursing Clayton. Why else would Bronco have that lethal look in his eye?

He jabbed a finger at her before flicking his thumb over his shoulder, beckoning her outside.

She couldn't move, and she might have squeaked a little while watching him thunder across the mat.

The shouts from her classmates did nothing to stop him from hauling her over his shoulder.

"What the hell do you think you're doing?" Twisting her body, she tried to hike a leg around his neck to choke him.

He tightened his grip. "What am *I* doing?" He swatted her ass. "That's a hell of a question to ask me, Harris."

As she bounced against his back, she glimpsed Spencer and the professor following them out, shouting for him to stop. "You need to let me go right now."

"Shut up." Bronco gripped her around the waist and plopped

her onto her feet.

Rachel brushed her hair out of her face, readjusting her ponytail. "Smooth, Murray. Real smooth. You don't see me coming to your training sessions and hauling your ass out."

"Man, you can't be coming in here and disrupting class." Spencer shot across the lot, then hopped on one leg, brushing at the bottom of his bare foot. "Damn, stepped on some glass."

Bronco merely raised a brow. "You're one to talk. You disrupted her life by cheating."

Based on the two male personalities in this current showdown, she needed to diffuse the situation fast. "Spencer." Rachel raised a hand between them. "I got this."

"Yeah, Spencer." Bronco flicked a hand at the building. "Head back inside."

Spencer shook his head, tightened the purple belt on his *gi*, and then glanced back and forth between them. "What'd she do?"

"Someone shot at her last night."

She was going to kill Clayton Kincaid. That traitor would never be her partner if he couldn't keep his mouth shut.

"What?" Frowning, Spencer grabbed her arm. "Are you hurt? What the hell were you doing?"

Great. Now two people were yelling, and all her classmates hovered outside of the gym to watch the drama unfold. She held her arms out at her sides, searching for patience with the overprotective men. "Do I look like I'm hurt?"

"Who was it?" Bronco growled.

"Someone with really bad aim." Rachel shrugged, because really, that was true. Or, perhaps they'd had great aim and just hadn't wanted to kill her.

"How can you say something like that?" Bronco threw up his hands and then braced them on his hips. "This isn't something to crack jokes about, Rachel."

"She has no thought for her own safety." Spencer addressed Bronco. "Just laughs off danger like she's invincible."

"What's her problem anyway?" Bronco continued.

"Mommy issues. Abandonment. Guilt."

Now *that* was enough. "Spencer, I suggest you shut up." She jabbed his solid chest with a finger.

Bronco smiled at Spencer, completely ignoring her. "Saw your last fight, West. Nice guillotine."

They bumped fists.

Seriously? What kind of bro-love was this? "Can I go back inside now?"

"No." They answered at the same time.

"I'll admit, Travers was tough, man, but I knew his weaknesses." Replaying the fight, Spencer mocked holding someone around the neck. "In that second round, after he got me a few times in the shins, I lost it. I charged and pinned him in the hold, and he just passed—"

Rachel cleared her throat. Loudly. "Can we move on to what you're doing here?" Exasperated with the play-by-play, she glared at Spencer before directing the same stare at Bronco.

"For a detective, you're not that quick, are you?" Spencer tugged on her ponytail. "You were shot at. Not cool, Rachel."

Bronco exhaled deeply. "Why didn't you call?"

He seemed to bristle with something, as if on edge, and his eyes were red. Had he been crying? Over her? Surely not. Still, his need to rush over like some knight in shining armor rankled. His expectation to know every facet of her life made no sense. Since when did anyone care what happened in her world? "Why would I call?"

After a hearty scoff, Bronco glared and then, after a short pause, nodded. "I see." He slammed a fist against the hood of his Audi.

Unclear where all his anger stemmed from, Rachel tried to ease his mind. "They weren't even real bullets."

"That isn't the point." Bronco rubbed his temples, dragging his fingers through his hair.

"I'm sorry, but I think it's very much the point. They were ballistic rubber media, made for shooting ranges and bullet traps." She shrugged. "So, in my estimation, they were fired to scare me. I've been working this case where—"

Bronco slashed a hand between them. "And did it work? Were you scared? Because knowing someone fired a gun in your direction sure scared the hell out of me."

"What's the big deal?" Rachel scratched her cheek. "My profession holds a certain element of danger. I understand that. I've accepted that." She glanced at Spencer, hoping for some back-up.

He just shook his head.

"I'll never accept it." Bronco's words rumbled out.

His tone was laced with something, an echo of whatever else was making him so angry. "I don't know what this whole scene is really about, Murray, but I've never asked you to accept who I am." She got right up in Bronco's face. "We've fucked a few times, but that doesn't give you the keys to my kingdom. I don't need a fantasy man charging to my rescue." Furious he thought to control her, or make her accountable to anyone other than herself, she held nothing back. "I am an investigator. And yes, my job is dangerous. But so is yours."

"I understand what your job is, Rachel. I'm not stupid." Bronco closed his eyes and took a deep breath.

When she connected with that clear blue-eyed gaze, she watched something shift within. She couldn't do this, have him worry about her, expect …whatever he expected. She'd only disappoint. Being alone was her penance, and she didn't want to love or need anyone. What if she let him protect her, and then one day he disappeared? No. She no longer took chances with her heart.

Tightening her brown belt around her body, she bit her bottom lip. Piercing through the thin flesh, she tasted the faintest blend of copper and sweat. Then, she aimed and shot more than a rubber bullet through Bronco's chest, because he deserved better than a heartless, empty woman. "I don't owe you any explanations. As you see, I'm all right. You had no reason to come here."

"No reason?" Bronco's jaw clenched and he narrowed his gaze. "That's your position?"

Rachel shrugged, knowing she couldn't speak the lie. Every reason existed. Every need to allow this man to mend the pieces of the shattered vessel that stood for her heart. But, over the past few days, she'd considered all their moments together. How, in truth, she couldn't keep making love to him, because she sank deeper under his spell each time, and she wasn't a girl who got hypnotized by hope.

She took a deep breath, shoring up her resolve. "Bronco, I think...it...ah...it would be best if we moved things back to a professional level." Unable to meet his gaze, she rolled a tiny stone under her bare big toe. "Had the bullet been relevant to your case, I'd have notified you. As it wasn't, I didn't." She sniffed and gripped the ends of her belt, holding onto something so she wouldn't falter and collapse into Bronco's arms. "So, as we move forward, I-I feel it would be best if you consider me only as under your employ."

"Under my employ? Is that what they're calling it, nowadays?"

"I'm not calling what we shared anything other than what it was. Friends comforting one another." She did meet his gaze now, because there was a level of truth to that statement. "I'm available in a professional capacity, Bronco. Everything else has to stop. Getting personal with clients is not...it's not wise."

"Fuck wise." Bronco jabbed a finger in the air between them. "For someone so skilled at digging into people's lives, you sure as hell don't have a handle on your own. You don't want to tell me anything? Fine. You don't want me involved? Fine."

Rachel fought for breath. This felt wrong, so wrong. What

was she doing? "Bronco, please if you could—"

"No, I'm not an idiot. I'm clear. Crystal clear." He rounded the hood of his Audi, but he stopped at the front and banged his fist against the hood again. "Call me when you have information on my case, Ms. Harris, or when you need a friendly fuck." After a round of various mumbled curses, Bronco hopped into his SUV and sped away.

Rachel watched the taillights fade and knew she'd rejected something from a good man, something he'd freely offered. But, what could she do?

Was this what love felt like, this regret and awful need when you'd hurt someone? A desire to turn back time, because you'd do anything to take back the words, the actions, everything? That man could bring her to her knees, and that kept her frozen, afraid to move forward or backward. Strong women didn't do fear. Strong women were solid. Capable. Aloof. She headed back to the gym and spotted Spencer leaning against her Jeep.

He grabbed her arm. "What do you think you're doing?"

"As if you care." Rachel shrugged him off.

"Don't." Spencer gripped her shoulders and gave her a shake. "Don't pull that sass-mouth with me. I've been on your side for a long time." His nose was practically touching hers, and his body vibrated with anger. "What we had…our relationship might not have been the real thing…but that was all your doing. You didn't want us to reach the next level, and I guess I knew that going in, but that guy"—he pointed to where Bronco's vehicle had retreated—"that guy loves you. Whether you believe that or not, he does. So get your head out of your ass."

"You're mental." Though, her heart did flutter at his words, an odd sensation springing forth from some dormant place deep within. Like a flower bulb left too long in arid earth that finally welcomed a little rain. But was the rain a gentle mist, or a torrential downpour? And with Warren Murray, weren't they one and the same? "He doesn't love me."

"You're smarter than that. A man doesn't beat down a door and come storming in for his woman if he's not feeling her." Spencer wrapped an arm around her neck and ruffled her hair. "Get your head straight before you destroy a good thing with a good guy. Let the past go, Rach."

She wrapped her arms around him and mumbled against his *gi*. "He deserves so much more than I can offer. I can't—"

"Then stay stuck." Spencer pulled away to cradle her face in his hands. "Stay unhappy, but don't start relationships with men if you don't plan on finishing them. Some of us do worry about you. Do love you." He kissed her forehead. "Deal with it, or we'll stop trying."

CHAPTER 19

"No, no, no. As if this day wasn't bad enough." Rachel sank onto her office chair and rubbed her eyes. Her stomach ached, and she wasn't sure if it was from her third cup of coffee, or digesting Spencer's words.

After class last night, she'd driven by Bronco's apartment but hadn't stopped. Just parked down the street and cried, screamed, and basically lost her mind for a couple hours before driving home. Raw emotion. Raw throat. Raw heart.

And now her office had been burglarized. Every file on the Khlebosolny brigade, as she referred to them, was gone. Her uncle's building had a state-of-the-art security system and her file cabinets were locked, but she wasn't surprised Marat's minions could break past every barrier. Looking for clues or security camera proof would produce a whole lot of nada. Hell, the footage likely showed her destroying her own files, or something equally ridiculous.

As nothing else in her office was disturbed, this theft must have been completed by a professional who got in and out, undetected, with exactly what he'd been assigned to retrieve. What Marat failed to consider, though, was that with her job and connections, Rachel had a fairly clear idea of who in town could've pulled off a robbery of this caliber, unless he'd brought in someone.

However, after following Marat to a few pawnshops, she'd begun to wonder if he was strained for cash. Perhaps he wasn't the head of the organization after all. Wasn't he the one doing the legwork? Running around, visible? Something wasn't right in that scenario. Plus, he was frequently alone. If he was the local brigade's leader, wouldn't he have guards assigned?

Lost to her considerations, she propped her feet on her desk and closed her eyes. The very fact her files were taken meant she was close. So very close to finding out what had happened to her brother.

A couple of strong knocks against her open door jolted her out of her contemplations, and due to either coffee or nerves, her heart jackknifed in her chest. She shot to her feet as she recognized Bronco's father, William Murray.

Always a gentleman, he smiled and remained just outside the door. "Good morning, Ms. Harris."

Rubbing her chest, Rachel nodded and swallowed past the lump in her throat. Was he here to read her the riot act for hurting his son? And didn't she deserve the verbal spanking, if he was?

He waved a hand at the padded metal chair before her desk. "May I sit?"

Finding her manners, she nodded again. "Yes, please, take a seat. May I get you some coffee?"

"No, thank you. I had a cup this morning." Mr. Murray settled into the chair and unbuttoned his suit coat. "I have beans shipped in from Columbia. A bit overboard, I realize, but I do enjoy some indulgences." He rubbed at his temples. "Forgive me a moment, I've had a splitting headache that hasn't abated."

"I'm sorry, sir." She grabbed her bag off the floor, digging around for her mini-Ibuprofen bottle. "I have some pain medicine in here somewhere."

"No, that's all right. Thank you. I took some before I came." He shifted in the chair. "I am sorry to interrupt your day. I require only a few minutes of your time, if you don't mind."

Rachel shook her head, now very clear where Bronco received his gentlemanly qualities. In her business, she had to read people immediately. Her gut instinct said Bronco's father was a kindhearted person, dignified, and refined, but with a steel backbone she believed few tested. He held a capable aura, one she immediately trusted to efficiently handle any problem. Wasn't that the exact description of Bronco? Except that mammoth man was a tad rougher around the edges.

Bronco's father cleared his throat. "There are things...a discussion I felt we should have...about Warren."

He seemed a slight bit flustered, with his black and gray hair a tad askew, as if he'd raked his fingers through his locks more than once this morning.

"My son...I know you've been working closely with Warren." William folded his fingers in his lap and directly met her gaze. "And he is my son, regardless of any test that says otherwise."

"I believe that to be true, Mr. Murray."

"I've always known Thomas Northman was Warren's father. I agreed to marry Gina, because I was...attracted to her. I also agreed with her mother that our family connections would further both our causes...financially and socially. After Thomas died, Gina was amenable, so we married."

Rachel held back the big question, waiting to see what all Mr. Murray would reveal.

"I had nothing to do with the death of Thomas Northman. I knew nothing of the man, until Gloria, Gina's mother, visited with the proposition of marrying her pregnant daughter."

"I believe you."

"Thank you." William nodded. "I understand Warren's need to look into his father's death. I also find Gloria Astor's involvement not a far stretch of the imagination." He dropped his gaze and brushed at non-existent lint on his perfectly tailored suit jacket. "I don't know that Warren will find the answers he needs, or if he'll find any peace in the results of this investigation." He sat straighter, squaring his shoulders. "I came here today to let you know I wish to help with your research. I wish I'd paid more attention to Thomas and Gina's relationship. But, Gina seemed unfazed by his death, and I had a new wife and child on the way, plus my career. So my focus wasn't on a dead man. An oversight on my part, surely, but you can understand why none of this flagged for me before."

"Mrs. Astor does have Alzheimer's, Mr. Murray. I'm not sure I'm completely sold on the story myself, but I'll continue the investigation for your son."

William nodded. "He means something to you, then."

"Ah…" Rachel sipped her now-cold coffee, but meeting Murray's gaze again, she found she couldn't lie. "Your son means…something."

With a grin, he tapped a finger on the chair's armrest. "He's worked very hard at bettering himself in the past few years. I'm very proud of him. He's a gifted athlete, but he finally realized he could be more at the same time." He squinted and rubbed his forehead. "I've got to see a doctor about these migraines, though I believe I'm aware of their cause."

Rachel searched her bag again for the mini-bottle of painkillers. Finding the plastic white cylinder at the bottom, she pulled it out and shook it, only to find it empty. "Sorry, I'm out."

"Speaking of pain, Ms. Harris, may I offer some advice?"

Sure his advice had everything to do with how to treat his son, she bit her tongue to hold back a sharp retort. He was simply trying to be a loving father, something she hadn't had for far too many years.

"Nestor Marat."

Surprised by this turn of thought, she shot her gaze to his.

"Steer clear of that man. My wife"—he cleared his throat—"Gina believes I've remained ignorant of her multiple affairs. I knew she married me at her mother's directive, but I felt we had some lovely years together. However, I would never go so far as to say we love each other. I've had my share of indiscretions, and lately…I've found… there was a woman that I should've…anyway…I've finally had enough and have set divorce proceedings in motion. Just this morning, in fact." He glanced out the open door, as if concerned prying ears would overhear. "The scandal, and the financial cost, will be immense. However, she's gone too far this time. Gina has placed her life, and our son's, in danger, and that I cannot allow. Marat is a vile man. I am very aware of his activities, and every dime that backs those endeavors."

"I could not agree with you more. You're wise to make this move. I only worry…" Rachel bit her lip. "I worry that your wife may be too involved. She may not have a choice in how she proceeds with Marat. I would look to your bank's interests, Mr. Murray, because I have no doubt that is the reason Marat is involved with your wife."

"He isn't the only one with connections, Ms. Harris." Jaw clenching, William gazed out the door again before sighing. "Warren is…he and his mother are at odds, I'm afraid. She's a selfish woman, and over the years, she's hardened, though I've never understood why. She seeks out equally hard men to do whatever it is she needs to fulfill her dark heart and equally dark desires." He shivered. "I no longer wish to play her games."

His cheeks had pinked, so she averted her gaze.

"She may be willing to destroy her own life, but she's hurting my son with her flagrant behavior while expecting him to fall in line and keep the family secrets, as she once did." William wiped a hand over his mouth. "Warren is his own man. His own person. But, I am his father, and my duty will always be to protect him and lead him into his future in the most secure way possible."

His convictions created a wave of sadness. Why hadn't her own father felt the same? Why had he abandoned her to her guilt and shame? And because of this, she was letting a man who could, and would, care for her slip through her fingers. Spencer was right. She did have her head up her ass. "Bronco is very lucky to have you as a father."

William smiled, a glimpse of the proud father shining through. "Thank you. I'd like to think so, too." He crossed his legs, relaxing and settling in for the moment. "What about you, Ms. Harris? Are you close to your parents?"

She refrained from answering that, no, she wasn't close to anyone and hadn't been since she'd let her brother slip away. Nor that her parents divorced because neither could handle the guilt of blaming her for the whole thing.

Though aware her response would seem rude, especially after he'd revealed portions of his life that he likely wouldn't share with another, Rachel still couldn't delve into her horrific childhood. Standing and shuffling some papers on her desk, she glanced at the clock. "Mr. Murray, I actually have an appointment with your son." She tapped a few papers against her palm. "Right now, in fact." Then to soften the dismissal, she rounded the desk and held out her hand. "I appreciate your stopping by. I'll take your words to heart, and my apologies for the…well, for your divorce."

"I hope to see you again, Ms. Harris." William stood and shook her hand. "If there is anything I can do to aid in Thomas Northman's investigation, or any other matter, I hope you'll contact me." He handed over a crisp silver business card.

Stopping at the door, he tapped the frame with the side of his fist before glancing back. "And you don't need to apologize for anything, dear. My mistakes are my own." He shot her a salute and then headed down the hall.

Wiping the absolutely-over-emotional tears from her cheeks, Rachel watched Bronco's father until he entered the elevator and the doors slid shut. "You're very wrong, Mr. William Murray. I have every reason to apologize, because my mistakes are my own, as well."

CHAPTER 20

Nerves buzzing, Rachel knocked on Bronco's apartment door. After stewing over her tête-à-tête with his father, she believed she owed Bronco a mammoth apology. He hadn't deserved her cavalier attitude the other night. The fact that he'd even buzzed her in at all seemed a good sign. Though she'd indicated she had news about his case, which wasn't exactly true, but if the lie got her in the door, she'd roll with it.

Her heart skipped a beat when he opened the door bare-chested.

Then he quickly slid a T-shirt over his muscular expanse. His feet were bare, and he wore a pair of green shorts with a faded Marauders logo.

Just what had she interrupted? If she found a woman in his apartment, though she had no right to do so, she'd rip that chick's hair from her roots. With a twinge of hesitation, she stepped past the threshold and looked around, hands clenching into fists.

He turned his back on her, though immediately his ingrained good manners took over, and he glanced over his shoulder. "Can I get you something to drink?"

"Sure, just a Coke or whatever." And a baseball bat to injure whomever else was in the apartment. "Did I come at a bad time?"

He raised a brow then shook his head as he continued into

the kitchen. "I've got diet Dr. Pepper. Would you like a glass with ice or will the can do?"

She chewed on the inside of her bottom lip, undone by his I-wouldn't-save you-from-a-burning-fire tone. "So, we're doing formal?"

"We are." Bronco popped open the soda can and handed it to her. "That's what you want."

"Nice place." Rachel walked around his spacious living room lined with a huge couch in a rustic brown color and a camouflage recliner off to the side. The décor had a decidedly cabin-like feeling, as if he'd trapped a little of the forest and plopped it in the middle of the surrounding steel buildings. "Warm room, like a cabin in the mountains, not what I expected in a downtown high-rise."

"Do you have word on my father's case? If not, I've got other places to be." He remained by the kitchen counter, pouring himself a tall glass of water from a Brita pitcher.

His blatant dismissal was the last straw. He mattered, even if they could only be friends. He had carved a place in her life and because of that he deserved an explanation and an apology. "All right, all right. Listen, I'm sorry, okay? I didn't...I'm not wired so well. I don't let people...close." She flicked her hands at her sides, expelling energy, emotion, whatever, to get through this reveal. "I don't like people crowding my personal space or thinking I owe them explanations for the way I've chosen to live my life."

"Yeah, I got that." He finished his drink in one swallow, and then tapped his temple. "Sharp as a tack."

"I don't want this between us." She waved between them and then rested her hands on top of his recliner. "This animosity."

"Neither did I."

"You're right. This current...situation is all my fault." She leaned against the chair, studied her shoes for a moment then took a deep breath and met his gaze. "I'm very, very sorry. The other night, you were being a friend, and I acted like a jerk."

Both hands braced on the countertop, he nodded. "More like a complete bi—"

"Okay, yes I was a bitch. I turn on bitch-mode when people haul me around and expect...things. When I can't handle how I'm feeling."

"I suggest you tone down that meter from now on, because I will continue to expect things. Whether we remain as lovers or not, we *are* friends, so cut the crap. I deserved a call."

"You deserved a call."

"Thank you."

"You have no idea how hard those four words were to admit." With her fist, she tapped the recliner's padded headrest.

"I have some idea." He winked and then chuckled.

"Changing the subject now." Rachel ignored his laughter at her expense. "Honestly, I think the shots were an attempt to scare me off."

"Of what?" Bronco rounded the kitchen island and leaned against the counter, mirroring her stance.

"My surveillance of Khlebosolny. Even after using two different vehicles, I got caught." She shrugged and placed her drink on a side table. "So, I'll lay low for a while."

"I think that would be a wise choice." Bronco folded both arms across his massive chest, his biceps defined by his tight T-shirt. "Anything else?"

"Your dad came to see me." Worried if she stood across from him much longer, she'd leap into his arms, Rachel kicked off her shoes, moved around the chair, and sank onto the couch.

"My father." Bronco ran a hand over his stubble-covered chin. "Why?"

"He wants answers."

"Don't we all?" He tossed a throw pillow covered with a bull moose onto the floor then settled in the opposite corner of the couch.

Still so far away—physically and emotionally. "Yes, Bronco

we do want answers. Even I want answers."

"What answers do you need, Rachel?"

And there it was again, that kindness, that openness, that willingness to let her express everything and stay by her side as she revealed all.

So she would.

She plucked the pillow off the floor, and traced the stitched pattern with her finger. "I see so much every day. Duplicity, pain, loss." And because he deserved more, because he was her friend, he was owed something deep. Something that hurt. He needed to understand why she pushed, why she just couldn't open her heart, even though she wished otherwise. "I do like you. I do, even though I'd prefer not to have all these feelings." Frowning, she fluttered her fingers by her chest. "I hate that I hurt you. How can I love someone when I don't know how to love...me?" She tapped a finger against her breastbone. "Or love anyone else for that matter? Is there some guidebook that explains love? Some way I can understand?" Bending forward, she braced her elbows on the pillow. "How do I express love? Because I don't know how, and until I do, I can't keep hurting you. You can't expect things from me, because I literally don't know how to show my feelings other than through sex. But that can't be all." She closed her eyes and sighed. "Sex can't be all. I know that."

"No, that can't be all. And I want it all." Bronco rested his arm along the back of the couch.

"Who says shit like that?" Rachel shot up and glared. "And why does it hurt when you do." She rubbed her temples. "I don't know what this is between us. I don't know relationships. My parents divorced when I was young, like nine or so. My mother and I, well our relationship is non-existent." Rachel raked her fingers through her hair. "She blames me for...something that happened. She can't forgive me, and I can't forgive myself."

"For what?" Reaching across the couch, Bronco drew her closer and massaged the back of her neck.

"Damn, that feels good." She leaned forward and flicked a finger along the binding of the HP Lovecraft and RW Hardcastle books on the table, holding back a secretive smile.

He lightly squeezed her shoulder. "For what, Rach?"

"My brother."

"You have a brother." He stopped his massage. "Wait, why haven't you mentioned this before? I mean I've grasped your unwillingness to discuss your parents but a brother?"

"Because...I-I had a brother, but I lost him."

Bronco was quiet for a moment, resuming his gentle caress up and down her back. "I'm sorry, when did he die?"

Overwhelmed by his touch, Rachel barely refrained from climbing into his lap. "He didn't, or at least...I don't know what happened."

"I'm confused. Family matters aren't really in my realm of understanding these days."

"My brother and I were at the park near the—"

Bronco's door intercom buzzed.

"Hold that thought." Bronco stalked to door and pressed the button on the high-tech security panel. "Yes."

"Mr. Murray." The doorman's voice came across. "Your mother is here to see you."

"Fine, send her up." Bronco slammed the wall with the palm of his hand. "Damn it. I told her I needed time."

A few moments later, a soft tap sounded on the door.

Heaving a sigh, Bronco opened the door then turned back toward the couch. "Hello, Mother."

Gina stepped into the room, sliding out of her trench coat and shaking it a little before draping it over her arm. "A bit of a late spring drizzle outside." The click of her heels across the tiled entryway came to a sudden stop. "Why is she here?" She directed her gaze at Bronco and then turned to glare at Rachel. "I told you to stop investigating."

Standing, while mentally rebuilding her emotional shields,

Rachel shrugged. "I'm not inclined to listen."

"I know who you are, and I suggest you back off." His mother padded closer, shaking her finger.

Rachel raised a brow over an action that treated her like a bad dog that hadn't yet learned to behave.

"This is a family matter. We'll work this out on our own."

"Mom, enough. Rachel is a friend." Bronco stepped between them. "I don't understand why you are here anyway. I told you I needed time."

"Rumors are already spreading." His mother rubbed her temple. "Your father's contacted a lawyer. He's divorcing me. My life is ruined."

"Ruined how?" Bronco leaned against the wooden table set behind his couch. "You've got everything. Now you're free to continue your activities with other men. Let Father go."

"We are a unit. A team. Everything was fine until you started digging."

Her blonde hair glinted under Bronco's recessed ceiling lights. A vision that on the surface appeared beautiful, but the farther you were drawn in, the more you saw the truth beneath.

Knowing Bronco needed her support, Rachel stood by his side.

"Don't blame your marital problems on me." Bronco's fisted his hands at his sides. "You created this situation with your infidelities, now you have to suffer the consequences. He truly cared for you and you played him for a fool."

"You think your father didn't have his own dalliances throughout the years."

Bronco huffed out a half-laugh, half-scoff. "I doubt any involved known criminals." He slashed a hand between them. "I won't do the whole choose between Mommy and Daddy crap. I'm not five, Mother." He rubbed two fingers against his temple. "Right now all I care about is learning more about my real father and whether or not he was murdered."

"Why? Why should any of that matter now?" His mother paced in the open entryway. "You have suffered nothing, you had a perfect childhood and life."

"Suffered nothing?" Obviously losing his cool, Bronco shouted his response. "I don't know who I am."

His mother clutched his shoulders. "You are Warren Murray." Her gaze was intense. Her declaration clear and concise.

"Mother, I need you to leave." Bronco shook her off. "Rachel and I...we were in the middle of an important discussion."

Gina sneered at her. "Just so you know, dear. He's meant for someone else."

"Mother, worry about your own love life, not mine," Bronco growled. "I think you should go, but know this, I won't stop searching for answers about Thomas Northman. You can either help or continue to get in the way. Either way, Rachel and I are doing this."

"Sunk your claws in deep have you?" His mother sniffed, and grabbed her coat from the chair.

Rachel made a show of looking at her nails, but remained silent, refusing to enter the argument. Some people she couldn't win against. His mother had her own rules for life, built on a social strata Rachel cared nothing about.

Bronco braced one hand against his mother's shoulder. "Leave her out of this."

"She's chosen to step in and I'll make sure she loses." Tossing that final volley, his mother exited, slamming shut the door.

Bronco stared at the door for a moment, then returned to the couch. Elbows on his knees, he buried his face in his hands.

Rachel hesitated before sitting beside him and taking his hand. "I'm sorry you have to go through all this."

He nodded, lifted her onto his lap, and then wrapped her in his arms.

Breathing in his scent, she wished she could also inhale some of his pain. Offer him a moment of solace. She could shuffle her hand lower, and massage the very hard erection she felt against her thigh, but she'd been down that road, and returning to that path wasn't wise. So, she'd just sit still for however long he needed.

Earning this man's trust and friendship seemed critical. Staying in the current position forever would be no hardship, and what did that mean? His overbearing nature would stifle her, meaning they'd never work long term. Not only that, she had a dangerous fight to finish. A struggle that overshadowed and ruined her every relationship. Her heart remained buried in too many layers of guilt. "I'm sorry you're hurting, Bronco." Rachel whispered against his neck. "I'm here for you and I *will* help find your answers."

If she could offer nothing else, at least she could use her professional skills to provide some sense of closure, and she would, no matter how long the investigation took. "We'll work this out together. I'm queen of the long haul. My life-long preoccupation into my brother's disappearance is proof."

"I'm sorry for you, too, Rachel." Bronco gave her a squeeze and kissed her cheek. "I'll help you, too."

Oh dear God, in the middle of everything, after all she'd said, how could he offer support? Suddenly, everything became very clear. This moment, this man defined...love. His kindness, his open heart, his willingness to forgive, his open arms—all added up to that four-letter word. While comfortable with all kinds of four-letters words, this one had, until this moment, remained elusive, but now a glimpse of what true love could mean exuded as heat from Bronco's body. The sweet smell of his skin had already drilled deep and filled her empty heart with an enticing aroma like evergreens mixed with fresh spring air. Obviously, his cabin decor had invaded her senses.

Though she fought the change, she felt a faint heat, a soft

pink glow emitting from the bottom tip of her black heart. These fanciful imaginings of a multi-colored heart weren't welcome in the least, but all the same they existed in a coloring book in her mind. All because of his strong hold on her body and the sincere words from his lips.

Out of every close scrape, every bullet fired, every crazed criminal, and indignant adulterer nothing in all those moments scared her more than her current position. In the depths of her heart, she knew this man did love her. So why couldn't she just fall with him?

She squeezed his burly body and mentally asked for forgiveness for the hurt she knew she'd inflict again. His heat soaked through her chilled skin, deep into her equally chilled, faintly-pinkened heart. He couldn't proceed in this relationship alone. She had a choice to make, and Lord knew her record in that sphere.

Rachel Harris—0.

Life—too many dark marks to count.

But maybe, just maybe with his strength on her side, she could win, just once.

Just once.

CHAPTER 21

Though swarmed by second thoughts over letting Rachel back in—into his apartment and his heart—Bronco felt they'd made progress. She'd stayed for dinner, and after watching TV, she'd fallen asleep on the couch.

So small, bundled in his soft, green blanket, like a pea in a pod.

He'd been done. Through. Over.

But, she'd come back. Apologized. Explained.

So, that action meant something, and he couldn't deny he still wanted her. Wanted to fix all her problems. Help her understand loyalty, commitment, and love. But they both had complications to surmount. His life was a mess.

She was a mess.

Did he really think he could assist anyone right now?

Rachel flipped onto her side. Even in sleep, she seemed restless. She'd been quiet after his mother left. If they'd spoken at all, they'd discussed the TV show. He'd mostly read while she watched, though she'd pestered him multiple times over what he thought of Hardcastle's latest story until he'd given up and shoved his napkin in the book to hold his place.

Eyelids drooping, he turned off the lights and moved to his recliner. He pushed the button to elevate his legs, and after getting the setting just right, closed his eyes. Rachel may believe they had taken steps back in their relationship, but the truth was, her coming here revealing truths about her feelings and her past, those actions led them further down the path. He'd stay beside her even if she broke his heart, because wasn't she worth the pain since she was the first girl who could ever rip him in two?

His cell phone rang and half asleep, he jolted to attention.

Worrying about the call waking Rachel, Bronco shot out of the recliner and answered. He glanced at the caller ID and noted the late night call came from his father. "Dad? What's wrong?"

"Hello, son."

No one started a 3:00 a.m. phone call in that tone if things were good. How much more could he take? "Dad, what is it?" Bronco's stomach churned and his heart slowed, as if preparing to go wild once his father revealed his purpose for calling.

"Warren, I'm afraid your Grandmother passed this evening."

"What?" He braced a hand against the wall. "When?" This was so much worse than he'd imagined. "You sure?"

"I'll come by your place after I take care of the details, all right?"

"But when?" He glanced around the kitchen for his wallet and keys.

"Son, I'm on my way to Oak Meadows now. I'll take care of everything."

"I'm sorry. I'm confused. How did this happen?"

His father paused for a moment. "They're saying natural causes."

"No." Bronco pounded a fist against the counter. "That makes no sense. What are the doctors saying?"

"I'm headed to speak to them now."

"Where's Mom?"

"Already there."

"I'm coming too."

"Not necessary." His father's sigh came across loud and

clear. "Warren, I don't know what I'm walking into, and I really don't want you to see your Grandmother in such a state. I'm worried about you...Right now isn't a good time for you to experience such a thing. You're dealing with enough."

"This whole *thing* is wrong." Bronco stormed into his bedroom, whipped open his closet door, and yanked a pair of jeans off the plastic hanger. "She couldn't just die. This makes no sense."

"People die, Warren. And your grandmother was—"

"No. I'll be there as soon as I can." Bronco hung up, quickly buttoning his jeans.

His phone immediately rang again, but he didn't pick up. No way his grandmother who was fine a few days ago, had just died unexpectedly. Though he hadn't heard her enter, he felt Rachel tug on his hand, all ruffled hair and heavy-lidded eyes.

"I overheard the tail end of your conversation. Who died?"

"My grandmother."

Her brown eyes flared. "How?"

"I hadn't been back to see her. I should have gone." He paced to the door then shot back again when he realized he needed socks. "She was fine physically. Mentally not so much, but...this doesn't add up."

"Don't do that." She leaned against his bed. "You can't make this more than it is."

Bronco sank onto the bed beside her, studying the socks in his hand. "I-I didn't...I didn't mean to upset her."

"Bronco, none of this is your fault." Rachel sank to her knees before him, grabbed his socks, and worked them over his feet. "Her death is just the natural order of things."

He studied the top of her head. A single lock of oddly angled hair stuck straight up. Once again, she was here for him, at his side when his world crashed around him. Though he knew he should be the one offering comfort, remaining strong, just knowing this solid woman stood at his side made him a better man. A complete man. "Will you drive? I…I don't think I can."

"Of course." Rachel nodded and stood. "Take my hand, Warren."

Somehow, he knew if he took her hand, if he clasped her pixie fingers in his, he'd be locked down forever. But wasn't he there already?

So, why fight their connection? He brought her fingers to his lips and kissed each knuckle. Then after hearing her breath hitch, he smiled and firmly took her hand, locking her fingers with his.

On their way to the parking garage, he slipped his phone from his pocket and dialed Tash.

She picked up after the first ring.

"Tash, what happened?"

"Whole lot a hinky up in here, Bronco. Whole lot a hinky."

CHAPTER 22

Executions, assassinations, so many ways to kill and over the years, Erik had learned painful, silent, bloody, and quick methods.

Marat's clear insubordination could not go unpunished, no matter what Erik had said to the marshals. Between leading his father's brigade and working for the marshals, Erik played a very dangerous game, one that frequently had him choosing sides. Tonight, in order to achieve his long-term goals, he'd stepped up to the plate and swung. Hard.

His hands would carry the blood of the men who would die. Maybe not tonight but soon.

Speaking of blood…he sighed as he studied his red, bruised knuckles, the remnants of his question-and-answer session with a man who felt hiding Marat's secrets was acceptable.

He had his plans and wouldn't allow Marat's side businesses to interfere or draw attention. After a few hours of serious physical influence against some key traitors, he now knew who was on his side, and who was on Marat's.

His next move would be a quick sweep of the filth that now soiled his organization. He'd have to perform a clean sweep. Messy, certainly, but necessary. He couldn't appear weak.

His brigade no longer ran women or drugs. Occasionally, they'd negotiate a weapons trade, but for the most part, they operated in conjunction with the world's most powerful banks. They held a gun to the head of those fixing the prices on adjustable-rate options like mortgages, credit cards, and interest-rate swaps. Peg the right finance guy and he could run a bid scam, and keep his interests masked behind percentage and points verbiage and half-laws any shrewdly-malicious broker could manipulate.

Wall Street held the real money.

Plus after watching what his mother had gone through, he'd made a promise never to deal in trafficking again.

Marat had crossed the final line by building his own empire.

Erik would take great pleasure in knocking down every brick.

No pity.

And certainly no regret.

CHAPTER 23

Three days after a nightmare visit to Oak Meadows with Bronco, Rachel's heart still ached over the single tear she'd watch fall down his cheek as he'd held his father. Poor fella had been through entirely too much emotional trauma lately. She appreciated he wasn't one of those guys who believed they were too cool to cry.

Now on her way to the after-funeral reception at the Murray's home, Rachel sat in the back seat of Owen's car. With a curse, she tugged her dress hem over her knees. This little black dress was over four years old, but still fit her perfectly and only came out for occasions like this. She had, however, dragged Ember along on her hunt for a new pair of sweet black heels.

"How's Bronco holding up?" From the passenger seat, Ember nudged Owen.

After sitting in the church for hours and then the grave site, Rachel was more than ready to lounge. She'd seen the Murray's outdoor pool and pool house on her last visit. Perhaps she'd find a lounger and prop up her blistered feet. New shoes were tough to break-in. Maybe not such a wise purchase after all. She glanced at her 4-inch heels. *Nah, perfect idea.*

The whole Marauders team had arrived in support of their fellow player. They'd all clapped Bronco on the back, and were uber-polite to his parents. Their sharp suits perfectly appropriate for the Murray family's high-dollar crowd, although most of the players also wore a splash of color, which livened up the event.

Arriving at the palatial ridiculousness where Bronco had grown up, Rachel hopped down and took Owen's proffered arm. She hadn't listened to Owen's response to Ember, too lost in her own thoughts, but now she wished she had. Owen had an inside track on Bronco's emotions that she hadn't achieved yet. Though, over a smattering of calls during the past couple of days, Bronco had said he was handling his grandmother's death. But how true was that?

Waiting a moment outside as well-wishers piled in, Rachel watched the steady stream of Manchester's social elite park cars that cost more than most people spent on a house.

In the entryway, Bronco greeted them, and then took her arm and drew her close. "Come with me for a moment."

"Bronco, where are you going?" His mother maintained her plastered-on smile, but glared at her wayward son. "Young lady, I will not allow you to carry him off. He will stand beside his family during this time of grief."

"Mother, I have stood beside you all day. Right now, I need a moment with my friend. So, you'll excuse me."

A bit of a stare down occurred before William cleared his throat. "Gina, you're holding up the line, dear."

"I suggest you keep it short." Gina snapped.

Bronco pulled her into a corner of the living room, smiling at everyone along the way. He blocked her view with his suit-clad body.

Mr. O-liner filled out a suit quite nicely.

"What's going on?" Bronco jabbed a finger against her shoulder.

"First off, ow!" She slapped his hand before rubbing the point of impact. "Second, what do you mean?" Rachel furrowed her brow. "I'm handling things on my end, following up on the list of names you gave me." She patted his clean-shaven cheek. "You need to deal with your grandmother's death."

"Finding answers *is* how I'll deal." He rubbed his temple. "Something's not right, and you know it."

"Maybe." In her own contemplations of his case, she worried his words were very true, and that he could be in danger. What if his grandmother hadn't died of natural causes? What if they were getting too close to finding out the truth about Thomas Northman's murder? Her hound dog nature knew this latest death only added to the scent and drew them closer to the real killer. "Listen, I'm still working to find answers, okay?" She punched his shoulder, just to keep things casual and him unaware of her concerns. "I plan on visiting a few people this week."

"I'm going with you." Bronco nodded.

Even though she felt like a jerk for arguing on the day he'd put his beloved grandmother in the ground, she still shook her head. "No."

"Yes."

"This thing with your grandmother…if you're right, it's dangerous." Rachel finally gave up sheltering the stubborn beast. Maybe common sense, or fear for his life, would crack his shell. "I don't believe in coincidences, either," she whispered, glancing around at the other occupants to assure herself no one could overhear. "Right now, I can't prove otherwise, but still…"

"Who are you interviewing?"

"Northman's sister."

Bronco's eyes widened, and he took a deep breath. "I didn't even consider he still had family." He clasped her shoulder.

His heavy hand against her body may help him remain standing, but what he didn't know was he'd likely topple her over, because these heels were killing her feet.

"I'm going with you, Harris. Don't leave me out of this, please."

On the verge of agreeing based on his simple please and the

look in his clear blue eyes, Rachel opened her mouth to answer, but was struck stupid when she glanced at a slender, tall, gorgeous blonde approaching.

So this was Heather.

"We'll discuss this later." Rachel squeezed his arm. "See to your guests." She nodded at the blonde.

Bronco growled, but followed her gaze, and then released her arm. "I am going, Rachel, and you will agree. Later."

# # #

Bronco watched Rachel go before turning to face Heather—figuratively and literally. The day's events were already chafing him raw, so he might as well get this deserved hardship over with, too.

Heather smiled, and then she turned to glance at Rachel's retreating back. "Who is she?"

"Tiny nightmare." Though unfair, he noted the contrast of Heather's tan skin to Rachel's pale hue, along with other subtle differences, like...well...basically everything. "I see you got some sun." He clasped her hands, leaned down, and kissed her cheek.

"No, you're not changing the subject, regardless of any sympathy I should offer today. I am very sorry, by the way." Heather kissed his lips, holding there for a moment before pulling away. "Ah...I see. So, it finally happened, did it?"

"What finally happened?" *Damn.* She knew him too well. Knew his evasions. Hadn't they both been dealing with his lack of clarity for far too many years?

"Hurts doesn't it?"

"At times, yes." He took Heather's hand and met her gaze, a few shades darker than his own. "I'm sorry."

She shrugged. "I knew. Still, let's not do this today."

Bronco wrapped her in his arms and kissed her forehead. "I'm still very sorry."

"I had fun while it lasted."

He couldn't hold back his knowing smile, because in truth, they had spent many great nights together, in friendship, and as more sometimes, too. Yet, each moment was filled with respect and care for one another.

Shaking her head at his smile, she took his hand. "Are you truly okay?"

"No." He huffed out a growl.

"I know Mrs. Astor meant a great deal to you, and I'm sorry for your loss. Seemed a bit sudden, yes?"

"Too sudden. I don't know what to think." His head ached like nothing he'd ever felt before, even after rattling around in a helmet for hours.

Heather nodded then glanced at the line of people pouring in. "We'll do lunch. I must tell you about my trip. You'll be positively envious."

Again, he kissed her forehead. "Believe me, an escape would be a blessing right now."

Though a tiny frown marred her perfect face, she nodded. "Let's talk later. I'll leave you to it."

He watched her work her way through the crowd and considered how she'd make some senator a perfect wife, someday. He'd always loved her, but not in a passionate sense. More of a familiar, comfy blanket sort of way, and wouldn't Heather just love being compared to a worn blanket? He kept his amusement over that revelation to himself.

After another hour in the greeting line, Bronco spotted Maude walking up with a drink locked in her elbow and one in her hand.

She bumped his shoulder. "Jason wants to talk to you." She handed over her phone and an ice cold Dr. Pepper.

"Couldn't make it back, man. I'm sorry."

"S'okay."

"You good."

"I'm here."

"All right. See you in a few weeks."

"Yep."

"We'll pound it out then."

"Sure." He hung up and handed Maude her phone, catching her in a dramatic eye-roll.

"What?"

"Men." She shook her red-brown hair. "Such communicators."

Bronco grinned and locked her in a headlock. "Thanks for being here today, Maudy. Where's Rachel?"

"They're all out by the pool." She combed down her ruffled hair. "Rachel said she needed some fresh air after being cooped up all day."

"Thanks" He tipped his soda in her direction before drinking the entire contents. Done with standing in the reception line, Bronco tapped his dad's shoulder. "I'm going outside."

His father gripped him in one-armed embrace. "All right, Son."

Ignoring his mother's glare, Bronco dropped his arm around Maude's shoulders and went in search of his people. Glancing around the pool, he caught sight of Rachel sitting with Ember, so he maneuvered Maude through well-wishers offering words of sympathy.

Rachel's short, but fit, legs were crossed on the lounger, and he noted the hot pink polish on her toes. Somehow, pink and his woman didn't add up, but then again, his pixie had layers he'd yet to uncover. Glancing at the high heels alongside her chair, he considered how she'd looked uncovered, with nothing but those shoes on her feet and her legs wrapped around his shoulders.

After chatting with Owen for a few minutes, he pulled Rachel from her chair and led her to the pool house.

"Ow, slow down. My feet are covered in blisters."

"My Aunt Bertha moves faster than you. Get a move on,

woman." He glanced over his shoulder before shoving open the door. Tugging at his collar, he undid his tie. "Why are you drinking coffee? It's a sauna out there. Muggy."

"I'm tired. I've been doing some late-night surveillance. Your dad made this for me using his special beans."

"Must be special, if he did that for you."

Rachel took a sip and hummed with pleasure. "Best coffee I've ever had."

"We Murray men know how to please a woman." Bronco pulled her onto the wicker couch and settled her on his lap. "Means a lot that you're here today."

"Why are we in here?" She waved at the pool hut.

"I needed to be alone."

"Hello." She waved a hand at herself.

"Alone with you." He scrubbed both hands in his hair. "I get that everyone wants to be seen and express their condolences, but I needed a break from all the limp hands and fake smiles."

"Everybody seems pretty nice. But I know what you mean. When I go to my uncle's firm's cocktail parties, I squirm under the pressure to chitchat. I'm impossible at it."

Bronco ran his hand up and down her back. "You're good at other things."

"Speaking of that, allow me to wrap up your father's case. Alone. You will be safer that way."

No," he murmured in her ear. "I want to be a part of the investigation."

She shivered. "This isn't like those suspense books you read. You could get hurt."

"So could you." He held her away, met her gaze, and then trailed a finger down her cheek. "Today hurts, Rachel. Yesterday hurt, hell, this whole past month I've been in a world of hurt, but if anything ever happened to you, that'd be beyond pain." He lightly kissed her lips. "I need to be a part of this. I've been left out of so much already."

"You're confused." She shook her head. "Looking for something to hold onto. Life is chaotic. I'm a stopgap, a provider of answers. What you think you want and my true place in your life are two very different things."

"No."

"No? You seem to like that word today." She frowned and squirmed in his lap.

"No." He chuckled, and then kissed her long and sweet. Taking his time, he set out to prove that when they were together life wasn't chaotic, and he wasn't confused. Once he had her laying pliant in his arms, he believed he'd made his point.

He pulled back from the kiss and just held her. "Whether you realize this or not, you're here. Always. You come when I need you and that means something. I know what that something is, and I'll wait until you do, too."

"Warren, I really—"

He silenced her with another kiss, because whether he'd admit this to himself, her, or anyone outside of this building, his world was spinning out of control. But, when he had her in his arms, everything stopped.

And he sure the hell needed this ride to end before somebody else got hurt.

CHAPTER 24

Fishing around in her second bag of fruit snacks, Rachel found the last orange one and popped it into her mouth. Not a good dinner, but after Bronco's grandmother's funeral yesterday, her stomach was off.

For the past five days, she'd donned a variety of disguises and borrowed cars to follow Nestor Marat, and she'd discovered a home where he trafficked young girls. The last girl, who looked barely seven, had been the last straw. Time to put a stop to this operation and damn the consequences.

Earlier this week, she'd spied Bronco's mother entering a ritzy hotel and leaving less than an hour later, mascara streaking, clothes in disarray, and her hair down instead of up. Nestor had followed her out, but Gina had slapped his face. That was one sight Rachel would leave out of Bronco's report.

No, she'd not think of him. Right now she must remove all thought of a future with that vibrant man, because she'd likely die tonight.

In her passenger seat, her backpack was laden with equipment purchased through back channels. She checked the mag in her 9mm, shoved the gun into her shoulder holster, and then yanked her sweatshirt hood over her head. Hopping out of the car, she checked the perimeter before jogging to the house next door to Nestor's horror shack.

Yesterday, she'd made a trial run, stashing the heavier equipment in an upstairs closet. The older woman who lived in the house was basically deaf, which Rachel had used to her advantage while setting up this sneak attack.

Shoring up her nerves by thinking about that young girl's terrified face, not to mention the nightmares that had likely been visited upon her own brother, Rachel jimmied open the back window after spraying the frame liberally with W-D 40. Once inside, she closed the window again.

The strains of an old country tune wafted from the kitchen as she tiptoed up the stairs and entered the empty bedroom, which had a window overlooking Nestor's house. The lights were on next door, though the shades were drawn. Knowing what vile, disgusting horrors the children and teens inside were likely enduring, even now, kept her on track.

As an extra precaution, Rachel slid her phone from her dark jeans and texted Clayton the address and a brief explanation of her plans before silencing her phone. Now that she'd notified him, she knew time was of the essence.

Adrenaline pumped as she crept to the closet and slid out the black battery box, equipped with an antenna, and a few other blue tubes along the top. Her electromagnetic pulse generator had set her back six grand, but if she saved one girl's life tonight, the expense was worth every penny. Hands shaking, she pointed the antennae end toward Marat's house, said a quick prayer, and flipped the switch.

Quiet ensued.

No more country tunes warbled up the stairs about lost love and drinking beer in pick-up trucks. Rachel glanced out the window, hoping the device was successful in disabling Marat's security cameras, alarms, and other electronic devices.

Cognizant Clayton could arrive at any moment, she scurried back down the stairs, pulling from her backpack her M203 launcher loaded with a smoke bomb. Racing around the outside of Marat's house, she launched smoke grenades through the windows, frantically reloading as she ran toward the back door.

Damn this thing was heavy.

She plastered herself against the side of the house as customers, merchants…filthy disgusting perverts streamed out, coughing and wiping their eyes. Donning her mask, she plowed past them and dashed through the open back door.

An older girl dressed in a stained white T-shirt grabbed her arm. "You must leave."

"Where are the little girls?" Rachel shook her shoulders. "Where does he keep them?" Breathing heavily within her mask, she ignored the shouts, pounding feet, and all-too-real fear she'd be discovered before saving anyone.

"They kill you." The girl's arms were lined with puffy red track marks, and she swayed on her feet.

Rachel grabbed her by the elbow and forced her outside. The lawn now crowded with men bent over and coughing due to the smoke, though most stumbled and lunged for their vehicles. Sirens wailed in the distance, but much clearer, and much more immediate, Marat's shouts rose over the din.

Pulling her 9mm from her shoulder holster, she scrambled inside again, tossing another smoke bomb ahead of her. Her breathing remained ragged inside her mask. She paused, leaning on the entryway's stair banister. *Calm down, Harris. Just breathe.*

Taking the stairs two at a time, she ducked in a doorway when she came upon a group of men in the upper hallway. Smoke swirled, distorting their features, and they coughed and wheezed as the smoke bombs delivered their payload. Taking advantage of the low visibility, Rachel opened and stepped inside the closest door.

A tiny girl with golden red-blonde curls sat on the bed, coughing and crying. An older girl stood beside her, stroking her arm, but upon noticing Rachel, the girl started shouting in Russian and flailing her arms.

"No." Rachel shook her head before realizing she still wore her mask. No wonder they were frightened. She whipped it off. "Friend." She pointed a finger against her chest.

Because the older girl continued her way-too-loud litany, she gave Rachel no choice but to knock her out. Rachel swept the hysterical child into her arms. "I'm here to take you home." She patted the girl's shoulder. Bony, suffering from malnutrition, and who knew what else, the girl's entire body shook. So very small and weak against the men who would destroy her innocence. "Don't be scared. I'm a friend."

Eyes wide and spent tears streaking her cheeks, the little girl met her gaze, and then lifted her threadbare pajamas to wipe her nose.

The action tore across Rachel's pounding heart. "No time for that now, little thing. We need to stay strong."

Shrieks from girls in the other rooms, slamming doors, and men yelling had the girl clutching Rachel in a death grip.

Struggling with the girl in her arms, Rachel inched closer to the door and opened it a crack.

A sneaky escape was no longer feasible as the smoke remained more of a filmy haze.

Two men hustled young frightened girls toward the stairway, and likely an escape vehicle.

Pressing a finger to her lips, she lowered the girl to the floor and whispered, "Stay here."

Though shaking in her thin white nightgown, the girl nodded.

Rachel slid through the open door and crept down the hallway.

The floor creaked.

Wincing, she stilled, but too late.

The men stopped their retreat, glanced over their shoulders, and then reached for their weapons.

Out of her mind with rage over the wrongs inflicted on so many young girls, she fired off round after round as she ducked for cover in a doorway. The percussion tore through her ears, temporarily deafening her.

Hearing only moans and curses, she blinked away the lingering smoke and opened the door behind her. Inside the bedroom, she detected two small heads peeping over the side of the bed: another young girl being comforted by a slightly older girl. Neither looked older than eleven. "Sick ass…" Curse words poured off Rachel's tongue as she grabbed them both by their arms and led them to the door. She peeked out into the hallway. The figure of a man flashed in the corner of her eye.

A well-dressed man.

Nestor Marat.

A stinging pain lanced through her thigh. "Damn assholes must have shot me." The front of her dark jeans pooled darker, and she detected a dirty copper smell mixing with gunfire and smoke. *To hell with it.* She was going out like Wyatt Earp at the OK Corral. Mouth dry, she mentally reiterated her purpose and resolve.

Marat had to end.

Tonight.

Disregarding pain and every reason to live, she took a chance and led the girls into the bedroom across the hall with the other little girl.

Police lights flashed blue and white across the walls. Sirens sang throughout the neighborhood. Clayton would arrive soon and halt her Q&A with the one man who held answers to her brother's disappearance. More than ready to die for the truth, she stepped into the hall to face Marat.

At the stop of the stairs, he stood beside a dark-haired man.

This man held one of the men she'd shot by his shirt and yelled in his face.

She lifted her gun. "Nestor Marat, I have some questions."

Marat spun in her direction, waving away the lingering smoke.

"Seventeen years ago, you took something from me." She cocked her gun. "At Millennium Park, 2:00 p.m. on Saturday, June 18, 1995. My brother, Erik Harris. I want to know where he is."

The dark-haired guy standing next to Marat dropped the man who'd been receiving his lecture and turned. "He's right here, Rachel."

Her whole world stopped, and she couldn't catch her breath.

A smiling boy with freckles and an infectious laugh.

No, a man. Brown hair, brown eyes.

A mirror of her father…of her.

This doppelgänger wore all black and pointed a gun at her chest while he strolled down the hallway.

"Oh my God, Erik?" She blinked, fighting to refocus as her world coalesced to a tiny pinprick featuring this man's face on the very tip. Lifting her hand to see if he was real, to touch him, she heaved in breath after breath.

"Idiot." With a shake of his head, he removed the gun from her limp hand.

Stunned by this vision from her past, Rachel didn't anticipate the right hook, but she certainly felt it.

Lights out.

CHAPTER 25

Sipping a second cup of his dad's special coffee, Bronco leaned against the kitchen sink and stared out the window of his parent's house, watching the landscapers prep the yard for summer. Planting flowers, trimming the bushes and grass. Normal things. Everyday things. Would he ever stare out the window of his own home? At a swing set? With his children laughing and bustling around his wife? Or see them sitting quietly in a lounge chair as his bride read them a book?

In his mind, Rachel starred quite clearly in that role. How much longer would she dismiss their connection as just friends comforting one another? She needed to trust him, he understood that, but the woman was driving him mad. Not only that, she hadn't returned his texts even though they were meant to confer about meeting Thomas Northman's sister today.

He'd stayed at the house this week to support his father. Plus he was still down over losing his grandmother and he needed to feel close to the family members he had left. Not to mention his fears his grandmother's death hadn't been due to natural causes. His mother refused to discuss anything further about Thomas Northman or Marat, which just about blew the lid off his top every time he thought of her unwillingness to provide answers. He'd been kind to her during the funeral, but he still felt awkward in her presence. He'd endure that though to be there for his dad.

After rinsing out his cup and placing it in the dishwasher, he heard raised voices coming from his father's study. Each word was a harsh beat against his thundering headache.

Tossing his half-eaten bagel in the fridge, he hastened to his father's study, halting in the doorway when he saw his father, his mother, and Joe Chogan.

Noting his father rubbing his temples, Bronco stepped across the room to stand at his side and tried to catch up on the heated conversation.

"I know a lot more than you think I do, Joe. Always have." His father stood behind his desk, raking a hand through his hair.

"You're making a mistake with this divorce." Chogan sat opposite the desk, holding Gina's hand. "And asking her to leave her home is equally deplorable."

"This white-knight persona you're wearing tarnished when you slept with my wife." Gaze cold, his father curled his lip in disdain. "And I must say, this continued devotion is a bit disturbing."

His mother sighed. "Joe and Claire have always been dear friends. What Joe and I shared ended years ago. Please, see reason, William. Divorce isn't the answer. We'll try counseling again."

"No. We won't."

"Her mother just died." Joe shook his head. "How can you abandon her at a time like this?"

His father huffed out a laugh. "I believe she's done quite fine by herself."

"I think you should leave, Joe." Bronco leaned against the desk. "And Mother, I agree counseling would be a good venue for you. Father and I have each other. We don't need other people"— he glanced at Joe—"telling us the basic tenets of common decency, which include not sleeping with your friend's husband or known gangsters."

"How dare you speak to your mother that way?" Joe shot out

of his chair, toppling it over. "You're just like your real father. Vile ruffian never comprehended the proper way to handle a true lady."

Bronco couldn't keep from dropping his jaw. "You knew my father?" Was this part of the puzzle? Did Chogan know who killed Thomas?

"He was a cocky jock, strutting around campus. Delving into a relationship with your mother without regard for the consequences." Joe flicked a hand in the air. "I'm glad he died. He was nothing but a *dumb* football player."

"You weasel!" Bronco rounded the desk and dove for Joe's throat. No other word could have pushed him over the edge quicker.

"No, Warren." Edging in front of him, his father grasped his arm. "Joe has been obsessed with your mother from the very beginning. Pay him no mind. He speaks only as a jealous ex-lover." William glanced at Chogan. "I want you out of this house. Warren will discover his own truths about his father. If anyone is dumb around here, it's you Chogan for thinking Gina would ever commit to you long-term. Have you forgotten your wife and children?"

"William, that's enough." His mother yanked a tissue from the box on the desk and dabbed her eyes. "You and Warren have always been a team. I've sat on the sidelines marveling at how that was possible when you aren't even his biological father. How could you be so close? Boys club the whole time. I was just the window dressing."

"You chose your position in this house."

His father's tone hit a level of lethal Bronco had never heard before.

"You left him to the nanny during his childhood. What did you expect?" William sighed. "Relationships take time and effort to develop."

"Come on, Gina." Joe pulled Warren's mother up from the

chair. "Let's get your things."

"I shouldn't have to move out." She remained standing by the desk. "This is my house. I did all the decorating and designing. I picked every detail." She jabbed a finger on his father's desk. "This house is mine and will be mine in the end."

His father shrugged and sipped from his coffee cup. "We'll discuss what's what with the lawyers very soon, dear."

"You're a fool, Murray." Joe chided. "She'd have been better off married to me."

"Whoa, Dad." This time Bronco held his father back, grasping him by his upper arms. "Don't. He's not worth it. The asshole will probably call the cops and charge you with battery."

"One shot?" His father growled.

Bronco loosened his hold.

His father kicked the padded leather chair out of the way. "You want a shot, Chogan?" He held his arms out at his sides. "Take it."

"This has been a long time coming." Joe hauled back and punched him in the face.

After accepting the blow, his father simply smiled and wiped the blood from his lip. "My turn." He punched Joe in the stomach before delivering an uppercut.

Joe tumbled over, bumping against the chair.

"What have you done?" Shooting her husband an icy-glare, his mother helped Joe to his feet, muttering obscenities the whole time she led Chogan to the door. She added an exclamation point to her displeasure by slamming the door hard enough to shake the frames on the wall. Gina Astor-Murray always got the last word.

Bronco clasped his father's shoulder, turned him, and then wrapped him in a bear hug.

"I wish you hadn't seen that." His father shivered, his skin clammy. "I'm so sorry, Son."

"Dad, you doing okay?" Bronco pulled back and studied his father. William's skin seemed pale and he kept licking his lips. "Do you have a fever?"

"I'm not sure." His father rubbed his temples. "I've had these headaches …but perhaps this thing with your mother…I'm not sure. Maybe I am a little heartbroken."

Bronco patted his dad's shoulder. "You'll get through this." Though, based on how ill his father looked, he wondered if maybe something more was wrong.

When his phone pinged with a text from Clayton, he jumped "Give me a sec." Pulling his cell phone from his back pocket, he read the message. After reading the unbelievable words, he stumbled backward, knocking over a side table.

Fine crystal crashed and splintered.

The smell of expensive scotch lit the air.

"Warren?" His father clutched his arm. "Warren, what is it?"

"Rachel's been shot."

CHAPTER 26

After driving at speeds likely illegal on Germany's Autobahn, Bronco whipped into the hospital parking lot, pulled into the first open spot, and then cursed as he got caught up in his seat belt. Finally free, he sprinted through Manchester General's Emergency Room doors.

Once inside, he bent over at the waist and heaved in a couple calming breaths.

Clayton shouted his name from the left.

Bronco spun on his heel and headed to where the detective waited by the ER entrance. "Where is she?" He barreled past Clayton and glanced around the desk and doctors, hearing moans and cries coming from various enclosures.

"She's asleep."

"I didn't ask that. I asked where she is."

"This way." Clayton jerked his head to the left then stepped down the hall before halting by a closed door.

His clothes emitted a smoky odor, as if he'd spent the night in a fireworks factory. He wore faded jeans and a white T-shirt with his gun holster strapped around his shoulder. His hair was in complete disarray, and if Bronco's wasn't mistaken, the detective had on two different shoes. "She's okay?"

"That's a loaded question."

Bronco nodded before entering the room. He'd find out what that comment meant later. Once inside the small space, he studied the still mound on the bed.

Rachel's left arm was attached to an IV bag, her left thigh wound tight with bandages, though blood's dark mark threatened to break through the binding. Seeing her so still and quiet drove him half insane. Her strong and capable persona silenced by a bullet. One shot that could have ended her life.

Lumbering to the metal chair beside the bed, Bronco sank down, rubbed his pounding temples, and glared at Clayton. "What happened?"

"Temporary insanity." The detective shook his head. "Your guess is as good as mine. Murray, come on, man, you were supposed to settle her down. Get all domestic and shit. But no, she's still unleashed, and now here we are." Clayton pulled the red-and-white swizzle stick from his coffee and chewed on it.

"I'd have better luck leashing a stray dog."

"You got that right." Clayton leaned on the end of the bed rail. "I got this text saying she's taking down Marat's trafficking house, and the address, plus an order to come quick."

"Wait. She texted you from the location?"

"Yeah."

Bronco held up a hand. "So, she was already there?"

"Yeah."

Cursing, Bronco shot out of his chair, which toppled over, hitting the floor with a clang.

"Believe me, I was just as pissed." Clayton ground down on his plastic stick. "We got there half an hour after her text and encountered total chaos. Girls running around in nightgowns, grown men fleeing down the street, smoke in the air. All the streetlights were out. Neighbors stood on their porches yelling about their TVs and cell phones not working." Shaking his head, Clayton huffed out a sigh and waved a hand at Rachel. "Gadget girl released an EMP. Not only that, she did this from the neighbor's house. So, along with an illegal weapons charge, I get to add breaking and entering. Not to mention trespassing. Then there's the pesky attempted murder charges." He heaved a sigh. "The list is so long, I'll run out of ink." Clayton combed his fingers through his dark brown hair. "If I'm here when she wakes up, I'm going to kick her ass then I'm arresting her."

"Who shot her?"

Clayton shrugged. "One of Marat's men must have hit her during the melee. I don't know how she got to the hospital either. She wasn't in the house once we gained access."

Pacing by the window, Bronco stopped and glanced at Clayton. "Did someone drop her off?"

Clayton dunked his swizzle stick into his almost-white coffee. "Must have. None of my guys saw her or brought her in." He pointed his stick at Bronco. "Not only that, the hospital's surveillance cameras from this evening have a blank of about fifteen minutes. Someone didn't want to be seen."

"Let's back up." Bronco lifted his hand, palm up. "What was she doing at Marat's place?"

"Saving some young girls from a gruesome fate."

"A trafficking house?"

"Pretty sick. The girl's ranged in age from 6 to 17." With the tip of his shoe, Clayton tapped the wheel of Rachel's bed. "In those situations, I doubt you think about anything but getting out the girls." He sighed. "And actually…actually her plan was sound. She created a diversion, disoriented her enemy, and then entered as everyone was exiting."

"Do not tell her that." Bronco stiffened and slashed a hand in the air. "Any plan which results in her getting shot isn't very sound in my playbook."

"One thing's for sure. She's in a world of shit." Clayton sipped his coffee, and then wrinkled his nose. "Civilians can't go all Batgirl vigilante and get away with it. She shot two men, though they're unlikely to press charges. She also now has the weight of

Marat's immense influence railing against her." He dumped his coffee into the white mini sink before tossing the empty cup into the garbage. "By going into that home, she drew a bright red target on her back."

Bronco contemplated Rachel's precarious position, and a thought formed that made him sick to even consider: maybe he could ask his mother to exert her influence with Marat. Did she have that kind of pull? "Honestly, Kincaid, I'd rather see Rachel in jail than bleeding out on some abandoned road after being abducted and tortured by Marat's men."

"I get that, but are you willing to visit her in prison? Because that's where she's headed after this stunt."

"Would you two at least wait until the pain subsides before you haul me off to jail?" Rachel's eyes remained closed as she mumbled out the words.

"Woman, you'll know pain when I put you over my knee," Clayton barked. "What were you thinking? Charging into a home loaded with mafia murderers?"

Bronco sat back and let Clayton vent. At this moment, any words that came out of his mouth would be unkind and would create a divide too wide to bridge. Plenty of angry words had ripped past his lips lately, especially after his mother's revelations and his grandmother's death, but this hit a whole different level. Rachel's actions and disregard for her safety seemed almost suicidal. But, why? He tuned back in to Kincaid's scathing reprimand.

"Not only that, Harris, one of those girls could have been killed in the cross-fire. Girls dead. You dead. Neighbors dead." Clayton glared from his position at the foot of Rachel's bed. "The people exiting the home could have been killed. And don't tell me you couldn't have waited another five minutes, because that's horseshit. You've completely fucked me...and yourself!"

"How many girls escaped?" Rachel fired back. "Where are the little ones? Did they get out? How many?" She sat up.

"Will you lie down?" Bronco mumbled a few foul curses, shifting his gaze out the window. Maybe if he didn't note her every wince and slight moan, he could lower his rage meter a millimeter or two.

Hardly likely at this point.

"Please, tell me," she pleaded with Clayton. "Are they all right?"

Bronco glanced over his shoulder at the damn pixie who cared more about innocents than herself. A tiny sliver of his anger dissolved.

"The girls are being treated downstairs. There were so many, but they all seemed calmer together, so they're being kept in the same section. We have officers on the floor, and the guys back at the precinct are combing through the missing person's database to match their photos."

"I'm sorry, Clayton…they're just so young." Rachel licked her dry lips. "I couldn't let them…or their parents keep suffering. I had to do something."

"You had to do nothing, Harris!" Clayton shouted so loud the vibrations likely shook the building. "The police would have handled this. But now we've got suspects scattered to the wind, and a bunch of scared and addicted girls with no homes."

Bronco considered his father's contacts, mostly bankers, but perhaps he had friends of friends who were power lawyers and could get his woman a deal. Nothing too sweet, but no jail time. Damn girl needed a tad bit of punishment to keep her in check.

"Something had to be done. I need my phone."

"What for?"

"I have a contact at Turning Pages, a facility which offers abused and trafficked girls counseling and a place to recover. I told her I'd call," Rachel mumbled. "I did have a plan. And my plan revolved around saving those girls. As far as I'm concerned, that's all that matters."

"What matters is you almost died." Clayton narrowed his

eyes.

"I hardly think a gunshot in the leg qualifies as almost dying."

"Rachel." Patience gone, Bronco turned and stood with both hands planted on his hips. "While your intentions were good, your actions were extremely unwise and deadly. How do you think we'd feel if you'd died? The fact that you didn't even give us a chance to help wasn't fair."

Rachel twisted her fingers together in her lap. "I texted him." She flicked a finger at Clayton.

"But went in alone." Bronco shook his head. "When will you learn? You don't have to work alone, anymore. Why are you punishing yourself and pushing the limits on this case?"

"I'm doing my job." Rachel sniffed and looked away.

Clayton jabbed a finger against the bed rail. "If your *job* is to break every law known to man, then you've succeeded. You've also managed to piss off your only ally." He jerked a thumb toward his chest. "This little escapade will cost you dearly, Rachel."

"I'm sorry, but I won't lie. I'd do it again." Blinking slowly, Rachel's voice had weakened to barely above a whisper. "They took her into that house...she was so little. I just couldn't." Her hair rustled against the pillow as she shook her head. "I couldn't."

Bronco crossed the room and took her hand, because he couldn't accept the girl's circumstances either. Because honestly, who could sit by while young girls were mistreated? Misused? Drugged? Just the thought churned his stomach "Rachel, calm down. It's okay now." He nudged Clayton's shoulder. "Enough arguing."

Clayton kept his gaze for a moment before huffing out a sigh. "I'll stop until she's better, but I'm not finished."

"I get that. I have plenty to say once she's up and walking around, too." He lifted his free hand and formed a fist in the air between them.

Clayton returned the fist bump.

That settled, Bronco released his first steady breath since hearing she'd been shot. Lifting her small hand to his lips for a kiss, he accepted what she'd done, and why. There wasn't anything either he or Clayton could do now but help her recover. "Get some rest, Batgirl. I'll look into hiring a good lawyer."

"I think I've got that covered." A short, dark-haired man wearing a tailored navy suit appeared in the doorway. Shaking his head, he glanced at Rachel. "Dear girl, you've done it this time."

CHAPTER 27

In an abandoned hotel five blocks from Marat's now-disrupted hellhole, Erik rested an ankle on his knee while sitting on a rickety wood side table. "What is it you thought to accomplish, Marat?" He wiped the blood from his knuckles. "Father thought well of you. But, I must say I never saw anything special. Just a little boy watching from the sidelines."

Marat remained incoherent in a chair opposite him, his face mashed to a pulp with blood trickling from his ears and nose.

Though Erik had promised himself no more death, he'd experienced an unstoppable rage after seeing those children exciting Marat's house. In each girl fleeing that house, he'd seen his mother's face. He'd flashed to memories of when he and his mother, who was barely fifteen years older, would whisper all their secret fears and darkest deeds in the dead of night.

His mother had been used until she'd become one of Pavel's favorites. Her breathtaking beauty had become a blessing and a curse, for though she no longer serviced customers, she remained at Pavel's beck and call. The man had known nothing of softness, but he'd reveled in cruelty.

Marat had completed Erik's actual abduction that fateful day at the park, so this revenge was long overdue.

"The thing about playing with the big boys, Marat. You need

to know how to win." Erik lifted his gun and shot him right between the eyes. "Looks like, you lose." With that bullet, he added another death to the long list blackening his soul. But, didn't some men deserve to die? Men who could put children in servitude? His father had condoned the same practices, but once Erik came of age, he'd ended that problem—personally.

"Dump him at his apartment." At the doorway, Erik glanced back at his men. "Then you know what to do." He waved a hand at Marat's tied-up accomplices before tossing his gun on the floor at a blubbering man's feet. "Pin him as the shooter."

Questions would be asked, but he'd blame Marat's and the other two men's deaths on this man they'd caught fleeing the house after partaking of the services. This revolting creature would take the fall. That's what he deserved for visiting children.

After being delivered back to his apartment, Erik immediately showered, allowing the scalding hot water to cleanse his outside, because an internal cleanse would never take place. Too late for that. All his chances to be someone else had ended seventeen years ago in a Manchester park.

While rubbing his bruised, bloodied knuckles clean, he thought of his sister. There she'd stood, raising a gun against the man who'd taken her brother. The expression on her face when he'd revealed who he was would become one of those rare happy moments he'd store deep in his heart.

His sister. A woman so vibrant and alive. Stubborn. Brave. A survivor.

Everything she had to be.

One different choice, and their lives would have remained side-by-side. But that dream had ended long ago. He could not interfere with Rachel again.

Too dangerous.

The past had to stay buried now that he walked so close to the finish line.

All his plans would come to fruition. If not, then what did

these past years mean? All the sacrifices. All the death and pain. Losing the one person he'd ever loved.

His mother died because of him. Because Otari Korzakov, member of the homeland's 12-person council, had visited and believed him too soft. Felt he needed to experience true pain and loss before he could become a leader in their world.

There was no discussion. No argument. No plea for her life.

Just an end.

Right before his eyes, he'd watched his mother take her last breath. Her eyes opened wide in surprise. Her small hand resting against the spill of blood, turning red upon her light pink top. A single strand of blonde hair covering her face.

That strand haunted his dreams. Because on that day, he couldn't brush it behind her ear.

Couldn't touch her.

He'd stood silent and still. Yet, internally he raged and swore revenge against the man who, with one bullet, destroyed his entire world.

At the end, he'd likely be dead, but so would Korzakov.

He had never been soft. Ever. Hadn't he proved that tonight by ending Marat?

No one followed a weak leader.

Pavel had raised him to be a brutal dictator, and so he was.

At times his feral nature—the injustice of everything, past pain and loss—simply overtook his reason, and he struck out. Tonight, Marat just happened to be on the receiving end, and good riddance as far as he was concerned.

Erik's life would continue along this same dark vein.

Because Otari Korzakov had to die.

CHAPTER 28

"You doing okay?" Owen stood behind Bronco as he completed his second set of squats.

"Yeah, I'm good for another round after this one." He wiped his sweaty hands on his shorts.

Bronco glanced at Ember pumping away on the elliptical in Owen's home gym. Her long red ponytail bopped up and down with her movements. He smiled at the look of determination on her face. She was a trooper in more ways than one. Owen was a lucky guy.

"You hear about Mario getting traded to the Hawks?"

"Yeah." Bronco nodded.

"Oh, for crying out loud." Ember erupted. "Weeks ago, his grandmother dropped a bombshell, then mysteriously died, his mom's having affairs left and right, his parents are divorcing, he doesn't want to hurt his dad by investigating his biological father. Rachel's been shot. Training camp is coming up. But no"— Ember tossed her towel at Owen's head—"you men don't discuss your problems. Just go ahead and act like the only important thing is Mervin going to the Hawks."

Owen cleared his throat. "It's Mario."

"I don't care." Ember growled. "What kind of friend are you?"

Owen shifted closer to the cardio machine, keeping his back to Bronco. Barely above a whisper, he bit out, "I asked him like you wanted, and he said he was fine, Stems."

"That's impossible." She stopped working her arms and legs and took a sip from her water bottle.

Owen shrugged.

"You're right, Ember." Bronco threw his pal a bone, unwilling to be the cause of them fighting. "I do have all those things on my mind, but I'll deal."

"I thought you two were friends?" Ember waved a hand back and forth between them. "Why don't you ever talk about anything?"

"Everything you said, I know he's dealing with." Owen patted her butt like he would a player on the team. "That's why I invited him over. We don't talk. We sweat."

"Yeah. This"—Bronco spun his finger in a circle—"is good enough."

"See." Owen slapped Ember on the ass again.

Crossing both arms over her chest, Ember glared before shaking her head, hopping off her machine, and stalking toward the door.

"Hey, Red?" Owen called after her.

"What?" She halted in the doorway and glanced over her shoulder.

"You're looking good in those yoga pants."

Ember flipped him off as she left the room.

"Excuse me a minute." Chuckling, Owen followed her upstairs.

Bronco heard shouting, followed by what sounded like a herd of elephants racing around, and then a woman's high-pitched squeal.

Then nothing.

He rolled his eyes. Ever since Ember had entered Owen's life, she'd turned his friend into a sex fanatic.

Half an hour later, as Bronco was finishing cardio, he mentally chuckled as an especially relaxed-looking Owen sauntered back into the room.

He brushed a hand through his sweat-soaked hair. "Ember wants me to ask how you're really doing."

"Worked that out of you, did she?"

"Thoroughly."

If Bronco didn't know any better, he'd swear his pal was blushing. "Good. Someone needs to knock 'King O' on his ass."

Owen grunted and shrugged. "Don't worry about my ass." He pulled the weights off the squat bar and settled them back on the rack. "I'm more worried about yours."

Tugging up his shirttail, Bronco rubbed the sweat from his face. "I was good until this morning." After scrubbing his neck vigorously with a small towel, he met Owen's gaze. "Clayton texted me. Nestor Marat was found dead in his home." He sank onto the weight bench. "I'm falling in an unending spiral. The kind of ride where you vomit afterward for hours on end. Plus, I've got these migraines. My dad looks like he's on the verge of a heart attack: shaky, sweaty, not sleeping or eating. We're both a mess." He rested his elbows on his knees, and then flicked his fingers through his hair. "I-I don't know…everything's just off."

"Let's back up a second." Owen handed him another towel. "How did Marat die?"

"Beaten, then shot. Pretty violent according to Kincaid." Bronco hadn't been kidding about the vomiting. His stomach felt like acid monsters were on a constant spin cycle. Twitchy skin and his heartbeat drilled 24/7 in his chest, like he'd just finished a 5K. Sleep remained elusive. Maybe all the mental stress was presenting as physical ailments, but that didn't seem right. Normally, he dealt with any struggle head on. Internalizing emotions wasn't on his playlist. Maybe he had the flu.

"So, that's good news in a way for Rachel's safety, right?" Owen nudged Bronco's foot with his shoe. "When is she getting out of the hospital?"

"She got out yesterday. I asked, but she wouldn't stay with me. I'm at Dad's anyway, but there's plenty of room, and Lada could have taken care of her while I prepared for training camp." Bronco rubbed his towel over his breastbone. Rachel's rejection hurt. Out of all the chaos that represented his life, he hated to admit what bothered him the most was her continued refusal to let him care for her. The past couple of days, his emotions had simmered on the raw side of rare, especially with his mom coming in every other day, boxing up shit and hauling it away.

The cure to all his ills was the tiny sprite, Rachel Harris. His only medicine—losing his mind inside her welcoming body over and over. Surely, this would erase his internal pain. To be held. Loved. He could have sex with other women, but only one would fully satisfy, and all those tiny bites weren't enough anymore. He wanted the full-course meal.

"Is Rachel safe where she is?"

Owen's question broke into his thoughts. "Her aunt is taking care of her for a few days. Based on the criminal defense cases her uncle takes, I'm assured the house is well protected." Bronco shot his damp towel into the nearby wicker laundry bin. "I went by their house last night, but Rachel was sleeping. Her aunt said she was taking it easy, watching trash TV."

"She got someone to handle her business while she's down?"

"Don't know." Bronco shrugged. "She keeps everything so secretive."

"Good at what she does, though."

"Good won't stop the crazy pixie from getting killed." He tapped a fist against the weight stand. "And as far as I'm concerned, her wings are clipped."

CHAPTER 29

"So, you think the guy that saved you at Marat's was your brother?" Maude perched in the recliner across from the couch Rachel had declared as her rehabilitation area.

"Yes." Rachel nodded. She held back a wince as she shifted her leg.

"Hmm...you were in an intense situation. Are you sure you weren't imagining things? At death's door maybe you saw a vision of what you wanted to see."

"At death's door? Let's not get dramatic." Rachel raised a brow. "This guy looked just like my father, *and* he could be my twin...but taller."

"So, what will you do?"

"Go back."

"What?" Maude's eyes flared wide. "Bronco and Clayton will skin you alive."

"Not if they don't know."

"Don't expect me to keep quiet about something that could get you killed. You almost died, Rachel. You. Were. Shot." Maude poked her index finger against the chair's puffy arm. "There was blood and bullets and a hospital visit. You're already in so much legal trouble it isn't funny. Didn't your uncle forbid you to leave the house?"

"Maybe." She shrugged and held back a sigh. Her uncle had indeed declared a halt to what he referred to as her 'vigilante' activities.

"And how do you think your aunt would feel...how Ember and I would feel, if you'd died?" Maude tossed a tissue at Rachel's head. "Not cool. Reckless and heartless, if you ask me."

"Well, heartless does fit."

"No." Maude threw the entire tissue box this time. "No, it doesn't. Stop saying stuff like that."

Rachel released a resigned sigh. "All right, but I need to know why he knocked me out instead of killing me. I want to know for certain that man was my brother. Finding him has been the reason for my existence for far too long. I have to know if he was the one who dropped me off at the hospital. And if so, why? Why not just kill me? I mean, he was with Marat. He said he was my brother, so why hasn't he come forward before now? So many questions, and I need answers." She fiddled with a throw pillow for a moment, holding back tears. Then she cleared her throat. "But, enough about me. What's up with you?"

"Fine, I'll let you change the subject but don't think I'm not telling Bronco you are a reckless idiot." Maude tossed her wavy red-brown hair over her shoulder. "Anyway...I'm seeing a new guy."

"Oh, well, I thought..."

"Thought what?"

"I thought you might pine over Jason for the rest of your life."

"That's still a high possibility." Maude sighed. "But I can't wait anymore. He thinks of me as Owen's kid sister, always has, always will. I've moved on." She took a sip from her water bottle. "What about you?"

"Me, well...I'll likely be serving time for the next sixty years. I doubt Bronco wants jail bait."

"That isn't what...I don't think that's what jail bait means."

"It does in this case."

"I wish I could love Bronco, instead." Maude plopped her feet on the coffee table. "He is perfect for me, when you think about it. He's studious. A quiet thinker. Heavy-duty muscles and burly body. Together, we'd conquer the universe."

Rachel narrowed her eyes.

"Touched a nerve, did I?" Maude huffed out a laugh. "Sheathe your claws." She nudged Rachel's arm with her sock-covered toe. "You need to decide what you want from Bronco. You're not being fair to his feelings, or your own."

"Why? He's got a lot on his plate right now. I'm giving him some space while he works out everything, and I heal." Plus, she felt an overwhelming amount of guilt for leaving him and Clayton out of her plan of action against Marat. The whole thing probably had been a bad idea, but for now, the girls were secure at the Turning Pages facility. In the end, that was all that mattered. She'd gladly do jail time if her actions kept girls from being horrifically abused.

"I do have to wonder though." Maude moved from the recliner to sit on the coffee table, and then squeezed her hand. "Are you healing? Mentally and physically? This thing with your brother...you're letting it consume you, and to be perfectly blunt, almost kill you. You went in alone and that's not okay, because you are *not* alone anymore. We all love you. So, while you're lolling around on this couch, get that straight in your head."

Rachel bumped Maude with the throw pillow. "Go away." With two fingers, she drew a circle around herself. "No psychoanalysis allowed in my zone." Quiet for a moment, she fiddled with a hangnail on her thumb. "Why doesn't anyone understand I just needed to save those girls?"

"No, what you needed was to save your brother. Those girls were just a representation of something you've tried to accomplish your whole life. But you can't win against those people, Rachel. You can't be a lone vigilante fighting for justice and displaced children. You must ask for help."

"I wouldn't bank on it."

Maude stood, shaking her head. "I'm not joking around this time. What you did was wrong. So go ahead and punish yourself and push everyone away, but don't expect me to sit here and say nothing."

Shocked by the serious turn in the conversation, Rachel couldn't find the words to respond as she watched Maude walk away.

CHAPTER 30

"Good morning, Erik."

Leonard's false smile and carefully controlled tone belied the polite greeting. "Leonard." Avoiding eye contact, Erik sipped from his coffee and wiped at the toast crumbs sprinkled on the table. Throughout his childhood, his mother had frequently brought him to this little diner. So now, when he was troubled, he came here to think. He wasn't a sentimental man, but everyone needed a place that brought fond memories. An escape from everything he'd become.

"Skipped out on our meeting yesterday, Kid." Tossing his cowboy hat on the table, Leonard slid into the booth beside him.

Erik wouldn't ask how the Marshal found this place. Likely they'd known of it since he'd offered his help in bringing down Pavel's brigade.

After placing his service revolver on the table, Leonard waved the waitress over and ordered a cup of coffee.

Sarah, the waitress who'd been serving him for years, avoided looking at the gun on the table.

"He's not going to shoot me, Sarah. I'm all right."

Sarah met his gaze for a moment before nodding and tottering off to get Leonard's coffee.

Poor woman had likely seen it all, anyway. This place wasn't known for serving chocolate chip pancakes topped with whipped cream.

Leonard tapped his knuckles against the table. "You realize this place is your tell."

"Didn't realize we were playing poker." Erik didn't drop Leonard's gaze.

"You've got a hell of a hand in this game." Jaw clenched tight, he shook his head. "What happened out there, Pavel?" Leonard hadn't raised his voice, didn't need to. "I believe the plan was for you to clear Marat's house. Next thing we know, your sister's storming in, dropping EMPs, and shooting up the place." He rested his elbows on the table. "She's pretty brave for such a tiny thing. Like to get herself killed though."

"I'd never allow that."

"What would you allow?"

The steel in his tone cut a jagged line through Erik. This man expected him to walk a line between two worlds and never get dirty? Well, that wasn't happening. They kept him in a position, knowing what he had to do to keep his crown, yet expected it to be easy. Clean. *No.* This man didn't get to question or judge him. "I'm allowing you to sit here." Erik glanced out the window. "Allowing your interruption to my morning meal." He waved a hand by his stomach. "Allowing you to disturb my whole digestive process."

Sarah returned, dropped off a cup for Leonard, and then refilled Erik's.

All this, done with a death glare at the man sitting across from him. Sarah had always had a soft spot for him. Poor thing was deluded.

"You didn't eat much." She held his half-empty plate in her hand. "You feeling all right?"

"Had a big dinner last night." Patting his flat stomach, he smiled and gave her a wink. "Food was perfect, as always."

She nodded, shot a final glance at Leonard and then headed back behind the counter.

"Appetite a bit off? Wonder why?" Leonard raised a brow then fiddled with the saltshaker resting on the table between them. "You've made a mess this time, Erik. I'm here to take you in."

"Let me ask you a question. During all the time you were observing Pavel, didn't you ever wonder how he suddenly had a son?" He let that thought, which had burned in his gut for far too long, sink in. "You may be all right leaving children to suffer. Me, not so much." He shoved his empty coffee cup across the table. "I'm not going anywhere. I have a job to do. If the mess you are referring to is the deaths of Marat and his men, then I heard someone already confessed to those crimes." Erik shifted his gaze out the window. "I've warned you against threatening me. You can't have it both ways, *Marshal.* The rules that apply on your side of the table don't exist on mine. I am who I have to be to get to the top. You either accept that, or let me go, and I'll finish on my own."

"Murder was never part of the plan." Leonard's clenched his fists on the table.

"Death is part of every plan. You live, you die. No exceptions."

"A whole lot of rage went into Marat's death, almost like someone had a personal stake in seeing him done."

"Then the man shouldn't have gone into the business of trafficking children. Retribution for actions like that does tend to get messy. And why shouldn't they?" Erik shrugged. "You live a brutal life, you get the same death."

"Erik." Leonard braced a forefinger and thumb against his forehead, ran those same two fingers through his hair, and ended by rubbing the back of his neck. "You can't take matters into your own hands. Arresting Marat and his men was the right call. They would've served time for their crimes. You are not the judge and jury. Working for us doesn't give you carte blanche." He leaned forward to sip his steaming black coffee, and then tapped the cup against the table. "I need to bring you in for the day. It's my job to ask you questions about what went down. You want someone else to take my place? You think I didn't get my ass chewed over this cluster-fuck? You may not have people to answer to, but I do."

"Guilt trips only work on people with a conscience." Erik sighed, because for a flicker there, he'd felt a slight twinge of something. "Say you take me down there, what's to say you don't keep me locked up for a very long time?"

"Well, like you said, someone else confessed."

"Where's your boy, Metro, today?"

"Metro would've shot you on the spot."

Erik rolled his eyes.

"Damn it, Kid. You're twenty years old, not old enough to order your own beer. You think I want you in this position? You think I want to watch you lose your soul?" Sighing, he glanced up at the ceiling, likely hoping a higher power would intercede. "I'm taking you in, and on my word, I'll let you leave. But, I want you to consider where you want to be. In life. In this world."

With a look in his eye Erik had never seen before, Leonard placed his palms together and tapped them on the table, as if offering a prayer.

"Let me pull you out of this. I've done and seen a lot of bad shit in my twenty-five years of police work, but this thing with you...no...I don't want this for you. Let's end it. Today."

For just one moment, Erik had a vision of white picket fences, a wife, maybe a couple of kids. Easy street. Then, a red haze covered the entire picture as the image of his dead mother's body filled his thoughts. "People live in this world doing unspeakable things to one another, for no reason whatsoever, every day. Someone has to stand against them." He held back the rage burning inside at the injustices of life. "I appreciate your"— he flicked a finger in the air—"whatever it is you wish for me, but I can't give you that. Out of all the people I've ever known, you are the only man I would ever say that to. The only man I've ever trusted."

Unable to meet Leonard's gaze as he spoke that truth, he kept his focus out the window at the gray morning quiet and calm, framed by grease-stained curtains. "To get where I need to go, I'll betray everything you want me to be, and more. I can't change course now, because I've seen just as much of the dark side of life as you. Black and red are the only colors on my palette."

Leonard shuffled out of the booth, placed his hat on his head, and then pulled a couple of bucks from his wallet. "That sister of yours. She's stirred up a lot of trouble."

"So, we'll scare her off."

Leonard halted with the money in his hand.

"I'm not killing her." Erik huffed out a sigh. "Scare tactics. The usual things. I'll have my guys drop off a package. She'll already assume she has a target on her back after storming Marat's operation." He smiled as he thought of her standing against Marat, smoke billowing around her as she hollered down the hall. "Foolish girl."

"She see you?"

"How would she have seen me?"

"You were there, right?"

"I don't know, Leonard." He arched a brow. "What's your surveillance say?"

"My surveillance says you dropped her off at the hospital. Guess your heart isn't so black, after all." Leonard tipped his hat. "And Kid, one last thing. If I had known about you, if there was intel regarding a child being raised by that monster, I can promise you no amount of payoff would have had me looking the other way."

After tossing down a twenty, Erik scooted out of the booth. "Pavel had dirt on a lot of supposedly clean people." He waved at Sarah as he followed Leonard out the door. Stopping before he crossed the street, he glanced over his shoulder. "And Leonard, regardless of what you might believe, if you'd known about me, you would have been owned by Pavel, too."

CHAPTER 31

For the next week, between visits to his agent, his offensive-line team meetings, and prep for training camp, Bronco could only see Rachel on those rare occasions when his schedule permitted. Another task requiring his time and attention during Rachel's recuperation was cleaning out his grandmother's room and saying goodbye to Tash. Both heart-wrenching moments.

Yesterday, he'd met with the lawyers about his grandmother's will. She'd left him the majority of her assets, which he planned to donate to Alzheimer's research. His mother was not pleased with this plan—an opinion she made clear during lunch after the meeting, which ended with him leaving before the main course was served.

Why should she care? They'd both been born with silver spoons in their mouths, and that spoon kept feeding him money. He made enough as a pro-football player to stay flush for the rest of his life. His family money was well invested for his retirement and any eventual children. He'd lived an entitled, carefree life, and had only just recently realized how all the materialistic trappings did not equal happiness. Although, in all honesty, having money did make life easier, but giving funds to medical research was the right thing to do.

Taking initiative had led him to this moment. He gripped

Rachel's arm as she hobbled along the sidewalk toward Thomas Northman's sister's home. One step closer to his aunt, Beth Conrad. No wonder his heart pounded, and perhaps that was why his head felt like a vise was crushing his skull. These headaches had to stop. Plus, no one dying, having an affair, or shooting at his woman for just one week would be nice.

With her injured leg, Rachel moved slowly, but other than that she was back to her sassy self. Her uncle had pulled him aside this morning and reassured him that he would handle her legal issues, but he was worried she might serve some jail time.

At the base of the concrete steps leading to a screen door, Bronco studied his aunt's small home adorned with dark grey siding and deep red shutters. A one-car garage sat off to the side with a grouping of bikes parked beside an old white Buick. The grass needed mowing, but the flowerbeds were spry and colorful. His aunt's home was located just across the railroad tracks from his parent's house. Literally. All along, the answers to who he really was sat close by, waiting. He shook his head.

The kids from this area no longer attended the same schools as those on his side of the tracks. The boundaries had separated them years ago. He withdrew from his musings and knocked on the door.

Rachel tugged his arm. "You're being very quiet. You sure you're ready for this?"

"I'm not sure. I mean, I wonder why she's never contacted me before." He rubbed the back of his neck. "But, I'm here now, and at this point, I have no choice but to be ready. And just so we're clear, from now on, I'm calling the plays."

"Is that so?"

"Consider yourself warned."

"I'd kick you, but then I'd fall so consider yourself kicked."

Bronco rolled his eyes.

Lucky for her, the door opened. His aunt was a tall blonde with a warm smile and tired blue eyes. She didn't say a word as she waved them inside, just kept both hands over her mouth and her gaze locked on his.

The smell of freshly baked cookies wafted through the air, and the homey scent almost had him in tears. His emotions were all over the place. "Thank you for agreeing to meet with us today, Mrs. Conrad." He cleared his throat and offered a small smile.

"Yes, Beth, we appreciate your time." Rachel shuffled into the house, leaning on his arm.

Still standing in the doorway, his aunt's entire body started to shake, then sobs tore from her throat as she released a quiet cry and launched herself into his arms. "I'm...I'm so sorry." Beth murmured. "You look so much like him and the whole thing...the whole thing is so unfair...he would have loved you so much." She held him tighter as her emotions unleashed.

Bronco kept his arms wrapped around her and gave comfort, but knew he'd not find his own. Unfair did not even begin to cover the situation. This poor woman hadn't deserved to lose a brother she so obviously loved. And he hadn't deserved to lose the chance to know his real father. Who had taken away that choice? And why? He glanced at Rachel and was surprised to see tears on her cheeks, as well. "See if you can find some tissues, Rach."

She simply nodded, not arguing.

Which meant she was more touched than he realized. She dug into her backpack and pulled out a tissue box like the ones his parents had loaded into his grade school backpack. He plucked free a few tissues. "Aunt Beth, let's sit for a moment." *Wow, a true aunt.* Neither of his parents had siblings, so the word was foreign on his tongue.

Beth nodded against his chest. "Right." Pulling away, she took his arm and led him into the living room. "I'm sorry. I thought I was prepared to see you, but having you here is like having Thomas home." She dabbed at her eyes with a few tissues before tossing them in a tiny trash can sitting by the couch.

The can was stuffed with cheese stick wrappers and, if he wasn't mistaken, a Barbie's head. He stifled a chuckle. Worn beige couches, kid's toys scattered across the floor, and warm chocolate painted walls. This was a home, not a magazine spread.

Had his life really been so shallow? Did he have any understanding of what people's lives were really like? The daily struggles? What did he have to be depressed about, really? He'd grown up perfect. But looking back, his childhood seemed empty without squashed cushions, throw blankets, soda spills on the kitchen counter, a peanut butter jar with two spoons sticking out the top, and the smell of baked goodness in the air.

If he had children, this would be their home. Not spic and span, but messy and filled with books. No video games, ever. *Well...maybe Madden.*

Beth settled on the couch. "I'm sorry I keep staring, but you look so much like him. I'm so glad you came to see me."

"Mrs. Conrad, we are grateful you've invited us to your home. Warren has hired me to look into the death of your brother. We feel more may be involved in the story, and would appreciate any light you could shed on the subject." Rachel levered herself onto the couch.

"Babe, you need some help?"

"No, I have to do this on my own. I can't have you following me around all day, dropping me from chair to chair."

Beth giggled. The sound seemed a perfect reflection of the happiness found in this place. Bronco raised a brow. "Ms. Harris, I do believe you need following so you won't run off on asinine adventures."

"And you'd be familiar with asinine things." Rachel offered a saccharine smile.

Beth cleared her throat. "Seems you two are already on an adventure." She winked at Rachel.

Rachel shook her head, cheeks pinking slightly.

Well now, this is interesting. Aunt Beth could already detect their connection. Too bad Harris was so slow on the draw.

"Warren, come sit beside me." Beth patted the loveseat cushion. "I dug out these old family albums." She set the album on his lap and flipped through pages filled with his father and his family. For over an hour, she took him on a journey through his father's past—and *his* past. Sadly, his grandparents were no longer alive. Page after crinkled page brought to life a man he'd never know.

After a round of cookies and milk, they finished the final group of photos and discussed Beth's thoughts on what had happened between her brother and the Astor women.

"Your grandmother hated Thomas. Threatened him." In a burst of what seemed nervous energy, Beth gathered toys off the floor and tossed them into a canvas tote. "Thomas was wild, but who isn't at that age? One day, he sat me down and told me Gina was pregnant." She paused for a moment, her gaze locked on the items in her hands while she mentally traveled back in time. "I worried about him, not only for his future, but over his involvement with such a powerful family. He was happy to marry your mother, because he did love her, but they were so different. Maybe that was the allure, I don't know." She shook her head. "I never understood any of it."

Seeming to come out of her haze of memories, she met his gaze and leaned against the couch. "Then, he died. The thought of so much vibrancy, fun, and charm gone forever...well, let's just say I miss him every day. Although I know this isn't very Christian, I wish he'd never met your mother. I'd always thought he drank that night because she drove him to do so, but then again, that never made sense, either."

Brows raised, Rachel shot her gaze to his before glancing at Beth. "Why didn't that make sense?"

All day, his pixie investigator's questions had been probing but not overly so. Rachel Harris was very good at disarming people. No mere fairy could hurt you. He huffed out a laugh. She sure had everyone fooled.

"Thomas didn't drink. Didn't do any drugs of any sort." Beth glanced at the clock on the wall. "My grandkids will be coming back soon. They went to the movies with Mike so we'd have some quiet time together."

Bronco gathered up all their dishes and took them into the kitchen.

"Is there anything else your brother may have mentioned, or perhaps you found odd at the time? Anything at all, just like him not drinking, what other moments have always been out of place in your mind?"

Bronco trooped back in from the kitchen, unwilling to miss this discussion.

Biting her bottom lip, Beth stilled, and then folded a throw blanket. After tossing it on the back of the couch, she tilted her head and met Rachel's gaze. "There's more to this, isn't there? What do you know?"

"Aunt Beth." Bronco took her hand. "I believe my grandmother, and another party, may have been responsible for Thomas's death."

Her eyes widened, and she slumped onto the couch beside Rachel.

"Bronco's grandmother mentioned something about help from a man." Rachel patted Beth's shoulder. "Do you recall any rivals for Gina's affections at the time of her pregnancy? Any old boyfriends that gave your brother trouble?"

"No." Beth rubbed her temple. "Nothing comes immediately to mind, but if I think of anything, I'll let you know."

A door slammed and voices streamed in from the kitchen.

"Oh boy, get ready, Bronco Murray." Beth smiled. "My grandchildren are huge Marauder fans."

The thought of having mini-fans warmed his heart. He always volunteered at Marauders kids' camps. So he was used to tiny monkeys climbing all over him.

A boy, likely ten years old, and a mini-Beth, likely six or so, stormed into the room and then halted as they took in his stature. At least, that's what he figured, anyway. He was a big guy. Though, he hoped they weren't frightened.

"Big Marauder terrorizing children. Good one, Murray." Rachel laughed. "Help me up, please."

A man with one cookie in his hand and half of another in his mouth followed the children in. He nodded at Bronco, wiped his free hand on his jeans, and then offered it in greeting. "Nice to meet you." His beefy hand encompassed Bronco's, and that was saying a lot.

After telling her grandkids they could have two cookies each, Beth stood beside the burly gray-haired man. "Warren Murray, this is my husband, Mike Conrad, and those two muffins are Thomas and Rebecca."

His gaze flew to Beth's when she spoke her grandson's name, and though he smiled, he had to blink back a few unwelcome tears.

Cookies in hand, Thomas and Rebecca stood before him once more, comfortable now, as they fired off question after question about the Marauders and Chewy. Of course, the quarterback, Charles Hendricks aka Chewy, got all the love. Still, their enthusiasm was infectious, and he and Rachel stayed for another hour, learning a bit more about the Conrads.

When he saw Rachel's lids droop, he knew the time had come to wrap up their visit. He stood and received hugs from them all, as did Rachel. At the door, he took Beth's hand. "Thank you. This won't be the last time I'll visit."

"Thank you, Warren." Beth nodded. "Your father would be so proud. You completed his dream, and I honestly hope you find the answers you seek." She hugged him again, but then pulled back to look him in the eyes. "While I hate to speak ill of the dead, I must tell you the truth. I do believe your grandmother capable of hurting Thomas. She made herself very clear he would never marry her daughter. I'm sorry I didn't attempt to contact you before, but even all these years later, I do not feel as if I can approach any Astor without being treated with disdain."

"I understand." Her honesty pierced his heart. "Even though, I am part Astor, I will view your family as my own. I promise."

"Thank you." She smiled. "And thank you for being so patient with my grandchildren."

"No problem."

Rachel squeezed Beth's hand again. "Thank you for the cookies, Mrs. Conrad."

Bronco's heart stung a little more for Rachel as he remembered she had no relationship with her own parents. Was today hard for her? Did these family moments tear at her heart?

After their final goodbye's, they walked down the sidewalk side-by-side. The cracks were full of grass tufts and highlighted by rainbows drawn in chalk.

"I'll take care of them. Send a group of guys to repair this house." Bronco glanced back. "Put on a new roof. She doesn't have time with babysitting her grandkids. Plus, with both her and Mike being retired teachers, I don't know that they can afford many home improvements. Maybe I could help with Mike's YMCA football team this fall." He scratched his chin, considering his upcoming schedule. He slowed so Rachel could catch up. All his musings had quickened his step. He caught sight of the Conrads' decade-old van. "Plus, I'd say they need a new vehicle."

"Okay, Daddy Warbucks." Rachel crept along. "How about you ask before you go all construction zone on this place? Maybe they don't want you to do those things."

"Remember, I've recently become flush with Gloria Astor's money." Bronco shrugged. "I had planned on donating most to research, but I'll have my advisor set aside funds for the Conrads' home repair. Quite an ironic turn of events, wouldn't you say?"

"Astor money going to Thomas' family? Hell yeah...I love it, though. Serves the old biddy right." Wincing, Rachel shot him a glance as she stopped by the car. "Sorry, probably too soon to disparage your grandmother. I should have said that in my head."

"S'okay." Actually, he hadn't decided where his feelings rested concerning his grandmother. He'd loved her, and though she'd potentially taken something precious from him, he still had a lifetime of memories with the woman. "Not everyone is as they seem. I understand that now. Believe me, the rose-colored glasses are off."

"I'm sorry for that, Bronco."

He combed his fingers through her hair and nudged her against the passenger door. "What else are you sorry for, Pixie? Are you sorry for putting yourself in danger? Are you sorry for avoiding me?" He leaned closer and whispered in her ear, "Are you sorry that injured leg is keeping me from making love to you?"

She shivered.

He kissed his way along her jawline, over to her lips. Holding her head in place, he delved deep into her mouth, taking what he could at this moment. After leaving that home full of love, he needed some of his own. Wanted the contentment exuding from the Conrad home to linger. "I've missed you." He rested his forehead against hers, then, as he considered the Conrads might be watching from the window, he stepped back. "I'm still really pissed you put yourself in a dangerous position, but I can't fault your actions. They came from your heart. Next time, though…call Clayton."

"I've attended this lecture already, I got it." Rachel nodded and licked her lips. "Listen, Murray, I have no idea what's going on between us. I feel like I'm in some time warp that keeps repeating." She shook her head. "This thing between you and I…I don't know if I'm cut out for the long-term. Don't draw blue clouds and fluffy kittens around me then post the picture on the fridge 'cause I don't do all that homey-lovey shit." She pointed at the Conrads' house. "That family unit in there isn't me."

"I never asked you to be like them."

"Every time you kiss me, you ask."

"No." Bronco brushed her hair over her shoulder. "The person asking those questions isn't me…it's you."

Pressing her plumped lips into a straight line, Rachel flicked a hand at the car door. "Shut up, Freud-face, and unlock the car." Then she jabbed a finger against his chest. "One more thing. If you do all your Home and Garden makeovers to this place, you'll make them stand out in this neighborhood. They may not want that. Don't assume you can barge your way into these people's lives."

Bronco held open the door while Rachel slowly sank onto the front seat. "Maybe you're right, but I feel like Thomas Northman would have given his sister everything. So in his honor, I'll do the same."

Rachel grabbed his arm and ran her tongue across his inner wrist.

"What did you do that for?" He stared at her mouth as he felt his cock weep with jealousy. "I've got other places you could lick."

"Really?" She rolled her eyes. "I was just checking to see if you're made of sugar."

"Funny." He leaned down, kissed her, and then held her gaze while he licked his own lips. "One thing is for sure: you're not." Crowding her space, he whispered against her lips, "Once you're out of that bandage, I'm going to spank the shit out of you."

"Gross." Rachel hummed out a laugh. "That might be kind of messy, not to mention embarrassing, if you literally spank the sh—"

He slammed the door and rounded the front of his SUV to the driver's side. *Literal wench.*

Once settled in the seat, he took her hand. "Come home with me." He waited to continue until she made eye contact.

"Everything calms when I'm with you. There's so much I need to say and share."

"With this leg injury, I'm not up for sex. Plus, antibiotics and birth control don't mix."

He brought her hand to his lips and kissed her knuckles. "No sex then, just let me hold you for a while. I have all these thoughts about what's happening, and I'd like to hear your theories on this case. Can we just be together as friends? I-I need to talk to someone, and I'd like that someone to be you."

"Wow, you know how to tear a girl's heart right out of her chest, don't you?" Rachel squeezed his hand. "Of course I'm your friend, and yes, I'll listen."

A weight he hadn't known existed floated out the open window. Slowly but surely, he'd win this girl, because whether she knew it or not, deep down, she loved him. Maybe as a friend now, but that was the basis of a real relationship, one that would last forever. And forever was what he wanted.

"Warren, wait!"

Beth's holler broke through his open window as she rushed down the sidewalk.

"I remembered something." She stopped by Rachel's door to catch her breath.

Bronco hopped out of the SUV and hustled to her side. "What is it?"

"I remembered that Gina spoke to Thomas about adoption one time." Beth took his hand. "Apparently, she knew of a company owned by a local businessman who had dealings with her mother. Gina introduced the man to Thomas before a football game. My brother was not pleased."

"This is great information," Rachel piped in from the open passenger window.

"Thomas adamantly disagreed with the adoption plans because he wanted the child, and because this older man seemed to have a sexual interest in Gina." Beth bit her bottom lip.

"Thomas was…he was very possessive of your mother."

Rachel braced a hand on the window frame. "Do you remember the older man's name?"

"No, I'm sorry." Beth shook her head. "But I do remember he owned a restaurant down on 38th Street."

"Was the name of the restaurant, Khlebosolny?"

"That sounds right." Beth nodded at Rachel.

"Was the man's name Victor Pavel?"

"Yes." Beth snapped her fingers. "That's it.'"

Rachel hissed out a breath.

"Who is Victor Pavel?" Bronco locked his hands on his hips. "Why is that significant?"

"I need to go to my office." Face pale, Rachel turned and stared out the windshield. "I need to think."

CHAPTER 32

On the ride to her office, Rachel tapped her nails against the door handle of Bronco's SUV, her thoughts in turmoil over this latest bit of information. Everything about this case seemed circular. Her past. Bronco's past. Both kept spinning round and round, crashing into one another but not quite sticking. What would be the final connection that would make all the other pieces fit?

How had the Astor family become involved with Pavel? Was the bank the connection? What about Chogan? How long had he worked at the bank? Had he engineered an introduction? He'd had an affair with Gina, but when did his interest in her begin? Since all her thoughts were wrapped up in Bronco, she hadn't had time to process each link in the chain.

With the answer almost clear, jumping free of Bronco's circle seemed the smart thing to do. But, she'd already tried jumping off the rails, and look where that got her. Weakened by a gunshot wound and likely serving time...and even worse, falling in love with the man beside her. Bronco was the one who belonged inside that neat circle. Her life was more like a lightning bolt, where each jagged edge cut deep and left her struck and lifeless on the ground.

But hadn't Bronco lifted her heart from the ashes and made

her whole? Until when, though? He'd leave, wouldn't he?

She needed off this track. Soon. Too bad her heart was punching against her chest, negating any future derailment.

Bronco turned down the radio. "I thought that visit went well. That last bit of information should help."

Rachel nodded and grabbed her bag off the floor, searching for some pain pills. She was not in the mood to talk now that she knew Pavel was involved, not to mention her thigh was throbbing.

"Who is Victor Pavel?"

"He was king before Marat." She sighed, really needing some quiet time so all the pieces in this case could align. "Mr. Pavel was kind enough to settle in Manchester with all his illegal endeavors, backed by the 12-person council in Russia." She shook two pills from the bottle and downed them both with her tiny water bottle.

"Maybe instead of going to the office, you should go home and get some rest."

"I will, after I look through some notes."

"I'll stay and help, then."

"I can't concentrate with you hovering."

"Try." He flicked on the turn signal and took the exit that led downtown to her office. "And one more thing: if you are planning to go anywhere near Marat's old haunts, you're wrong."

Keeping her gaze out the passenger window, Rachel shrugged. "Clayton says they've pulled up stakes since Marat's death, anyway."

"Still, I suggest watching your back."

"About that..." Rachel shifted in her seat and then cleared her throat. "There's something I should tell you."

He turned off the radio. "What?"

"I saw my brother."

Bronco swerved a little then straightened the vehicle. "You saw your brother?" Frowning, he stopped at a green light and studied her. "How?"

The car behind them blasted its horn.

Bronco rolled down his window and waved them around before weaving back into the lane, which led to the parking garage.

"That night in Marat's house, I saw him." Rachel leaned against the cup holder set in the middle of the front seat, redistributing her weight off her left leg. "The vision is vague now, and perhaps I imagined seeing Erik, but then, how did I get to the hospital? The last thing I remember was facing down Marat, then a man who…well, he looked like my father…and a lot like me." She drew a deep breath, seeing her brother's face again in her mind. His severely angry face. Actually, she'd been frightened of that man.

"So, you think he took you to the hospital?" Bronco maneuvered his SUV into a spot on the third level by the elevator doors. "Why would he help you if he was working for Marat? That is, if the man was your brother at all."

"I've always wondered if Pavel had something to do with Erik's abduction. He snatched children all the time, but…just go with me here, what if Pavel kept the boys for a different reason?"

"What reason?" Bronco slouched against the door.

"To have children of his own." Rachel closed her eyes and settled against the headrest. "No records exist that indicate Pavel had his own kids, which is why, when he died, Marat took over." She looked at Bronco. "But that man…that night…I-I believe he was my brother."

"Okay, let's consider this a moment." Bronco tilted his head. "How could he know who you are? Know you enough to save you? And why would he deliver you to the hospital when you'd just crashed the Marat house? Wouldn't he be working for them if he was, in fact, Pavel's son…or whatever?" Rubbing his fingers along his jaw, he shook his head. "Perhaps one of the girls took you to the hospital."

"No. He…uh…he incapacitated me."

"He what?" Bronco straightened from his slouch. "What

does that mean? Incapacitated how?"

"He tapped me on the jaw."

"I see." Bronco's tongue poked out the side of his cheek as he considered her words. "Tapped your jaw. Is that right?"

"Listen, I don't honestly know what he was doing, or why. I just know that man was my brother."

Bronco nodded. "Okay. I believe you."

A wash of relief flowed through her, quickly followed by exasperation that his support meant so much. Now that Bronco believed her, she finally believed herself, and what in the world did that mean? Since when did she need anyone's approval?

"So, Pavel took your brother. And years ago, he offered my mother the adoption option. Did he have a legitimate adoption business? We should check. Let's get you out of this SUV first. We'll stay here for a couple hours, and then I'm taking you home."

"Just help me to the elevators, Murray." She wouldn't argue but wouldn't agree either. One hour would likely be enough to get her work done, anyway, plus her leg pain was now shooting up her back. Just like lightning. Good to know pain could jump free of the circular loop.

Taking slow steps, she followed Bronco across the lot. The cool early-summer air was wrecked by exhaust filtering up from the cars bustling around on the streets below. "I have back-up files on Pavel's activities. I'll check his connections to your family." Standing outside the elevator, she clutched his arm. "Bronco...Pavel's men were hired for jobs. For a price. Do you understand what I'm saying?"

Bronco led her into the elevator and punched the floor for the crosswalk. Once inside, he kept his hand on her elbow. "You're saying Pavel could have hired someone to kill my father." He raked his fingers through his hair before once more taking her arm when the elevator opened.

"Yes, Pavel hiring someone at the directive of another,

specifically your grandmother, is a possibility."

After working their way across the lobby, Rachel nodded at the guard and handed him her access pass for her uncle's floor. Weaving her way through the well-wishers and some disapproving glares, likely due to her impulsive and very illegal actions, she finally managed to hobble to her office.

A manila envelope leaned against her door.

Bronco bent down to retrieve it.

"No." She yanked away his arm, tripping in the process, but was saved from a face-plant when she landed in Bronco's arms. "Don't touch it."

"All right. Calm down." He brushed the hair away from her face. "Did you hurt yourself?"

"No." Yet, she remained in his embrace. Shameless, but this man held her steady in more ways than one. "We need to call Clayton."

# # #

After sucking down three diet Cokes, Bronco felt bloated but his headache subsided a little. He still felt jittery, like creepy-crawlies were vacationing under his clammy skin. He positioned himself across the police station lobby from Rachel because he felt so gross. He'd likely have to visit the doctor, because he'd noticed his heartbeat either raced or skipped. Not only that, his stomach constantly hurt. All this emotional stress must have manifested into physical ailments. Yet, something else felt off. He'd never been this ill.

They waited while Clayton investigated the envelope's contents, likely in some CSI room. Bronco had basically begged to tag along, since scientific analysis of crime scenes fascinated him, but Clayton had shot him down with a very serious, "Hell no".

"How long do these things take?" Bronco shifted in his seat, seeking comfort for his acidic stomach. Perhaps he'd ask one of the cops for an antacid. Surely, they ate the things like candy.

"They take as long as they take."

Rachel seemed just as grumpy. They both needed a nap. Yet, at this point, he'd prefer to sleep alone. He didn't want her getting sick, too. *Damn, is it hot in here?* With a shaky hand, he wiped his dry mouth. Seriously, this had to stop. Tomorrow, he'd schedule time with the team's doctor. He rubbed his pounding temples and studied the brunette across from him. Poor thing was leaning on her right side. "Why don't you go home?"

"I'll wait." She kept her gaze on her phone.

So focused, she seemed intrigued by whatever she was reading. "So, what do you think's inside the envelope?"

She shrugged, still intent on her cell. "Warning."

"Great." Just when he thought she'd reached an all-clear in the safety zone, he watched her get smacked with some psycho's cryptic message.

He winced when his phone pinged with a text from Owen.

U R late for practice.

Rachel received death threat. He texted back that golden nugget.

Surely that would be enough to stem Coach's fury. Bronco didn't know the envelope's contents for sure, but based on Clayton's frown when he opened the package, his guess seemed likely. No way would he leave while his woman was in danger. In four years, he hadn't missed a day of practice. They could give him a break. These weren't even official practices yet, anyway, so they couldn't fine him. If they tried, they'd hear from his agent.

Owen texted back. *I'll cover.*

Coach pissed?

A tad. I'll have Jason distract.

That'll work. His pal, Jason, was a smart-ass who knew how and when to push just the right buttons.

Need me? Owen responded.

Not yet.

Let me know.

Rachel pulled some mini-computer from her bag and was typing away, lost to whatever was on her screen.

Maybe she'd let him see. He should've brought in his latest library book. Bronco sighed heavily, which earned him a glare from Ms. Typing Pixie.

Clayton sauntered down the hallway, tapping a yellow folder against his palm. He kicked Bronco's chair.

"Man, don't jostle me. I might toss my cookies right here."

Clayton stepped back. "You are looking a little gray. You need some water?"

Bronco closed his eyes. His heartbeat had suddenly decided to drive Mach 90 in his chest, and he couldn't catch his breath. He rested his elbows on his knees. "What was in the envelope?"

A cool, small hand rubbed his neck. "Bronco, you've got a fever. We'll get you home after this."

He opened his eyes and saw four legs, but they were fuzzy around the edges. He blinked, breathed deep, and clenched his jaw, his head feeling like he'd just been steamrolled by fifty defensive linemen.

"Typical 'black hand' tactics. They used to send a letter with threatening signals and a warning. Now, they send photos."

Clayton's words came across as if spoken in a tunnel. Photos flashed before his hazy vision. One of Nestor Marat's dead body. Two with Bronco kissing Rachel—one outside the bank and the other outside his parents' house. The last one featured Rachel's uncle at what was likely a business lunch.

"These people go after everyone, Rachel. You've stirred the hornet's nest."

A soda can popped open.

Sure he was on the verge of losing his breakfast, Bronco stood, swayed, and clutched Clayton's shoulder. "I think...I'm going down."

As he fell, he barely registered the pain of his arm slamming into the metal chair along the wall.

Blinking, Bronco raised a hand against the glare of the fluorescent lighting. "Wh-what happened?" A cold brush of something wet trailed across his forehead.

Rachel sat at his side, holding his wrist in her hand.

Was she checking his pulse? "Why am I on the ground?" He tried to sit up, but quickly rejected that idea as black spots danced before eyes. As he became more aware of his surroundings, he realized Rachel had his head cradled in her lap.

"Just rest here a minute. You passed out."

That cool brush went over his cheeks this time.

He licked his dry lips. "I did?"

"Yeah."

"I might have the flu."

Rachel nodded. "I think so, big guy."

Clayton's face appeared in his line of vision. "I'll take you home. Unless you think you need the Emergency Room?"

"No, I'll see the team docs tomorrow. Take Rachel home. She's not safe." What kind of cosmic cluster-fuck was this? His woman was once more in danger, the target truly painted on her back, and he was too sick to stand up.

"I'll have a patrolman take you home, but I'll keep Rachel with me until I can get out of here. She and I have a lot to discuss."

Bronco cursed but conceded. If there was one man he could count on, other than his O-line teammates, that guy was Kincaid. Plus, the man was very handy with a gun. Bonus point for the Copper. "Keep her safe, Kincaid. All this death: my real father's, Grandmother, Marat. It's all connected, somehow. We need to figure it out."

"We will."

Resting in Rachel's lap, he gazed into her deep brown eyes. "Is it my fault? Should I have left the past alone?" The thought churned his stomach even more.

"No." Rachel again brushed the cool towel along his cheek. "The past always finds its way into the present. There's no escape for any of us."

CHAPTER 33

For some reason, John Mellencamp's song "Crumblin' Down" played on repeat in her mind all day after Bronco left. Perhaps the repeated tune had to do with watching the big man fall, or maybe the words of the song reflected the current state of her life. Either way, the walls were in fact tumblin', tumblin', crumblin', crumblin' down.

Sitting in her uncle's overly-leather-and-cigar-scented study, she glanced at her quiet phone on the table. No texts from Bronco for hours. Maybe he had gone home and crashed. Hopefully, not literally.

She texted him again.

Hey, you make it home okay? How are you feeling?

She pretended to read through a file on Pavel while waiting for a response that still didn't come after ten, fifteen, now she was getting pissed at thirty minutes.

Clayton stretched beside her. The man needed a keeper. He had mentioned preferring blondes once. Perhaps she'd search her friend database and see who might fit, or maybe she'd ask Maude. That bubble of happiness had a lot of friends.

"So, Harris, how do we explain your familial DNA markers found by Nestor Marat's body?"

Her nerves already past the point of sanity, she spilled the whole story about seeing her brother at Marat's. Especially, since Erik was likely the reason for this discovery.

"Why are you just now telling me this?" He shifted forward in his seat.

"I was shot, Kincaid. I needed time to decide what was delusion and what was real."

"And this was real?"

"Yes."

"Unequivocally?"

"Yes." Still no text or call from Bronco, and Clayton was fraying her last nerve with his questions. "This is why I didn't mention seeing my brother before, because I get that face."

"What face?"

She waved at his stoic stare. "That cop face that reveals nothing, but secretly means you think I'm insane."

"After a statement like that, I'm suggesting that you are, in fact, insane." Clayton raked his fingers through his dark brown locks.

She growled out a sigh. "What was my brother doing with those mafia men? Why didn't he just kill me? Did he recognize me? And deep down I'm wondering, what if..." She bit her lip and dropped her gaze to the floor. "You know Pavel didn't have any kids, right? So, what if...?"

"What if your brother took over Pavel's operations?"

She nodded. Then deciding she'd shared enough, she changed the subject. "Have you heard from Murray? He's pissing me off with this silent treatment."

"I'm not sure about this brother angle. We have nothing on the man. He's a ghost." Clayton tapped a pen against his bottom lip. "Do you think your brother could have ordered Marat's death?"

"Well, that would explain his DNA at the crime scene. This also proves he is my brother."

"Maybe."

"No maybe. DNA is DNA, Clayton....duh." She smacked his arm. Still, had her brother killed Marat? If so, why?

Clayton's phone buzzed.

Rachel glanced at the screen to see if the caller was Bronco. *Nope.* Blocked appeared in big bold letters. Must be serious cop business.

After answering, Clayton shot out of his chair and scurried off to another room, shutting the door between them. Five minutes later, he came back in, fingers dragging through his thick hair again. "The FBI and U.S. Marshal Service are at the station. They are requesting everything we have on the Marat case, stating the information is part of an ongoing investigation into Russian mafia crimes."

"Is that so?" She raised a brow. "They can request all they want from you. Me, not so much." Didn't matter what they requested, because her backups had backups. She wasn't stupid. But, while federal intervention was not surprising, the involvement of the Marshals struck her as a bit odd. *Very interesting.* Why would they be at the station? They typically dealt with prisoner transport and witness protection.

Clayton cleared his throat, sat beside her, and took her hand. "We can still search for your brother, but if he's involved with Marat's brigade at all, he's likely gone underground after your raid. And, if that's the case, I'm sorry, but I say good riddance. We don't need that kind of poison in our city."

"Oh my God." Rachel shot up, wincing as pain lanced through her thigh.

"What?"

"He isn't sick."

Clayton stood beside her, shifting so he blocked her from the study's door. "Who isn't sick?"

"Poison. How could I miss it? So stupid." She tried to bonk herself on the head, but wavered and clutched Clayton's shoulder.

"What poison?"

"Listen up, Kincaid. We were never convinced Bronco's grandmother died of natural causes. And now Bronco's sick. A man as healthy as a horse, who eats kale, broccoli, and all those other green things. His illness makes no sense." She waved a hand in the air and almost toppled over. "You said poison. You were right. He's being poisoned."

Clayton gaped at her, opening his mouth and then shutting it again.

"Let's go, Fish Face. The pieces will fall into place on our way to his house." She faltered by the door as a wave of fear crashed through her, making her head spin. "He'd better not be dead. I will kill him if he's dead. He can't go around kissing me, sexing me up with A-plus bang sessions, and making me feel all this fluffy pink crap in my chest, and then die from poison."

"Good catch, Harris." Clayton stormed past her and opened the door. "Let's hope we're not too late."

CHAPTER 34

Rachel jerked awake. Surely, the nightmare she'd just experienced couldn't be real. Surely, she hadn't busted into Bronco's father's house and found William covered in vomit on the kitchen floor. Maybe she'd only dreamed of seeing Bronco collapsed on his bedroom floor, his entire body shaking and covered in sweat.

But no, this nightmare was real. She should probably call his friends. Ember. Owen. Somebody.

She typed a quick text to Ember.

Bronco in Manchester General. Caffeine poisoning. Have Owen handle his work contacts.

Rubbing her eyes, she considered all she and Clayton discovered and all she'd have to explain once his inquisitive friends arrived. Did she really have the patience for that? Bad enough, Bronco's mother had been alerted somehow, and now sat in the corner of the lounge, holding Joe Chogan's hand. *Seriously, lady?* The man had a family of his own. Using great effort, Rachel refrained from rolling her eyes.

After a preliminary analysis, the doctor had discovered both Bronco and his father suffered from severe caffeine overdose. He'd lectured her and Clayton on how studies had shown not to consume more than 200 milligrams of caffeine in a single serving, or more than 600 milligrams per day. Both their levels were way over those limits.

Clayton had returned to Bronco's parents' home with a forensics team and ordered William's special coffee blend bagged and sent to the lab. Powdered pure caffeine was available online. Easy way to poison someone, especially someone who used his own beans.

All night, the doctors worked to control the Murray men's convulsions and fought to keep their airways open. Just the thought of Bronco struggling for air created a tight cramp in her chest, as if she couldn't breathe until she knew he could, as well.

When Rachel got her hands on whoever was poisoning Bronco, she'd squeeze their necks until *they* couldn't breathe. She'd been running around, lost in her own past, while Bronco's snuck up and bit him in the ass.

Great detective work, Harris. Should have seen the signs sooner, and she would have, if she hadn't been trying so hard to avoid her personal feelings for the man, instead of focusing on his case. But, no longer. This was more than she could handle. Game over. Time to get back to a professional level, no matter what the mammoth cock made her feel. Too much was at risk.

One thing was clear: poisoning was a personal act. Her first two suspects were sitting in the room. Gina and Chogan. Both had much to gain from William's death. Unfortunately for them, they'd almost taken Bronco with him. Whether this was a vicious prank on Gina's part or a true attempt at death, Rachel would determine the facts, no matter what measures were needed. Her eyelids grew heavy and she drifted off once more, but she was jolted awake by the shaking of her shoulder.

Clayton stood beside her.

She heaved a sigh and closed her eyes again. "You're lucky I don't have my gun. Don't sneak up on people while they're sleeping, Jerk."

He chuckled and sank beside her. "Any word?"

"Yeah. They're breathing better, not as jittery."

"Poison." Clayton huffed. "Easiest thing to trace, and the suspect list is never very long. Stupid criminals."

"Yep. Guess I'll have to dust off my book of common household poisons and study up."

"How are you holding up?" He nudged her knee.

Yawning, Rachel shrugged. "I hurt for him."

"Wow." Clayton's sea-blue eyes went wide as saucers. "You love him."

"Probably, but I'm quitting."

"Quitting?" Clayton sighed and shook his head. "Not the girl I know."

"Well, you don't know much," she grumbled, closing her eyes again and trying to rearrange whatever was going on in her head—and heart. "I'm going to love watching you fall for someone." She smirked. "Greatest day of my life. Then you'll see all this"—she waved a hand at her chest—"is not worth it. So, I quit."

Clayton grunted. "You must have low expectations if *my* finding love is *your* greatest day."

"It'll be my greatest something, all right." Opening her eyes, she bumped his knee. "Let me know when you're through talking about all this foo-foo stuff and are ready to get back to business."

Clayton stretched that trim swimmer's body, crossing his legs at the ankles.

Rachel closed one eye, but shot him a glance with the other. "I don't get why we never...ya know..."

"Picking up dates in a hospital waiting room? Desperate, Harris. Very desperate." He tugged her out of her seat. "Let's go see this man you don't have any foo-foo feelings for and are bound and determined to quit."

She continued her train of thought. "I mean, you're tall, gorgeous, but..."

"I'll place a bet right now. Five hundred dollars says you are

Mrs. Warren Murray within a year."

All teasing flew from her mind as she halted in the doorway to Bronco's room and took in her fallen mammoth. So silent. Hooked up to all kinds of monitors, his sweaty blond hair sticking to his face. All this pain could have been avoided if she'd been paying attention. Well, she was now. "I'll take that bet, Kincaid, because I'm never putting myself in this situation again. Hurts too much."

Clayton shook his head. "You know what they say, Harris. That's how you know it's real."

# # #

Disgusting.

The smell of vomit coated him like someone had dumped a vat of guacamole and sauerkraut, mixed that together in his mouth, and then spread it all over his body. Shivering with cold sweats, he realized that whatever was wrong wasn't the flu.

By the resigned masks on Rachel and Clayton faces as they walked into his room, he knew he was right. "What was it?"

"Caffeine overdose." Clayton settled into a chair beside him.

Rachel remained by the door, leaning against the wall. What was going on inside that brunette's head now? "Caffeine, really? How?"

"Likely mixed with the grounds of those beans your dad favors."

Bronco nodded. "Makes sense. Who?"

Clayton pulled his black notepad from the back pocket of his jeans. "All right if we ask you some questions?"

"If you can stand the stench. Plus, I'm not going anywhere in this fashionable blue gown."

Rachel didn't even crack a smile.

"How's my dad?"

"Same as you."

"Is he safe?"

"We have an officer outside his room."

Bronco shifted in the bed and pushed the button to raise his back. "I want to see him."

"Answers first. I'll need you to compile a list of who has been in your home recently, and try to remember when your symptoms first occurred."

He rubbed his temple, massaging the ache. "We had that reception after Grandmother died. Any one of those people could have left it. I mean, that caffeine stuff, or whatever it was." He glanced at Rachel. "How was this in the coffee? I'm not quite grasping anything right now."

"Whoever it was used pure powdered caffeine." Rachel responded. "You can order it online."

"We have people testing the grounds now and tracking the source." Clayton tapped his pen against his chin.

"Everyone knows Dad uses that special blend." Bronco ran a shaky hand over his stubble before pouring water into his plastic cup. "I've been staying with him during this transition, and we usually drank a cup together before he left for the bank each day. I do remember it tasting bitter, but I just added more cream."

"Who would want to poison your father?" Rachel questioned. "Who knew you were staying there?"

"The staff. My friends. The Chogans…and my Mother. "

"You think she's capable?" Clayton raised a brow.

"Might run in the blood." Rachel tossed in.

Clayton made some notes. "To what end, though? Was it a ploy to get her to come home and take care of him? Or a way to get his money?"

"My mother has enough of her own money." Bronco shook his head, sickened by the thought his mother could be capable of such a thing.

"Maybe she *was* part of the plan to kill Bronco's biological father in order to marry within her social sphere. Maybe she used her Russian mafia ties to do her dirty work. Maybe she's been after you, Rachel, because you're digging. Your mother is all over this from many angles, Bronco." Clayton shrugged. "I'm sorry."

"We need to keep digging into Gina's past." Rachel scratched her chin.

Bronco studied Rachel. He wanted her closer, needed her tiny hand held tight in his. Why was she so far away? She'd been so panicked back at the house, shaking him awake, with tears pouring down her cheeks. What happened between now and then? He wouldn't ask with Clayton in the room. "What's the word on Marat's people?"

"They've moved out. Khlebosolny's been emptied."

"So, Rachel's clear?"

"I couldn't say, especially after that package of photos arrived at her office."

Sighing, Bronco rubbed his temples again. "That's if the photos were even from Marat's people." Too much all at once, and he was stuck in a hospital bed, stinking and sulking. "I'm sorry I brought you two into this mess."

"This mess is unraveling. The poisoning was a grave miscalculation, which will lead back to the perpetrator. The puzzle pieces will align soon, Murray. Just give Harris and me some time."

"Speaking of that, could I have a few minutes with Rachel? I need to talk to her for a moment."

Clayton stood.

They bumped fists before he walked out.

"I know I stink, but why are you so far away?"

Rachel bit her bottom lip. "Bronco, this situation could have been avoided if I'd been paying attention." She flicked a hand in the air. "Poisonings are like private eye 101. I can't believe I missed this. All the signs were there, but I was too caught up in you."

"Why do I think that's not all?" Bronco briefly closed his eyes as the pain in his heart superseded the pain throughout the rest of his body.

"Because, it's not."

"Come here."

"I'm not." Rachel shook her head. "I-I can't. I'm quitting."

"Can't is right. Once you go team Bronco, there's no escape."

"I'm serious, Warren."

"I believe that you are, *Rachel.*"

"Holy crap, who needs a breath mint?"

Jason, his buddy and teammate, chose the exact wrong moment to enter the room. Bronco fisted his hands in the sheets.

"Whoa! What's with the faces? Somebody die? Sure smells like it."

CHAPTER 35

Seated on a light blue floral couch, Rachel shifted her weight off her aching thigh and studied Eva Stone as she poured mint tea into a dainty cup. A lovely older woman with light brown hair and clear blue eyes, Eva was the type of woman who should have had five or six kids and been surrounded by grandchildren. But her home in a northern Manchester suburb was tidy and...empty. "These lemon bars are fantastic, Ms. Stone."

"I enjoy baking." Eva smiled. "How is William holding up? Do you see him much?"

Interesting questions. Rachel's Cupid meter shot into the red zone. "William and Warren are returning home this afternoon. They've suffered through their withdrawals, and neither was pleased, to say the least. Though, I think perhaps William is more upset about losing his precious coffee blend." Rachel winked. "He's sworn off caffeine for the rest of his life."

"He did love his coffee. Poor man." Eva chuckled, and then quieted as she stirred a sugar cube into her tea. The spoon clinked softly against the edges of the thin, flowery china. "Gina cared for those boys in her own way. She made sure I took very good care of Warren. Many times she mentioned how much he looked like his father, which was strange, because he didn't look anything like William."

Rachel nodded. She'd scheduled this meeting with Bronco's former nanny to ascertain what the woman knew of Gina Astor, but she hadn't assumed Eva knew anything about Thomas Northman. Hopefully, Eva would divulge what she knew on her own without much prompting. Forceful questioning always led to defensiveness. She'd never understood why people agreed to meet with her, only to clam up after a few probing questions. Rachel refrained from sighing as she led Eva farther into the past. "What are your thoughts on Gloria Astor, Bronco's grandmother?"

"That woman ruled over them all." Eva's lips tightened into a straight line, and she clanked her cup against its saucer. "At first, she was cold with Warren, but once he started crawling, she seemed to accept him more, and even stopped by for more visits. He became...a pet, of sorts." She sniffed, and then restacked the diminishing lemon bars into proper order. "Eventually, Mrs. Astor doted on him. Sometimes I'd catch her just watching him with an odd smile on her face. Of course, she never spoke to me directly. But if she saw anything amiss, she made sure I'd hear her concerns from Gina the next day."

"I'm sure you were wonderful with Bronco." Rachel smiled before sipping her tea.

Eva's cheeks turned a slight pink. "I cared for Warren as I would my own. He was so vivacious and eager to please."

A bright smile, likely filled with memories of a toddling Bronco, filled her face.

"After giving birth, Gina became busy with her new position at William's bank. Her coworker spent a lot of extra time training her."

The word coworker was uttered with a slight pursing of her lips, a look of distaste Rachel had seen many, many times. "Would that coworker be Joe Chogan?"

"Yes." Eva tipped a bit more tea into her cup. "Would you like more?"

Rachel shook her head. *Time to probe.* "So, Gina spent a lot of time with Chogan?"

Eva flicked a crumb off her slacks. "Well...I just felt...you see, I believed that man was in love with her. Oddly so." She folded her hands in her lap. "The way he looked at Mrs. Astor-Murray sometimes, especially when she cuddled with Warren...I-I used to shiver at the look on his face."

"That does seem odd." Best way to keep 'em talking was to agree with everything they said.

Eva met her gaze, then lowered her voice to just above a whisper. "I heard them arguing once."

Rachel nodded. "Arguing about what?"

"Mr. Chogan told her he would do anything for her." Eva took a deep breath before spilling the rest. "That he'd loved her, and only her, since the first moment they met. Gina said he was a fool to think she would change her situation and told him to go home to his wife. Then, Mr. Chogan said, 'I'll kill her and him'." Eva's eyes widened. Her cup rattled against its saucer as she placed them both on the coffee table. "I tell you the truth, Ms. Harris. A chill went down my spine. But Gina laughed off his threats. She claimed to have friends who would kill him and his whole family if he touched a single hair on Mr. Murray's head."

Now this was interesting information. Rachel shifted closer and took Eva's hand. "It's okay, Ms. Stone. All of this will help. I can only imagine how you felt to hear such words. I agree, something is off about that man."

"I-I was shocked by the whole conversation." She squeezed and released Rachel's hand. "I was so disturbed, I went to Mr. Murray." She lowered her lids and worked her fingers together in her lap. "He assured me he'd handle things. I felt awful for revealing such a story about his wife, but when I heard them speak of murder, I-I...I feared for William's life." Eva looked up, her eyes filled with tears.

How many times had this woman cried over William Murray? Had he known she cared for him? Had he seen her as a woman at all, or merely an employee?

"William was a good man, *is* a good man, and I couldn't allow such a thing to happen. He deserved to know someone meant him harm."

"Mr. Murray is a very kind man."

Eva pulled a few tissues from a box on the side table to dab her eyes and nose. "He spent every spare minute with Warren. He loved that boy so deeply…even though he isn't…he's not…"

"So, you know?"

"Yes. His father told me one night, when we both happened to visit the kitchen very late. The conversation started innocently enough. He asked after Warren, and then we laughed over his antics. Then his demeanor changed, and he seemed sad. I brewed some decaf and asked him to share his troubles." She smiled, blushing slightly. "Once he was through revealing the truth about Warren's father, he asked that I never speak of it again. You understand, Mr. Murray didn't care he wasn't Warren's biological father. In his mind, Warren was his son." She sniffled into her tissue. "I was in awe. Such a gracious man. And the love he felt for his child. So deep." Shaking her head, Eva wiped at her eyes again. "I'm sorry. I tend to get emotional when speaking about those Murray men." She reached over and squeezed Rachel's hand. "Please understand, I'm only speaking of this because I fear for Warren's safety after this poisoning…I won't have him harmed again. Neither him, nor Mr. Murray."

Rachel bit her lip to keep from requiring a tissue herself. All this love for the Murray men was making her heart hurt. "You loved William Murray?"

After a moment's hesitation, Eva nodded.

"I'm sorry." Rachel patted her hand. "Those two are easy to love."

"I stayed another few years, but when things…I began to feel things too strongly."

"Did Mr. Murray reciprocate your feelings?"

"I never asked."

Rachel shrugged. "He's a free agent now."

Eva gasped, and then laughed. "Oh, dear, I think those days have passed."

Oh, no, she wasn't letting this kindhearted woman miss out on love again. Nope. Not happening. "Is that ever true, Ms. Stone? Shouldn't you both find out? Why not ask? Those Murray men, they've got something. It's kind of annoying, actually. They draw you in with their kindness, and you keep waiting for the other shoe to drop, and then it doesn't, and you get all pissed off because that shoe is up there, you just know it." She glanced at the ceiling and shook her head. "But nope, they keep on being nice. Who's that nice? And then someone goes and poisons them, and you hurt so badly you can't stand the pain, and you have to leave, because they've sucked you into their world, and…" She looked up, realizing she'd been babbling. She opened her mouth to refute everything she'd just said, but she couldn't lie to Eva. This ex-nanny had some kind of magical influence. She'd likely been contaminated in the Murray home by whatever craptastic magic those men had.

"I see." Eva simply smiled, lifting her tea cup before taking a small sip.

Rachel cleared her throat—and her head. "Do you recall any other events with Joe Chogan after that?"

"He and Gina took many business trips together, and I believed…well, you understand what I believed."

"I do understand." She fought not to cringe at the thought of Chogan and Gina together. "Do you recall any other odd happenings during that time?"

"No, just that one argument." Eva set her tea cup on the side table and grabbed a few more tissues. "I was relieved of my duties after Warren turned five."

"A five-year-old Bronco." Rachel shook her head. "Seems hard to imagine." She shifted against the too-soft couch.

"I'd bought him a little jersey and a plush football. I dressed him up in the shirt and took him to the park. When I came back, I indulged him as he ran around the house, so very excited to show everyone his new clothes, and that he could play catch." Her smile dimmed. "Mrs. Astor was visiting and became enraged. She fired me on the spot."

"William argued my case, but Gloria Astor's word was law. So I packed my belongings and left." She sniffed and wiped at the tears trickling down her cheeks. "Forgive me for becoming so emotional."

Damn it. Rachel leaned over and grabbed a few tissues for herself. Stupid magic Murray men, making people cry.

"Mr. Murray was very apologetic." Eva paused for a moment, calming her emotions. "I told him I believed the time had come for me to move on, anyway. They expected a lot out of the boy, and wanted me to become more of a tutor. I felt he was too young. He didn't listen when I read his books during the day, just played with his toys. Which is normal. However, Warren did listen when his father read, but that was usually at night, when he'd worn himself out." A tear dripped onto her navy blue blouse, leaving a dark circle.

"I'm sorry I've upset you."

"No, I loved him…them…very much." She took another sip of her tea before clearing her throat.

"Has Warren been to see you?" Rachel hoped the story hadn't ended with Mrs. Gloria Astor's royal decree.

"When Bronco turned sixteen, he called and said he remembered me, and then asked if I'd like to have lunch. Every year we have lunch on my birthday, and a few times in-between."

Rachel wiped at the stupid tears forming at the corners of her eyes. Stupid sentimental kindhearted bastard. These kinds of Harlequin moments pushed her into some unknown emotional zone where Warren became her perfect prince, not that flawlessly-coiffed freaks like that really existed, but he was pretty close. Who visited old nannies on their birthdays? Assholes, that's who. Assholes with hot, heavy bodies, and mammoth cocks. A mammoth cock she hadn't seen in far too long.

"Will Warren be all right?"

Rachel jumped, embarrassed by her wayward thoughts. "Yes. Actually, Ms. Stone, I'm not sure. He's pretty shook up." Shaking her head, she laughed. "And cranky."

"Hmm...what is your involvement with the family? You said you were an investigator?"

Clever lady. Subtle, yet direct. Good tactic. "Warren hired me to look into his paternity. As you've indicated, you knew his father is not his biological parent."

"Oh, my." Ms. Stone dropped her teacup onto the table, spilling a little over the edge. "How did he take the news?"

"Perhaps you should give Bronco a call, ma'am. I'm sure he'd find some comfort from your presence." She tapped a finger against her bottom lip. "You know, they have a housekeeper, but they really need someone more...personal taking care of them. You should stop by. I think Bronco...and William would appreciate a visit." Rachel hid her smirk. "Take him some of these lemon bars. They'll match his sour mood."

Shaking her head, Eva chuckled. "I'm aware of what you're doing, Ms. Harris. For an investigator, you should be more subtle."

"Subtle has never been my style." Rachel grinned

"Is Warren your style?"

Oh, this woman is good. She gave a brief nod, indicating her approval of the parley. "Warren and I...started something, but in the middle of all this mess...this danger, I missed a very important clue, and so I don't believe continuing is wise. Just because he's unstoppable on the football field doesn't mean he can't get hurt. I didn't catch the poisoning, and all the signs were there. I know better than to let my job become personal."

"Your job, at its core, is very personal. The things you see and reveal to people are very raw and real. Why shouldn't you feel the same, when that job is someone you care very deeply for?"

Rachel opened her mouth, but then closed it. Eva saw too deeply into her heart, which wasn't helping her choose sides in her internal war. And why would she be clear on anything when she'd been hit by a Cupid's arrow, tipped by some magical potion that made Warren Murray irresistible?

"Warren has been shielded his whole life. From every hardship, even school work. All he cared about was football. You should have seen him when he found out he'd been chosen for the Marauders, so happy and proud."

"I imagine."

Eva sat forward in her chair, her gaze intent. "When Warren cares, he cares deeply. If he's hired you, he believes you are now a part of his world. Under his protection. I wonder, Ms. Harris, what you'll do with that? You seem so reserved, contained, as if you've never known softer emotions, or perhaps..." She glanced at Rachel's empty plate. "Perhaps you were hurt by those who were meant to show you affection."

Why did this investigation keep veering into her personal life? "Ms. Stone, with all due respect, this investigation is about Warren, not me."

"I'm a fifty-two-year-old woman, and as a nanny, I've been in and out of many families' homes. Some happy, most not. So, let me offer a bit of advice." She clasped Rachel's hand. "Let him love you."

Rachel shook her head, biting down hard on her bottom lip to stave off tears. "We're not...I—"

"My dear." Eva tipped up her chin with a finger. "Not *all* of those questions you asked were for investigative purposes." With the same finger, she tapped Rachel's nose. "Now, let me show you some photos of baby Bronco." She chuckled as she rose from her seat and headed for a china cabinet.

With all the tipping and tapping of her face, Rachel worried the magical nanny had turned her into a pumpkin. For another hour, she stewed over Eva's words as she finished her tea and viewed multiple photo albums. She refused to let her thoughts stray to having her own baby Bronco, someday.

After thanking her and leaving with a Tupperware container full of cookies, Rachel walked to her car. Halfway down the sidewalk, she glanced back.

Eva stood in her doorway, smiling, and then gave another little wave.

A gesture like some fairy godmother casting a spell. Sweet Jeez, what was with all the fairyland magic crap?

She refrained from tossing her cookies, for real, and checked her phone. This visit today served as a reminder of all she'd never had: no mother figure baking cookies, patting her hand, listening to her spill about a man she...No! Nope. She really hoped Ms. Stone visited the Murray boys, because that woman deserved a happily ever after.

If Mr. Murray was smart, he'd scoop up Eva and never let her go.

Rachel would have to do some recon, lay some groundwork, and drop some not-so-subtle hints to make that situation happen. No way would she let Eva's love go unrequited. Flipping through her phone, she noted Clayton had texted five minutes ago, asking to meet at the firing range.

On occasion, they doubled up at the range and then hit the Cajun place next door, ribbing each other over spicy beans and rice about who'd shot better. Though, she was full of lemon bars, she wouldn't pass up the smell of gunpowder or po'boys.

She texted back: *I'll be there in 30. Get the middle lane if you can.*

More than ready to take out her emotional turmoil on the bullseye, she hopped in her Jeep and headed to the range. After taking the exit that looped around the city, she noticed her Jeep's tire pressure light flashing in the dash. Easing off the gas, she heard her tires pop and she swerved.

Narrowly avoiding a minivan, she jerked the wheel toward the side of the road. A raw scream tore from her throat as she watched in slow motion as a huge Dodge truck whipped to the right to avoid the minivan and clipped the back of her Jeep.

The jolt was enough to flip over the lightweight vehicle. The loud scrape of metal on pavement, her body jerking against the seat belt, and her laptop flying out of the passenger seat to slam against her cheek all added to the live-action nightmare. She blinked away the pain as the Jeep flipped again, righting itself.

Her entire body shaking, she glanced around, orienting herself. Smoke poured from her engine. The loud hissing sound joined the pounding of her heart. She wiped at the wetness on her cheek and fumbled to unsnap her seat belt. After pulling free, she basically rolled out of the Jeep and then dragged herself off the highway to lean against a narrow tree.

Dizziness overtook her, and she glanced at her bloodstained hands. "Where...where..."

"Ms. Harris, are you all right?"

Startled by the male voice behind her, she stumbled and fell into the ditch, landing in putrid water left over from last night's rain. Gagging, Rachel tried to stand. As she wobbled to her feet, she felt someone take her hand.

The smells of smoke, blood, and whatever foul brew existed in the ditch choked the breath from her throat. Attempting to escape the stench, she tried unbuttoning her shirt, but her bloody, shaking hands wouldn't work.

"Ms. Harris..."

She blinked and shook her head as the pain in her face and ribs overwhelmed her odd sense of needing to flee.

The last thing she saw was Joe Chogan's face, as she blacked out.

CHAPTER 36

After settling his father in his bedroom, Bronco took a deep draw from his water and grabbed his phone off the coffee table.

Jason and Owen had driven them home from the hospital.

Maude and Ember had hot grilled cheese sandwiches and tomato soup waiting when they arrived.

"Who are you texting?" Jason finished off the last of his sandwich and jerked his head toward the phone. Tan and even more blond after his tropical trip, he lounged in the La-Z-boy.

"Rachel."

"She back to work?"

"She took off yesterday, but today, she was meeting with my old nanny, Ms. Stone." His phone rang. Hoping the caller was Rachel, he quickly swiped up his cell. "Hello?"

"Warren, how are you?"

"Ms. Stone?"

"Yes."

"I'm doing a lot better. Thanks." He rose from his sprawl on the couch and headed for the windows, avoiding the noise his friends were making in the kitchen. "How are you?"

"I just spoke to your girl, Rachel. She's a sharp one."

"Yes, she is, Ma'am." Bronco refrained from adding, in more ways than one.

"I planned on dropping by later with some of my chicken and noodles and some cookies. Would that be all right?"

"Nothing is better than your homemade chicken and noodles. I'll be here all night." Bronco wrapped up the call, happy to hear from his old friend. She was like a dear aunt. Someone who baked him cookies and listened to his problems without judgment or censure.

Owen slapped him on the back. "What's up?"

"Just talking to Ms. Stone." Tired and in need of a long hot shower, he punched Owen's arm as he headed back to plop onto the sofa.

The doorbell rang.

Before he had a chance to ask Owen to check the door, he saw Maude bolt from the kitchen. "Wait, Maude, don't..." He glanced at Owen. "She shouldn't be opening the door with poisoners and whoever else roaming around."

Owen nodded then trailed after his sister.

"Is Ms. Stone coming over?" Jason piped up. "Is she bringing food?"

"Not that you'll get any, but, yeah."

Jason threw a pillow at his head. "She loves me. She'll probably bring something special, just for me. Did you tell her I'm here?"

Maude caught Bronco's eye as she slid into the room with some blond guy. "Warren, I'd like you to meet Brady Stephens. He stopped by to take me home."

Bronco nodded before standing and shaking the guy's hand. His bud's sister was growing up, but he trusted Owen to vet the dude properly.

Jason flipped up the handle on his La-Z-Boy and stepped into Brady's space. "Didn't I see you at Rockies the other night?" He braced both hands on his hips.

Bronco shook his head. Poor Brady would learn the hard way. Maude had not one, but three older brothers.

Brady shrugged. "Probably. I was out with friends, but Maude met up with us later." He wrapped an arm around her shoulder and kissed her temple.

"I've seen you around…a lot." Jason cocked a single brow.

Maude stepped in front of Brady and poked Jason in the chest. "You're one to talk about being seen…*around,* Jason."

"Then I'd know about certain people's reputations, wouldn't I? And I'd have a right to interfere if anyone could disrupt *your* reputation." He tugged her away from Brady.

Owen clasped Jason's shoulder, working his way between the two. "That's enough."

"This guy is bad news, Big-O." Jason nudged Owen's hand off his shoulder. "I ain't having it."

"You aren't having it?" Maude huffed. "May I remind you that, over way too many years, I've met hordes of girls with obscene reputations who were hanging on your arm? But, I've held my tongue. And the one time I ask you to do the same, I get this?" Maude almost barreled over her brother to get to Jason. "You're an ass!"

Owen held her around the waist. "Calm down. He's always been overprotective. You know why."

Maude glanced at her brother, and sighed. "Fine." She shot a final glare at Jason before leaning down to give Bronco a hug. "I'm so glad you're better. You're my favorite brother."

He squeezed her and whispered in her ear, "That boy better be good to you."

Smiling, she kissed his cheek. "He is."

Bronco sipped his ginger ale, happy to see his little Maude had moved on from her crush on Jason. Not that Jason had any clue.

The couple left, and Ember followed Maude and her new guy to the door.

Owen punched Jason's shoulder. "What the hell was that?"

Jason toppled back into his chair. "The guy's a dick."

"If he is, then she'll figure that out on her own." Owen sank onto the corner of the couch opposite him.

"Big mistake. And when I find out he's hurt her, I'll kick his ass, and then I'll come kick yours for letting her date him."

Bronco tuned them out as he watched Ember enter the room and slide alongside Owen. Seemingly without thought, Owen wrapped his arm around her and pulled her close. Like two magnets.

His heart ached, which pissed him off because most of the poisoning symptoms were gone, yet this pain remained.

Perhaps Rachel was right, and she wasn't the kind of girl who could give him affection, home, kids, and reliability. So, he'd adjust. He wouldn't believe she didn't care for him. They could make their own brand of relationship work. He wasn't the kind of man who could handle an overly-needy woman, anyway. Not with his job's travel schedule.

He had lived in a structured, privileged world. Spoiled and untouched by anything dark or sinister, but now, his eyes were open. The real world had entered in all its shadowy shades, but Rachel was a glimmer in the darkness.

No longer would he sit back and wait for the future to come. He'd set goals and reach them. No more easy street for a kid who lived on a road paved with gold that had lost its shine.

His phone buzzed on the table. Once he read the text, he shot off the couch, that pain in his chest now piercing like glass shards throughout his entire body.

Within seconds, Owen was somehow standing beside him, clutching his arm. "What's wrong?"

"Rachel's been in an accident."

CHAPTER 37

Rachel tossed her keys onto the kitchen counter. "Thanks for bringing me home, Kincaid."

"I'm not pleased about doing so, since you should have stayed at the hospital." Clayton shoved his hands into the front pockets of his jeans.

"They wrapped up my ribs and checked my cheek. I'm not hurt that bad. I just need a shower."

"Yeah, you do stink."

"Would you...would you mind staying until I'm done?" Her body may be in working condition, but after that accident she remained a bit shaken...and majorly stirred.

"Bronco's on his way."

"Okay."

"Wow, you must really be messed up."

"Pretty much." Rachel headed for her bathroom, more than ready to wash free of 'eau de drainage ditch'.

Flicking on the faucet, she stretched her arms over her head. After studying her bruised face in the mirror, she heaved a sigh and got out a washcloth. Entering the shower, she breathed deeply as the scalding water helped clear her senses. Had someone just tried to kill her? Why was Chogan at the scene? Had he followed her from Eva Stone's house? Was he the real threat?

The door creaked open.

"Who's there?" Her heart pounded as she tried to make out the bulky form through the steam.

"Just me." Bronco opened her shower's sliding glass door.

"You should be home in bed." Rachel waved her shampoo bottle at him.

He stripped down.

"Hey, you can't just—"

"No." He placed a finger against her lips. "I don't want you to say a word."

Though bruised and bumped, her aching body thrummed with need. He was here. Naked. Hard. And so very, very wet. All she wanted was to slide up and down that big frame, so she provoked him. "Word."

He took the bait. Swooping down, he kissed her, engulfing her with his thick, heady presence. Steam rose from their meshed lips and from the heat of the water.

With each abrasive stroke of his lips, each greedy plunge of his tongue, she surrendered that final piece of her heart. The broken shards mended, but each stitch still caused pain. This man now held the frayed edges together.

And he knew, the bastard.

He eased back from the kiss and flashed a way-too-sure grin. "Are you all right?"

"Perhaps you should check my temperature. Got a thermometer handy?" She ran a hand up and down his thick shaft.

He chuckled. "We filming a bad porn in here?"

"Oh, it's going to get crazy pornographic." She squeezed his balls. "My plan is to get you very dirty in this shower."

After a hard kiss on the lips, he met her gaze. "You have got a mouth on you, that's for sure, but a side of you exists that wants the hearts and flowers. You want softness."

Rachel shook her head. "I don't want the softness." She gripped the head of his cock. "I want this."

"You want love. And, after all I've been through these past few weeks, I do, too. The rough stuff exists outside of this sphere, Rachel, but between you and me, we'll work this out. I could have lost you tonight." He tucked her hair behind her ear. "Clayton said your Jeep flipped. I need to feel every inch of you in order to be sure you're whole and still with me."

"I don't need all this romantic babble." She arched against him and kissed her way down his chest.

With two strong fingers, he lifted her chin from its descent. "Pink towels in your bathroom, Pixie? A bit romantic, aren't they?"

"They're actually fuchsia." She grabbed his fingers and bit them.

"Hell." He laughed. "That's even worse...you always sing along with the love songs on the radio." Bronco backed her into the shower's corner. "You want romance. You want me."

"Pure cheese." Rachel avoided his gaze.

"Is it?"

Wrapping her arms around his neck, Rachel kissed him just to shut him up. "Be gentle with me. I've just been in an accident."

"You're a walking accident," he grumbled, kissing the tip of her nose.

She locked her legs around his waist, buried her face against his neck, and mumbled into his ear, "I was completely freaked out. My tires popped, and then the Jeep tumbled." The memory made her shiver. "I was actually more scared of hitting the minivan full of kids in the lane beside me."

"That's my girl." He shook his head. "Worried about others while your life is flashing before your eyes."

She took a deep breath before giving him more than she'd ever given any man. "I'm not scared now. I'm right where I want to be."

"I know where you want to be." As he kissed her, he lifted her up, and then plunged deep into her body.

She held his head in her hands as she returned the kiss then, with a gasp, she arched back. Her hair brushed against the tiles as he worked her up and down along his thick, hard length.

All the day's fears and pain receded as pleasure followed each slow thrust.

Drawing her upper body closer, he teased the tip of her nipple with his teeth and tongue. His breathing grew harsh, and his groans echoed off the shower's walls.

When her bruised ribs protested, she clenched his biceps. The power and strength in those arms rocketed through her body and lit up her core. Tiny waves undulated, and she gasped as she crashed into satisfaction. Gripping him tight, she shouted her release, biting her bottom lip as each spasm tightened and released.

Heightening the length of her orgasm, Bronco maintained the smooth glide one, two, three more times before he stilled and murmured her name. His thick length pumped his release into her body, filling her with warmth.

Like always, he erased the lonely coldness, the fear of what might come. He was ever there for her. And that scared her as nothing had before. Unfair, but she couldn't stop the unease that slid in after the bliss. Why did she have to be like this? Why couldn't she let go and love him back? And she did love him. So very much. But, what did that mean?

Loving him was unwise with someone out to kill her...and him. Who was responsible for all this chaos? Obviously, the person was ramping up his efforts, perhaps out of control now. She needed to step back and think, but right now, she just sank against Bronco's warm, wet body.

"You okay?" He ran a hand up and down her back.

She clutched him close, holding his head against her neck. Not saying a word, she remained draped like a very wet curtain, because she wasn't okay. Not at all. She kissed his wet head, then his temple, then his mouth. Thanking him the best way she knew how, she poured into her kiss everything she felt.

He returned the kiss with equal fervor and quickly hardened inside her once more. Without asking, without stopping, he rocked into her slick core again, all while kissing her with his hot, wet mouth.

Burying her fingers in his hair, she moaned as his hands worked magic on her body, making her forget each ache and pain.

He cast his spell over each rosy nipple, her ass, her clit, until she exploded again, but softer and more drawn out this time. Her head lolled back against the tiles as she gasped out her release.

Bronco clutched her bottom in his hands and pounded into her, harder and faster, until he groaned and spilled inside her once more. He licked a long trail along her neck before plunging deep into her mouth, kissing her with gratitude and a bit of steam that matched the white wisps floating throughout the shower.

She followed his lead, not soothing, but allowing him to release his savage side, letting him wallow in the pleasure he'd found within her body.

He pulled back and lightly kissed her lips over and over before clutching her tightly in his arms. "I love you, Rachel Harris."

She froze, a lump forming in her throat. "Bronco, I-I...I don't—"

"Shhh, it's okay." He jostled her in his arms so she rested at eye level. "I'll wait until you can say the words back."

Trembling with joy, with fear, *who knew,* Rachel disengaged her grip on his body. What if she never said the words? Didn't he deserve to hear them? *Oh God.* Why couldn't she just spill her feelings to this man?

Steadying herself on the bathroom rug outside the shower stall, she grabbed a couple towels from her cabinet and handed him one.

He dried his hair before the rest of his body.

Rachel tried not to appreciate his robust form even though

she wanted to jump him and never let go. She rubbed herself dry, then tucked her towel under her arm.

"Look at us. We're a mess." He flashed a lopsided grin. "We should spend the next week in bed."

"We're getting close, Bronco." Rachel squeezed a dollop of toothpaste on her toothbrush. "Close to something, and the person behind all this is out of control." She glanced at him in the mirror as she brushed her teeth.

"What do you mean?" Bronco's brow furrowed. "Who's out of control?"

She rinsed out her mouth and handed him her toothbrush. "My Jeep accident wasn't an accident. And the weird part was, Joe Chogan was there."

"Joe was there?" Using her toothbrush, he took his turn at the sink.

"I know. Odd, right? He pulled me off the side of the road after the crash and called 911."

"What did Clayton say about him being there?"

"Chogan told him he was just driving back to work, and the accident happened right in front of him."

"That does seem like an odd coincidence."

She leaned against the sink, trying to ease some of the pressure on her leg. Shower gymnastics probably wasn't the wisest form of exercise after being shot and wrecking her Jeep.

Bronco finished swishing out his mouth then met her gaze in the mirror. "Maybe we *should* spend a week in bed. Safer that way."

"Safer for whom?" Rachel scoffed.

Bronco turned then backed her against the sink. "You like to play it safe, don't you, Pixie?" He trailed a finger along her cheek to trace her lips. "We're not safe outside, or from what's in this room, so stop building barriers. I'll just break them down."

"Bronco." She braced her arms against his chest. "Someone tried to kill you and your father, and now someone came after me.

So, yes, I'd like to play it safe."

He bumped his hips against hers. "My bed is safe."

"Again?" She shook her head. "You're not feeding that mammoth blue pills are you?"

"No, I believe he likes eating Pixies."

Laughing, she shoved at his chest again.

He lifted her onto the counter and tugged at her towel.

"Stop." She gripped his wrist.

"But he's hungry." Bronco's lower lip jutted out.

"Stop referring to your dick as a he, it's killing the mood."

"You started it." After yanking away her towel, he licked her very perky nipple.

Apparently, her body was jacked up on adrenaline or something, because she wanted him again despite her injuries.

Taking the initiative, she flicked away the towel from her prize and squeezed his rigid cock from root to tip. "One more time, and that's all."

He grunted, kissed her, and then proceeded to satisfy her hunger once more. *Okay…twice more.*

Apparently, near death experiences were an aphrodisiac. *Who knew?*

# # #

Thoroughly relaxed and wearing clean clothes, Rachel finger-fluffed her semi-dry hair and followed Bronco to the kitchen to scrounge for nourishment after all that lovely exercise. The cat-in-the-cream smile on her face would not fool the grouping of friends lounging in her living room. And who cared if they could read everything in her smile? Why not?

Jason smiled from his slouch in her recliner.

Stopping by his chair, Rachel jabbed his shoulder. "Hey, Jason. How was your trip?"

"Better than yours, obviously." He smirked.

"True."

Bronco bent and whispered in her ear. "What do you want to eat, Rach?"

She shivered. "Just a sandwich, because that's all I've got. Sorry."

He grunted. "Stay in here. I'll see what you've got."

"Why don't we order pizza?" Jason grumbled.

"Too late. No one's open." Owen sighed from his perch on the couch.

After fidgeting beside Owen, Ember shot up and pounced. "Rachel, are you okay?" She wrapped her arms around her and awkwardly patted her back.

Girl, if you knew the gymnastics we just performed in that bathroom, you wouldn't worry at all. Rachel drew Ember closer. "The wreck scared me, but I'm okay. Just bruised and sore."

Ember took her hand. "Bronco was really worried."

Owen rested his head back on the couch. "So, what happened?"

"Tires popped." Rachel winced. Owen would take that as a personal affront. He took car care very seriously.

"Huh?" Owen furrowed his brow. "I just checked your Jeep. Tires were fine."

"Yes, they were."

"Oh no!" Ember's eyes widened. "Was the accident deliberate, then?"

Rachel nodded. "Most likely."

Jason straightened in the recliner. "So, who's out to get you?"

Ember ran her hand up and down Rachel's arm. "Yeah, what did Clayton say?"

"He believes as I do that foul play was involved. The cops have my Jeep and are looking it over now."

"Why you?" Ember took Rachel's arm and led her around the couch, nudged her into the corner, and covered her with a blanket. "Look at your poor cheek."

"I'm okay, Ember. Really." Smiling, she squeezed Ember's hand. "As to what happened to my Jeep, could be regular wear and tear, or someone believes we're too close to the truth."

"I won't lose you." Ember braced her hands on her hips. "You must be careful. Whether this is related to Owen's case, or your brother, or even some case you've investigated before, you need to be alert." She sank next to Owen and dropped a kiss on his cheek.

He raised a brow before drawing her closer for a much longer kiss.

Good Lord, those two need a room.

Bronco came back in and handed Rachel a sandwich. He munched on his while standing.

Grabbing Rachel's hardback book off the coffee table, Ember thumbed through the pages. "When did this come in? I love the cover. I see your publisher went with the red dress."

"New cover?" Bronco took the book from Ember.

Rachel's heart pounded. She could practically see the light bulb going off above Bronco's head.

"R.W. Hardcastle?" He stopped chewing and glanced at her, then back at the book, and then at her again. "It's you, isn't it? You are R.W. Hardcastle."

No way to avoid this one. Rachel glared at Ember, avoiding the confusion in Bronco's gaze, as well as the coming confrontation.

"I don't understand." Bronco set his half-eaten sandwich on the table lining the back of the couch and scratched his chin. "You know I read these books. I've gone on and on about how I'm a fan." Head tilted, he handed the book back to Ember.

Rachel shrugged, sure her cheeks were bright red as she tried to come up with an answer. What could she say? How could she explain why she had always kept her writing to herself? Why she rarely, if ever, shared her creative side? R.W. Hardcastle truly was someone else. An escape from reality that had served since she was a lonely, abandoned girl. In fiction, she could escape. Be someone else. But her secret life now gleamed bright in the spotlight. *Never a good place to be.*

"Why didn't you tell me?" Bronco's voice had softened, as if he were afraid to hear the answer but was too curious to keep everything inside. "R.W. Hardcastle is the whole reason I started reading this genre. *You* are the reason. Why keep it a secret?"

"My pen name is a secret. No one knows who I am except the publishing company, and that's really only a select few. I have…a lot of fans." She waved a hand through the air, ignoring the churning in her stomach. "Nosy fans aren't conducive to my work as a private investigator, and now that they are making a movie out of the second series…well things would've spiraled out of control."

"I'll accept that." Bronco ran his fingers through his hair. "But you could have told *me*. I wouldn't have told anyone."

Rachel shifted in her seat, unhappy with all the accusing stares. Why was this such an issue? "I gave you plenty of clues," she mumbled, twisting her fingers in her lap.

"Did you?" Bronco mock laughed, waving his hand in the air. "You know everything about me. My life has been ripped open." He pounded a fist against his chest. "I've shared everything I am with you, and you couldn't give me this one thing."

Owen cleared his throat. "Bronco, maybe we should leave you two—"

"Did you think holding this secret over my head was funny? Were you laughing behind my back at how dumb I was because I hadn't figured it out? And when you listened to me go on and on about how much I loved your books, was that some kind of ego boost?"

"I don't know." Rachel rubbed her ribs because her pounding heart was jostling other organs in her body and making her nauseous. Why was he so irritated? And why were her friends staring like she was some vile betrayer? "Bronco, I mean, come on. I dropped so many hints, you'd have to be stupid not to figure it out. I practically told you every time you brought up my books."

"Oh, Rachel." Ember gasped, clasping her hand over her mouth.

"What?" Rachel cleared her throat and glanced at her friend. "So, I don't want people to know. What's wrong with that? I can't really tell anyone anyway, because I do have a contract stating I need to keep my mouth shut. And I am the one who put that bullet point in the contract to begin with, so I can't be running my mouth off about how I'm R.W. Hardcastle."

Ember shook her head, stood, and grasped Bronco's arm. "I'm sorry, Bronco, I thought you knew."

What is this?

"No, I didn't." Bronco patted Ember's shoulder. "But, I guess I'm just too stupid to figure it out."

His tone and words struck like venom, which had somehow entered her eyes, because for some reason she was tearing up. How had they gone from fucking like rabbits to him not even looking at her? And then her best friend was consoling him, when he had no right to need consoling. What had she done wrong? "Bronco, listen. I'm not quite clear about wh—'"

"No." He closed his eyes and took a deep breath before standing right in front of her. "I know who I am. I know what my limitations are." His voice seemed flat, and his arms hung slack at his sides. "I may be stupid, but I am smart enough to know why I do what I do. You don't trust anyone, and you push away all those who could love you in order to punish yourself for something that took place long ago. Not me. I've learned from my mistakes." He cleared his throat. "I made the choice to move on. I worked on me." He pointed a finger at his chest. "What have you done but reject every facet of who you really are?"

"Bronco." More scared than she'd ever been in her life, teetering on the brink, she found her footing and shuffled to her feet. "What is this about? I was only...I can't legally tell anyone my author name…so…"

"That's just an excuse." Bronco shook his head. "You're full of reasons to never let anyone close. Do I even know you? The real you?" He stepped back. "You've lost more than a fan tonight, R.W. Hardcastle." Bronco's jaw clenched tight, and he dropped his gaze to his feet.

His next words were barely above a whisper.

"I gave you everything. But all your warnings were true. You gave nothing in return. So yeah, maybe I am stupid. But the thing about stupid people is, we can learn. You? What can you do?"

Rachel jumped as Bronco exited, slamming the door hard enough to rattle the frames on the wall.

While also rattling her carefully concealed world.

CHAPTER 38

Seriously off-kilter, Bronco tossed his keys into the bowl on the entryway table. Never had he been so humiliated. He felt as if he had stood in front of the classroom and answered every problem incorrectly. A fool, when the answers were written in ink all along. As a funny smell shot up his nose, he sneezed.

Wailing cries sounded from the living room.

His father shouted murderous words at someone.

Bronco hoofed his way down the hall.

In the doorway, the scene was so odd he took a moment for his brain to calculate what his eyes were seeing.

Joe Chogan crying.

His arms wrapped around Gina's body.

His mother's face and hair smeared with blood.

His father being held back by Ms. Stone.

Ms. Stone turned and spoke to him in words he couldn't hear.

A dull hum had taken over his mind.

Thrumming.

Thrumming.

Joe Chogan rocked his mother's body.

All the furniture was askew.

A dark stream of blood spilled down Chogan's arm.

"Wh-what...?" The single word served to question the entirety of the full-colored nightmare. He took a deep breath as rage filled his heart. "What have you done?" He charged across the room, bent down, and grabbed Chogan by the shirtfront.

"Warren. No." Ms. Stone gripped his bicep.

Why was she here? She shouldn't be here, in the middle of all this death. She was kindness and purity. "Ms. Stone. Why? Wh-where?...I-I don't..." He dropped Chogan and removed her hand from his arm. "You shouldn't be here. It's not safe." His heart thundered as he glanced around the room. What had happened? Were there intruders still in the house? Why was everyone just standing around? And would Chogan just shut up already? He couldn't think. Couldn't reason.

"Warren, please sit down." Ms. Stone came into view again as she wrapped her cool palms around his cheeks.

Then, somehow he was sitting beside his father on the couch, which wasn't in its proper place. Everything was misaligned.

Wait.

His father.

"Dad." He shook William's arm. "Are you all right?" He quickly looked him over, and then braced an arm in front of his father's chest as he gazed around the room.

"Warren, calm down." Perched on the coffee table before them, Ms. Stone squeezed his knee. "William, I'm calling the police now."

His father nodded before slumping back against the couch.

Bronco waited until Ms. Stone finished her call. Each word spoken to the 911 attendant was like a nail being hammered into his head, and he had no choice but to take each blow.

"Wh-what happened?" He scrubbed a hand over his face. His face, overly dry from the few tears he'd shed after leaving Rachel.

Don't go there. Things were bad enough with the sound of

Chogan's crying, his father's muffled tears, and his own pounding heart. Too many sensations. Had he walked into some TV drama? Was any of this real?

He glanced at Chogan, still holding his mother. Yeah, still way too real. He swallowed back the half-sandwich he'd eaten at Rachel's. There was no coming back from this moment.

Chogan's face displayed pure agony.

What had he done?

Bronco shifted to stand.

"Warren Murray, look at me." Ms. Stone's schoolmarm tone always drew his attention. "Your father and I went out for dinner, and when we returned, we walked in on this." Though her cheeks flushed pink, she sniffed and straightened her spine. "From what I can gather, Mr. Chogan's wife, Claire, found Mr. Chogan and your mother in an indiscretion at their home." She cleared her throat. "Your mother fled, but they both followed her here. According to Mr. Chogan, a scuffle occurred, during which your mother fell face-first onto the glass side table's corner. The steel leg...it pierced...it pierced her throat."

A heavy drum pounded through his ears, skyrocketed by his heartbeat exploding in his chest. "Chogan did this?" Bronco turned, ready to kill the man with his bare hands.

"Warren, more violence isn't the answer. While Mr. Chogan does carry some blame, he stated the altercation was primarily between the two women."

"Where is Claire?" Bronco glanced around the room again.

"Your father and I passed her as she left. She escaped just as we pulled in. Chogan's story rings true, or else, why would she flee?"

"Dad recognized her car?"

"Yes, Son." His father clamped a hand on his shoulder and shook his head. "My God, I can't believe she's gone."

"After all I've done for you, Gina. Why? Why?" Chogan moaned. "We were so close to finding our happiness. So close to being free. I've waited so long, for nothing. Sacrificed for nothing."

The whole idea of this man and his mother churned Bronco's stomach. And this display in front of his father and himself was completely inappropriate. Bronco sank to the floor and buried his face in his hands, taking deep breaths, doing what he could to think of other things. Football plays, sunny beaches, winning the big game—anything to erase the vision of his mother lying bloodied in Chogan's arms.

Ms. Stone combed her fingers through his hair.

That soft touch pushed him over the edge. He couldn't help his outburst of sorrow and anguish. He sobbed like a child who'd lost something precious.

And he had.

He'd lost his mother.

CHAPTER 39

Erik maintained a stoic mask as the man seated across from him continued his banal financial speech about percentages and ways he could invest or manipulate.

Joe Chogan's appearance was hardly acceptable in this private men's club on the north end of Manchester. With his wrinkled clothes, unshaven face, red-rimmed eyes and disheveled hair, the banker looked like the lunatic he was destined to become. He'd barely touched his steak, but had certainly enjoyed the club's high-end bourbon. Seemed the man was indeed stricken by the death of Gina Astor-Murray.

Not that such things mattered in the least. That woman had been teasing the raw side of life for far too long.

The only reason he was fouling his air with Chogan was because he'd been seen deflating Rachel's tires.

And though, he'd prefer to stay out of her life, he'd always been disturbed by Chogan. Always slithering in and out of his father's office like a snake. But the snake could, and would, lose its head if it kept trying to kill his sister.

Chogan shouldn't play instrumental parts in hooking up hit men with desperate old women if he wasn't willing to be found out. Stupid man hadn't even bothered to cover his tracks, believing Astor money covered the trail.

That was never true. Every act eventually caught up with you.

Erik sliced a piece of his asparagus in half, lifted it to his mouth, and slowly chewed. Then he took a small pat of butter and slathered half his roll. "Mr. Chogan," Erik interrupted the sweating, blathering man. "I must confess, I brought you here under false pretenses."

Chogan's blood-shot eyes widened, and his mouth dropped open. "Wh-what? Why?"

"You are aware of who my father was."

"Yes, of course."

"Then you understand I am intimately aware of all his dealings, present...and past." Erik raised a brow, sipping his water.

Good Lord, had the man showered in cologne? He cleared his throat past the stench of whatever foul brew Chogan had drenched himself in. "You see, you've been playing with knives. Using them to puncture rubber on my friend's vehicle. And I find I'm slightly disturbed."

With a shaky hand, Chogan wiped the sweat from his forehead. "I didn't know...I didn't—"

"Shut up." Erik raised a hand between them, palm up. "Just please, enough. I'm not going to kill you...in a crowded restaurant." He smiled and took a bite of his perfectly-prepared steak. "Aren't you eating?" He waved a fork at Chogan's full plate. "I don't like wasteful people."

Chogan downed his bourbon in two swallows before glancing at his plate. He lifted his fork, but then his cell, which sat beside his drink, rang with some musical chime. Chogan's jaw clenched as he answered the call. "Where are you?"

Erik glanced at his man standing behind Chogan and gave a subtle nod. Based on Chogan's lethal tone, he'd likely just found his wayward wife.

"You'll regret this, Claire." Chogan ran a hand through his

greasy hair. "Tell me where, and I'll meet you." A few seconds passed, and then his face went beet red. "I'll be there shortly." He shot out of his chair.

Oh, does he really think he gets to leave so easily? "Excuse me, Chogan but where do you think you are going?"

"It's...my wife...she just called and I need to...um...leave."

"Do you?"

Chogan glanced at the door.

Surely, the man wasn't considering making a run for it. "Sit down," Erik ordered.

Chogan clenched his hands into fists. "I need to leave."

"And I won't ask again." Erik used an even tone lined with every menacing vibe imaginable. "So, your wife called, did she? Ready to turn herself in? Or is her plan to make you pay for past indiscretions?"

Chogan sat but didn't say a word.

"You weren't stupid enough to tell her what you'd done, were you?"

"I know things...things about you." His gaze narrowed. "Don't sit there and threaten me."

"I don't threaten, little man. I finish." Erik leaned forward, tapping his steak knife on the table. "Where is she?"

Chogan shook his head.

Erik glanced over Chogan's shoulder and jerked his head at his associate.

His man pulled out an empty chair and sat close to Chogan.

Erik raised a brow.

"She's at William Murray's pool house," Chogan spat out. "Says she's going to spill the truth about Thomas Northman to that bit—private eye."

"A much better word choice, Chogan. Good to know you can learn."

Hopefully, his sister wasn't stupid enough to meet with Chogan's wife alone. *Damn it!* He'd have to save her ass, again.

Because based on the look in Chogan's eye, he wasn't letting anyone walk out of that pool house alive. Still, he couldn't haul the man outside at gunpoint. *Unfortunate, that.* He'd have to follow him to Murray's place and call in Leonard. He was in enough trouble with the U.S. Marshal as it was, but that didn't mean he wouldn't get a head start.

"What are you waiting for, Chogan? Your sweetheart awaits."

In his rush to leave, Chogan toppled over the chair, causing patrons to stare his way.

Erik really hoped he didn't have to kill the man after being seen by so many witnesses. He waved down the waiter. "I'll need my check."

Once the man left, he glanced at his driver and right-hand man. "Night's far from over, my friend. Far from over."

CHAPTER 40

"So, there's an ABP on Claire Chogan?" Rachel rubbed her temples, hoping to stave off the headache that had only gotten worse in the three days since Bronco left.

"Rachel, at this point, the Manchester PD have taken over this investigation." Clayton tapped papers together on his desk and slid them into a yellow folder. "I really think you should get some rest. You've been shot and been in an auto accident. Go home."

"I need to keep busy." She sipped from a semi-warm Coke she'd bought from the police station's machine. "They need to turn up the temp on your soda machine."

"They need to do a lot of things, but none of that matters, because you're going home."

Dog with a bone, that was Clayton Kincaid. She didn't want to go home, or be alone, because then she'd visit that headspace that said Bronco was right. She hadn't revealed anything. But, she'd never had a chance to develop those sharing skills. Did she want to learn? Could Bronco show her? Was she too late to mend their relationship?

Maybe she should see a psychologist. She was totally mental. And now, she was empty and alone.

Bronco was in the police station, meeting with another

detective, giving his statement. They'd given him additional time while he prepared his mother's funeral.

She only knew this information through Ember who, after Bronco left her apartment, had tanned her hide with more words that hurt. Rachel had fences to mend all over town. She snuck a glance at the interrogation room and noted everyone was standing. That was her cue. "You're right, Kincaid. I'll head out now."

He nodded, but then narrowed his eyes. "I don't believe you."

She sighed and meandered over to the coffee machine, waiting for Bronco to exit.

As he stepped out of the room, he exuded that usual raw masculinity, yet he seemed ruffled. Hadn't shaved, was dressed in a T-shirt, and faded jeans. Lack of sleep evident by the dark circles under his eyes.

"Bronco, you got a minute?"

"Harris." He nodded, but he kept moving.

She followed him out, but she didn't speak when they shuffled onto the full elevator.

On the way to his SUV, he halted in his tracks and braced his hands on his hips. "Why are you following me?"

The muggy, early-evening air clogged her lungs as she tried recalling everything she needed to say. "I want to talk, and you haven't answered my calls." She gripped his arm. "Bronco, please let me apologize. But first off, please let me say how sorry I am about your mother." She kicked a loose rock across the pavement. "I've made a mistake...this whole thing with you, I've messed up everything. I don't know why I say things sometimes. I think I'm being funny, but the words come out snarky, and not everyone gets my jokes."

He shook his head and stepped toward his truck again. "Not in the mood to hear your excuses today."

She fought to breathe, feeling stifled and rejected. He couldn't leave. "Bronco, please, don't leave. I just want to—"

"Rachel! My mother just fucking died." He spun on his heel and swiped a hand in the air between them. "Everyone around me is dying. My real father, my grandmother, my mother. Who's next? So, whatever you feel you need from me—forgiveness, understanding, an ear to listen—I'm not offering right now, got me?" Bronco rubbed the back of his neck. "I'm out. Done. So just don't. I get who you are. We're good, so let's both just move along with our lives, all right?"

Her mind raced to find just the right word. When words were part of her living, why did they not surface when she needed them most? What did he need to hear? And how could she remove that cold and flat tone from his voice? "But, Bronco, I want—"

"Sometimes there aren't second chances, Rachel. Hell, I gave you more than that, and now...now I don't have the strength to give you another shot at my heart. I'm bleeding enough."

And once more, the door slammed as he drove away.

Rachel wobbled over to open her car door, collapsed onto the seat, and burst into tears.

What had she done?

CHAPTER 41

Later that night in his father's home office, Bronco shifted his weight in the leather chair. His father had opened a rare bottle of Scotch. Not really his drink of choice, but he sipped anyway and had to admit the liquid went down smoothly.

He'd tuned out all the football talk surrounding him, which was at odds with who he was at his core. Football was his life, yet over the past few months, death had taken over the playing field.

Owen lounged back in William's leather recliner. "Did you see we signed Lance Hunt yesterday?"

"Maybe he'll keep Overocker from getting the drop on you this season."

Owen flipped him off. "Overocker's insane."

Bronco's father chuckled. "Sounds like the season's shaping up. I know Warren's anxious to get back on the field."

"He's always ready." Owen shrugged, taking a small sip from his snifter. "Coach and the boys will be here tomorrow, after the funeral."

While Bronco knew he should be concentrating on their first game of the season, he only had regrets swirling in his mind. Regret that he'd lost a chance to know his real father. Regret for feeling that way when he loved the man sitting across from him. Regret he hadn't visited his grandmother more often. Regret his mother had died when harsh words still remained between them. Regret he'd taken his emotional baggage and dumped everything on Rachel when she'd only meant to apologize. If nothing else, he'd promised they'd remain friends.

He finished off his Scotch and reached for the bottle.

"Warren, that's heady stuff. Meant to be savored, not used to drown sorrows." His father uncrossed his legs and stood, placing a hand on his shoulder. "We'll get through this, Son. We'll get through the funeral tomorrow, and all the days after that. I know I don't say this often enough, but I love you."

Bronco lumbered out of the chair and wrapped his arms around his father. "I love you, too. I'm just so damn sorry about everything. I feel like, if I'd just let the investigation go, we wouldn't be here. Mother would be alive."

His father held him tighter. "None of this is your fault. We'll find answers together." His father pounded his back a few times before turning to leave. At the doorway, he glanced over his shoulder. "One other thing I want you to know...regardless of everything, I did care for her."

Bronco nodded. "I know...so did I."

As his father left the room, Bronco heard the clink of a bottle against glass.

Jason nudged Bronco's knee with his shoe. "Sit down and drink this, Big-B." He handed over the snifter filled halfway to the top with Scotch. "That was some touching shit."

Bronco halted with his glass partway to his lips and chuckled. "Yeah, it was. So succinct with your words, Jason."

"Hey, I didn't grow up with that kind of love. I don't like seeing you, or your dad, suffer. You're my family, Bronco." He pounded a fist against his chest. "I'm hurting for you."

Owen was just as slack-jawed over Jason's comments as he was.

"Oh, come on." Jason glanced between the two men and huffed. "You think I can't have feelings?"

"No, man." Bronco leaned over and ruffled his bud's hair. "You can have whatever you want. I feel the same way. You two being here right now…means a lot." He cleared his throat. "So, what did Coach say about my ideas on the new blocking schemes?"

For the next couple hours, he sat around with his brothers, drank expensive Scotch, and talked football. His lids started to droop, but he jolted to attention when his phone rang with Clayton's ring tone.

"What's up, Clayton?"

"Claire Chogan has been located. She called Rachel, said she had some information about Thomas Northman's death."

Bronco shot out of the chair, rubbing his eyes in hopes of sobering up. "Where are you?"

"I'm heading to your house."

"My house? Why?"

"Claire Chogan is in your pool house."

"Why the hell would she come here? I haven't seen any cars pull up."

"Hell if I know, Murray. Maybe she's been hiding there all week, or maybe she's just returning to the scene of the crime. I have no idea why people do what they do. One thing I do know, though, you better stay in the house. She's cornered and scared. Who knows what she'll do?"

"Where is Rachel?" His heart pounded, and he raced over to look out the back patio windows.

"She's with me."

"She doesn't go in alone, Kincaid."

"Affirmative. See you in ten."

CHAPTER 42

Four huge male bodies hovered over her tiny frame.

Rachel held back a sigh. They were wasting time.

"Absolutely not. You are not going out there alone." Standing in the dark shadows under the back patio awning, Bronco shook his head and glared. "Kincaid, she isn't going out there to meet that woman without backup."

Tired of all the male posturing, she grabbed Bronco's arm and pulled him back inside his father's house. "Listen, Claire called *me*. She's expecting *me*." Pacing across the tile floor, she raked her fingers through her hair. "I get it now. I understand that you're not keeping me from being who I am, and I'm sorry I've kept so much from you. Though we don't have a lot of time for this, I just want to say, I'm really sorry...about everything. I have no idea how to conduct a relationship or whatever, but I'd like to try." He couldn't know how hard those words were to say. He'd turned her into a puff-head who doodled pink hearts and traced their initials inside with red crayon. But, playing with crayons was fun sometimes. Maybe this mammoth man could replace all the love she hadn't received during her childhood.

"I don't want to change what you are." Bronco cupped her cheek in his hand. "But I do need to understand *who* you are, and if you leave out big pieces, well then, we'll never be whole."

Fighting back tears, she wrapped her arms tight around him. "I want to be whole."

"I know." He kissed her cheek. "I do, too, and we will be." Pulling back, he tipped up her chin. "But, listen, I don't like this. That woman in the pool house is like a coiled snake. Push too hard, and she'll strike."

"Clayton is with me. I'll be okay." She leaned up on her tiptoes to kiss him. "I need to go." She reached for the handle to the back patio door.

Bronco grabbed her elbow. "You better play it safe, because I need you to finish the April Archer series."

"I'll finally be able to give my characters their happily ever after. I never knew what to write"—she squeezed his hand—"until you."

"Ah, Rach." Bronco drew her close and kissed her.

A hard press of lips that asked for more, and she finally relented, giving back more than comfort, but a promise for the future.

Clayton opened the door. "Rachel, you ready?"

Just as she pulled away from Bronco, she jolted as the sound of gunfire pierced the air.

"Son of a bitch." Clayton took off toward the pool house.

Rachel followed, limping slightly from injuries not yet healed. If she got shot again, she'd throw in the towel all together. These bumps and holes in her body were stacking up.

Clayton stationed himself alongside the pool house door, hollering, "I am Clayton Kincaid with the Manchester Police. I'm coming in. Do not shoot." After a count of three, he opened the door.

Rachel peeked inside.

Joe Chogan had a steel grip around his wife's throat—and a gun jarred against her temple.

"How the hell did he get here?" Rachel murmured.

"Drop the weapon." Clayton crossed in front of her and

entered, training his gun on Chogan.

"No." Joe shook his head. "Get out."

Hearing rustling that wasn't coming from her skittering heart, Rachel glanced over her shoulder. Bronco and his crew, which now included his father, had joined their party. *Oh, hell no.*

She waved them back. "Stay back. He's armed."

William grabbed Bronco's arm.

"Stay behind Clayton, Rachel," Bronco ordered. "I mean it."

Sirens sounded in the distance. The neighbor's dogs started barking madly, and the summer heat created tendrils of sweat down her back. The whole situation seemed just one flinch away from a full-fledged shootout.

"We'll wait out here." William pulled Bronco beside a flowering tree planted amongst the pool house's landscaping.

Rachel turned her attention back to Chogan. After taking a steady breath, she sidled up to Clayton, stepping just past the threshold.

"I said get out!" Chogan waved his gun.

Sobbing uncontrollably, Claire rested on her knees, cursing her husband and calling Bronco's mother some very colorful names.

"Quiet." Chogan smacked her with his gun, effectively silencing her.

Rachel swallowed past her fear and mentally prepared her game plan. Keep 'em talking. In heightened situations, she'd learned to either get people to spill their secrets, or the bullets started flying. "Time for answers, Chogan. Did you kill Thomas Northman?"

"No. Although I wanted to." Spittle flew from Chogan's mouth, and sweat poured down his face.

His handsome mask slipped, revealing the true evil within. Momentarily sidetracked by his pulsing hatred, she almost forgot her next question. "Did you kill Gloria Astor?"

"They made me." His icy glare cut across the room. "But I

didn't mind, that old witch made me promises years ago and never delivered."

"Who made you?" Clayton inched farther into the room, keeping his gun leveled on Chogan.

"Years ago, I brought in Victor Pavel as a banking client, because of the man's friendship with my father. Pavel had Northman killed, per a directive from Gloria. Gina deserved better. She deserved me." He jerked a thumb at his chest. "Gloria gave me the money. I passed it to Pavel. But Marat was the one who made sure Northman ran off the road that night." He snorted out a laugh. "What would Bronco think of that? His mother sleeping with the man who killed his real father."

"How do you know this?" Rachel asked, wondering how much of this Bronco could hear, and how he was handling each revelation.

"I arranged the meeting."

"With Pavel and Bronco's grandmother?"

"Yes, you stupid bitch." He waved his gun in Rachel's direction. "I already said that."

She tensed and glanced at Clayton.

"How did you kill Gloria?" Clayton took over the questioning, drawing away Chogan's attention.

"Pure caffeine. Only took one heavy dose to kill her. Pretentious hag deserved to die." Chogan sneered. "At Gloria's funeral reception, I poured the rest of the powder into William's coffee grounds. He deserved to suffer for hurting Gina."

"Did you kill Gina?" Rachel studied Claire's prone form, searching for evidence the woman had been the recipient of the gunshot they'd heard earlier.

"Gina." Chogan's voice cracked. "W-we finally had our chance. But Claire ruined it." He kicked his wife's side and once more aimed the gun at her head.

"Joe Chogan. Did you kill Gina Astor-Murray?" Clayton's cop tone startled Chogan enough to delay what Rachel believed was inevitable—Chogan *would* shoot his wife. There was one way to stop him, and she was prepared to do so. She glanced at Clayton. He appeared ready to do the same.

"Of course, I didn't kill Gina." Chogan's incredulity rang clear in his bellow. "I loved her. There was...she and Claire...there was an-an-an altercation. So much yelling, and then she just...she just fell." His gaze lifted and focused on something over her shoulder.

Damn Murray men! Rachel stiffened, knowing without turning who had decided to join their party.

"Well, well, William. Come to witness the end, have you? You had Gina far too long. I deserved her. I gave her to you, and Gloria promised she'd handle you, but then she never did. Many times throughout the years, I considered taking matters into my own hands."

William crowded behind her. "Consider me paid back in full, Chogan. You've damaged my life irreparably."

With a disgusted huff, Chogan kept his gaze on William. "No, you've not suffered enough. I wasn't the rich William Murray." He waved a hand in the air. "I wasn't enough for Gina, but once she was on her own, she saw how much I cared. She needed me." He aimed the gun at William. "Who's the one with the power now? If I'm going, I'm taking you with me."

"No!" Jumping backward, Rachel shoved William out of the way.

Shots thundered through the air.

Rachel stilled from her position on the floor atop William. Ears ringing, and the percussion still vibrating through her chest, Rachel detected a tinge of copper mixed with the sharp scent of gunpowder.

Gun in hand, a dark-haired man stood where Chogan had been only moments before.

"Drop your weapon!" Clayton shouted.

"Clayton, wait." Rachel scurried to her feet before helping

William stand. Gazing at the man holding the gun, she blinked, her vision hazy. "Erik, is that really you?"

"Funny." Brow arched and his lips in a tight line, he answered, "You've been looking for me all these years, and now that you've found me, you don't even recognize me."

"I-I...wha-what are you doing?" Biting her bottom lip against the outpouring of emotions too long held deep, she barely remained standing.

"Saving your ass...again." He frowned.

She tried speaking, but she couldn't decide where to begin. His face gave away nothing. Something wasn't right. This reunion was unlike any she'd ever dreamed. "I don't understand. Who are you?"

"I'm your brother."

"But...that's not...where have you been?" How could she expel the zillion questions in her head during the chaos of a shooting and everything else that was happening way too quickly?

The whop-whop of sirens sounded loud enough to have her almost checking over her shoulder to see if they'd pulled up alongside the pool.

Clayton stepped in front of her. "Listen, *Erik*, I appreciate the assistance, but I need you to lower your weapon, brother or no. Slowly, set it on the table."

With a smirk, he nodded and did as he was told.

Drawing closer to her brother, Rachel side-stepped Chogan's body, laden with one bullet hole in his forehead and one in his chest. She shuffled past Claire's unconscious form until she stood before Erik.

Her brother.

She lifted a hand to touch his face, intending to verify he did, in fact, exist.

He flinched and turned away. "This isn't the time." Erik shook his head. His hair was the same deep brown as her own, his voice the most welcome sound she'd heard since losing him seventeen years ago.

He was alive. Not dead, not buried in an unmarked grave in some creepy wood. Alive. Here. *But why?*

"I'm not even supposed to be here." He glanced at the door to the pool house's bathroom.

Was he deciding if he could slip out as easily as he'd slipped in? No. He couldn't leave. Not yet.

"For someone so small, you get in way too much trouble."

What could she say to that? His words rang all too true. "Was it you that night at the Marat house?"

"So, you do remember?"

"Yes."

"We'll have to fix that."

"How?"

He pinched the bridge of his nose. "This can't keep happening."

"What can't keep happening?"

He shot her a look that suggested she'd lost her mind before waving his hand across the room. "Seriously?"

Allrighty then, no warm reunion for the Harris siblings. Though she continued casting furtive glances at her brother, she stepped aside as police officers spilled into the pool house.

After things had settled, Clayton cuffed her brother and led him to a police car.

Chogan dead. Claire unconscious. Bronco's case over.

But, now what? For her. For Bronco. Where was that man, anyway?

And why, in this moment, did she need him more than ever? Why did she crave his calming presence? The certainty of her brother being alive was now overshadowed by her fear she'd lost another man.

Standing off to the side of the pool house, she flinched at the tap on her shoulder.

A man in a cowboy hat with a toothpick hanging out the side

of his mouth squeezed her fingers and tugged her toward the back of the pool house. "Ms. Harris, we finally meet."

"Who are you?" Rachel jerked away her hand.

"I'm Leonard Moore, U.S. Marshal in charge of your brother's case."

"And why should I believe that?" She glanced at him before continuing her search for Bronco. Would he go with her to the police station? Would she be ready this time to speak to her brother? Should she call her parents?

The Marshal heaved a world-weary sigh. "If I were you, I wouldn't know what to believe either, but I *am* working with your brother. I need you to come with me. He's waiting in my car."

"How is that possible? I just watched him leave with Clayton."

The man raised a brow and continued chewing on his toothpick.

"I'd like to see your badge."

Again, he sighed, but then pulled it from his suit coat pocket. "We ready now?"

She nodded, but halted halfway to his car. "You really have my brother in there?"

"Yes."

"I thought I was ready, but now I'm not so sure. What happened to him? My brother? Why is he...so hard?"

Scrubbing a hand over his face, the cowboy tossed his toothpick into the grass. "He's Victor Pavel's son."

"No, he's Carl Harris's son."

He patted her hand and led her closer to the car supposedly holding her long-lost brother. "Honey, that's where you've been wrong all along. Harris might be Erik's biological father, but that boy is pure Pavel."

CHAPTER 43

Along the side of his parent's house, Bronco stood by his father and Clayton as Joe Chogan's body was loaded into a coroner's van. Owen and Jason had left an hour earlier after Clayton told them they were crowding the scene.

The entire area was decked in crime-scene tape. No one was allowed back there except investigators.

"Dad." Bronco glanced at his father. "You all right?"

"I'm heading upstairs." William rubbed the back of his neck. "I need...I have no idea what I need. I'll see you in the morning."

Bronco watched as, with slumped shoulders, his father headed back into the house. Guilt over this whole debacle crept up his spine and threatened to drop him to his knees. He'd never wanted this. All this death and pain. Never wanted to see his father looking so dejected and alone.

He hadn't seen Rachel since the shooting. When she pushed his father out of the way, she'd stopped his heart. He just knew that bullet flying through the air was directed at her pixie head. When that percussive boom sounded, he'd nearly died himself.

Her brother. Of all people to save the day, the hero just had to be her long-lost brother.

How was she handling that bit of information? Sure, she believed she'd seen him that night at the Marat house. But now that he'd made an actual appearance and plainly stated he was her brother, was she okay? Were they reconciling? And where had he been all this time? "Clayton, where do you have Rachel?"

Clayton glanced up from his phone. His eyes went wide as he scanned the area. "I haven't seen her." He scratched his chin. "That girl needs a leash."

"Tried that, didn't work."

"Try harder."

"Where's her brother?" Bronco headed toward the front of the house to see if Rachel was waiting out front.

"I put him in a car earlier." Clayton followed alongside. "By now, he should be downtown. He's got a lot of questions to answer about tonight, and about Marat's death, not to mention that house Rachel plundered. He's the one with all the answers and, regardless of who he is, I won't go easy."

Bronco nodded. Though he and Rachel had dealt with their share of difficulties, he'd be at her side through this whole mess. "Huh, I don't see her." He bent and glanced inside a couple of the squad cars. "I'll check if she's inside."

"You do that, Murray. Then tell her to get her ass down to the station."

"Will do." He took two steps away then halted as he caught a glimpse of three black sedans pulling up the drive.

Men in suits poured out and immediately headed over to the police vehicles.

"What the hell?" Clayton dropped his phone into his pocket. "Looks like this investigation just went federal."

CHAPTER 44

In an interview room at an office downtown, Rachel sipped some actually decent coffee. Seemed U.S. Marshals got the good beans. Though, the steaming brew barely made it to her mouth, as shaky as her hands were from the evening's events. Damn, that was close. Maybe she should retire and write full-time. Dodging bullets wasn't such a swell job anymore. Plus, she'd likely lose her private investigator license after storming into Marat's house, anyway.

Sitting in a twirly office chair, she twisted back and forth as Erik received a very thorough verbal spanking from an extremely pissed U. S. Marshal.

Her brother hadn't backed down, simply stood head-to-head against the short blond guy's wrath.

She sighed. Her brother. Alive, thriving, and quite handsome. Throughout all her time searching, she'd believed that once she found him she'd feel closure, or some sort of relief. But right now, she felt neither. What would her parents think of his return? Not that Humpty Dumpty could put everything back together again, but his reappearance might provide some comfort.

After a jaw-cracking yawn, she took another sip of her coffee. All this time, he hadn't needed to be found. Or maybe he had? She wasn't quite clear on who he was. Or how he had arrived at the pool house. What part was he playing in this game? She had gleaned he was under the Marshals' protection, but somehow also working against Marat and Pavel's organization. Like a protected informant.

The well-groomed man continued his verbal assault, chastising Erik for blowing his cover, and threatening to send him to South America.

Her brother seemed so young to be embroiled in such dealings. What schemes were these Marshals using him for?

Mr. Cowboy Hat aka Leonard had yet to say a word.

She really needed to use the bathroom. Hopefully, all this chest-beating would end soon.

"Pavel is dead, Erik." Leonard entered the fray.

"I know." Her brother smiled and cracked his knuckles. "But the brigade has bigger fish."

"Not fish, sharks that will swallow you whole."

"Fine by me." Erik sniffed and shrugged.

"You're compromised." Leonard shook his head and tossed his hat on the table.

"No." Erik braced both hands on his hips. "No, I'm not."

"Yes, you are. Listen, you've done as we've asked." Leonard clapped him on the shoulder. "Pavel is dead. Marat is dead. We've splintered this brigade and brought in two other mafia heads due to your intel. We've done some good here."

"Those charges won't stick." Erik paced beside the table, his fingers now locked in his thick dark hair. "Their influence runs too deep."

"We've done what we can."

"I can do more."

"You will die."

"Erik, please," Rachel whispered. She couldn't take any more death. "What are you doing? If you've helped these men, let that be enough. Haven't you lost enough? Haven't we all?"

"You're done, Erik." Leonard crossed both arms over his

chest. "Accept this."

"We'll pull all the files and any information on this case," the overly-tan shorter guy announced. "Bury everything and get you someplace safe." He turned his gaze to Rachel. "Ms. Harris, all charges will be dropped in relation to the proceedings at Marat's house. But, let me warn you now…" he jabbed a finger against the conference table. "Stay away from the Russians. You've done enough damage by dragging your brother in to save you."

As those words sunk deep, Rachel took a deep breath. "I did need him to save me…in so many ways," she whispered, running her hand back and forth across the smooth wooden tabletop. "I'm sorry…it's been a long couple of months, and those words, though you didn't mean them that way…they really struck a chord." She glanced first at her brother, then Leonard, since he seemed to be the one in charge. "Do you think you could give us a few minutes alone?"

The marshal nodded. "Make it quick."

After the door shut, she didn't know where to begin. "How did you know where to find me tonight?"

"I was meeting with Joe Chogan."

"Chogan?" She tilted her head. "Why?"

"He tried to harm what's mine."

Her heart pounded at that admission, though she wasn't exactly sure what he meant. "Do you mean Chogan tried to harm *me*?"

"After all this time, we're talking about Chogan?" Erik arched a brow.

She cleared her throat. Awkward was too small a word to describe this encounter. Wasn't he happy to see her? "How did you know who I was?"

"My mother."

"Your mother….did…" She rolled a hand in the air between them, hoping he would continue.

"She was taken as a child, just like me, and then she was

forced to raise me once Marat brought me in." He paced beside
the table again. "She paid attention to things. Knew who I really
was, because she listened. They never gave her enough credit. She
could have ruined them all."

"You loved her?" This was a small crack, but one she'd barge
through just to understand him a little.

"Love sometimes isn't enough to describe the depths of a
feeling, Ms. Harris." Both arms crossed against his chest, he
leaned on the conference table. "The question you should ask
yourself is: would you die in their place? Sacrifice every piece of
who you are for that one person? Define *that* with a single word,
and you will have your answer."

"Answers," she scoffed. "You standing here isn't giving me
any."

"Why did you ever think it would?"

"I suppose I believed *you* would be the answer...but I-I still
have questions. And a lot of them start with why." She clamped
down on her teeth to keep from crying. This hurt. A lot. "You
look well." Erik shot her another of those looks that suggested he
believed she'd lost her mind. Apparently, he did carry the little
brother gene, annoyed by everything his older sister did.

Clearing her throat again, she tapped her folded hands on the
tabletop. "It's just, I had all these nightmares of what you were
going though. Torture, buried in someone's basement. The usual
imaginings, but here you are, alive and whole. I have no words,
really. Other than I'm grateful you're alive."

He huffed out a laugh. "Not that I really want to burst your
bubble, but I was raised by Victor Pavel."

Her stomach churned. Based on what she knew of Pavel, she
couldn't imagine being raised by the brute. "What does that
mean?"

"It means I'm Pavel's son. He raised me to follow his lead, to
take over the organization once he'd gone, so don't imagine I was
raised to be a Boy Scout."

"I'm so very sorry." She dropped her gaze to her hands. "I've waited years to tell you that. I shouldn't have left you in another's care that day at the park. I've regretted my actions ever since." She swallowed against the hard lump in her throat. "I-I'm sorry, Erik."

He nodded. "Apologies are generally made to make the person speaking feel better, because words don't erase actions. Although, you have nothing to be sorry for, whatever you may believe. Pavel took what he wanted."

"The guilt I feel will never diminish, because you are correct: words are only that, and I can't turn back time." Rachel sniffed and glanced around the room, searching for a tissue box. "I don't speak to our parents. Well, rarely, anyway. They wrote me off long ago, but I'd like to tell them you're alive. Do you have any idea what they went through, what I went through, when we lost you?"

"No, I don't." He shrugged. "I barely remembered you, and I did what I had to in order to survive. Your parents are not mine."

"That isn't true." Struck by his indifference, Rachel studied him, looking for something in his eyes that reflected compassion. "Are you so heartless then, that you'll leave them to their imaginings?"

He tugged on the cuff of his black shirt sleeve—his dark jeans and shirt a match for his dark heart. "I'm a product of my environment. Besides, they not only lost one child, but they've obviously abandoned another. Why should I care for their sufferings?"

"Because you are a human being." Rachel shook her head, saddened by his lack of empathy. "What did Pavel do to you?"

"Enough!" Scowling, he slammed a fist on the table. "You know nothing of who I am. I am not your brother. I am not an investigation. And I certainly don't care what *your* parents believe of my existence. I was placed into a role at a very young age, and I will see it through." He stepped closer and jabbed a finger on the desk before her. "You will stop your probing. You've been satisfied I'm alive. I'll even accept your apology, if that is your wish. But, do not seek me out again." He paused until she met his gaze before he leaned closer. "I will not ask again. Nod if you understand."

She glared for a moment, but then she nodded. Rachel didn't think she could speak past the knot in her throat, anyway. Not after spending her whole life searching for someone who didn't want to be found.

Years wasted searching for a brother who'd obviously died long ago.

CHAPTER 45

Stepping out of the room, Erik waved off Leonard. "Give me a minute to take a piss."

As he trudged down the hall, he fought to catch his breath. After that verbal altercation, he needed a few minutes to deal with this foreign feeling clogging his chest. A searing pain, of loss, and something...indefinable.

He'd had no choice but to wound Rachel, to warn her off forever. His path was dangerous, and she could never follow. He punched open the bathroom door.

She had to stop digging. If not, they'd kill her.

He'd never forget that heartbroken look he put in her eyes as he made sure she understood he was nothing. Felt nothing.

After splashing cold water on his face, he gazed into the mirror and took a moment to wonder just who he had become. His mother had begged him to stay strong. Too fight to the top. She'd helped him survive through all those years of mental and physical pain. Enough that he'd buried any softer emotions beneath years of Pavel's iron fist.

Yet tonight, he'd jeopardized years of work to keep Rachel safe. She'd likely never understand what he'd done by pulling that trigger, nor how much he'd exposed. He couldn't turn back the clock and give her the perfect family unit. Two parents, one boy, one girl.

None of that could happen now.

He'd never again be her brother. Not in any real sense.

That stung a bit, because he'd lost the dream, too. After discovering her investigation, he should have shut her down in the beginning. So, why hadn't he?

In this moment, his dealings with Rachel Harris were complete. No matter how much he admired her spunk and drive, he would not continue any observations of her life. "I am not her brother. I am…no one." He gazed into the mirror again, shoring up his resolve. "I am a fly creeping on Otari Korzakov's web. Nothing more."

Tonight's mere breeze would not sweep him from his goal.

Intricate spindles wove through the Korzakov organization. Layers so thin, if a person wasn't careful he'd fall right through.

He'd made his place in the web, and he'd continue until he arrived at the center. For now, he'd allow Leonard and Metro to hide him away for however long they needed. Then one day, when he was smarter and stronger, he'd have his revenge.

And the spider would fall.

CHAPTER 46

Stretching her arms above her head, Rachel blinked awake and caught Bronco staring down at her. He'd arrived at the Marshals' office last night, stormed into the room, scooped her up in his arms, and left. Without a single word, he'd driven to his apartment and deposited her in his bed. And though she tussled with him, and perhaps grumbled a bit, she was glad he'd carried her away.

Right now, she had no idea what time it was, or even if they'd slept away three or four days. "What time is it?"

"Time for our reckoning, Harris."

She nodded, though she knew pulling all her feelings to the surface would sting. "This story didn't end the way I wanted it to. If I'd written the ending, then my brother, he wouldn't...I don't know. It's so messed up." She shuffled against the pillow and rested her forearm over her eyes. "I'm so confused, and I-I hurt."

"I hurt, too." Bronco's deep baritone sounded right beside her ear. "But, I've come to believe that sometimes life's greatest mysteries aren't mysteries. Life is right in front of us all the time: greed, lust, jealousy, but there's also love. Are you done searching? Seeking the answer for why you got to live, or why you weren't the one taken? Your brother is alive." Bronco tugged on her hair. "So, I need to know. Are you done blaming yourself for your own existence?"

"I hope so, but I still feel guilt, especially…he was so hard." She opened her eyes and gazed into his calming-blue depths, gaining comfort. "So indifferent. I thought, maybe…maybe he could be my brother again. But that won't happen."

"I'm sorry he can't be who you want. But, we don't always fit into the roles others have assigned to us. We do what we can. The question now becomes, can you let him go?"

"When my brother was abducted, he took part of me with him." She hugged the camouflage comforter closer to her chest. "All those years ago, when I came out of that park bathroom and found him gone, I lost the part of my inner being that accepted me for who I am. From that point, I didn't like me. Some days I still don't, but I'm getting better. None of us deserved what happened on that day, and yeah, I'll have to live with the guilt for the rest of my life. But, at least now I have an answer. I don't have that empty space in my soul. Erik is alive. And I'll have to accept that's all I'll ever have."

"No." Bronco shook his head. "You'll have more. Who we end up becoming is on our own shoulders. We make the choices. Sure, they are in some ways dictated by who raised us, but in the end, the only ones responsible for what happens in our lives is ourselves."

"I want this." She braced a hand on his shoulder. "What's between us. I want to try. I know we'll fight, but I know, at the core of everything, I love you enough." She pressed a hand to her chest. "I love *me* enough to make this work. I want that mammoth cock forever. No sharing, just mine."

"The mammoth cock was the deciding factor, was it?" Bronco arched a brow.

"It really tipped the scales." She stifled a giggle.

"Mmm…" He nuzzled her neck and then lightly kissed her lips. "So, you're really ready for this?"

She gazed into his eyes, knowing he meant more than just

making love. He meant everything. Foo-foo-frilly pink candles, love songs, and seriously sappy walks on the beaches. "Yes, because I love you. I've held in those words for too long. You said them once, and I ached inside because I couldn't say them back. But I do love you, Warren 'Bronco' Murray, with every piece of my broken heart." She rained kisses all over his face and then, frantic for skin against skin, she whipped off her shirt and tugged down his shorts. More than ready to seal this deal with sweat and wet kisses.

"Whoa." He tugged on her hair. "Not a race, pixie. Slow down, and let's see if we can fly together."

And then he kissed her. Used those big hands to touch her in every possible way, then made love to her until she came, shouting and gasping with release, and a heart full of relief. This was making love. Touching someone not only physically, but also emotionally. This was a connection sealed by their bodies and their hearts.

After multiple heated sessions, where she was more sated than she'd ever been and comforted when he held her against his side, she trailed her finger up and down his heaving body. "I already know the acknowledgment in my next book."

"What's that?"

His voice rumbled in her ear, though the vibrations seemed to come more from his chest than his mouth. "'To my Mammoth. I promise I won't get so lost in the rainbow's shadow that I lose sight of the pot of gold.'"

He squeezed her side. "How did you know you loved me?"

"I didn't *know*." She kissed his chest, and then, with a way-too-wide smile she decided he needed a repeat of the Rachel Harris-customized rendition of the well-known Journey classic. "Just a small town girl, livin' in a lonely world. I took the midnight mammoth goin' anywhere." And, as she shot up and danced on the bed, singing her crazy lyrics, she knew with this man by her side, she'd never stop believing.

EPILOGUE

Nerves crackling up and down her spine, Rachel chugged along behind Bronco, Clayton, and Maude. Kincaid was her lead security for the day, and her mammoth man and Maude her lead supporters.

"You ready for this, Rachel?" Maude eased along beside her.

"I hope so. Did I tell you my mom called last night?"

"Oh, yeah?"

"My parents...I don't know, my mom anyway, she's making amends. Isn't easy, though."

Bronco squeezed her hand.

She met his gaze, and immediately all the old pain flitted away. He'd become her rock and her sounding board, never wavering from her side. They had fought together to overcome all the strain and heartache endured last spring. And as a new spring began, they were stronger and more secure in their own lives and with each other.

Her author posse stopped beside the metal stairs, leading up to a stage set up on the Manchester Marauders' football field. This was the only area large enough to accommodate so many people.

Good grief, her stomach hurt. She inhaled and released a few deep breaths as Bronco had suggested on their drive here, but nothing worked.

The crowd waiting out on that field had gathered for her. She'd finally spilled the beans, or shared the pen name, or whatever. Today, a week before her movie released, she was doing a big reveal in the form of a book signing and question-and-answer session.

Now that the threat from Marat and prison time were gone, she'd decided to work only a few cases per year and concentrate full-time on writing. Her partner, Clayton Kincaid, now handled the majority of cases.

She shifted from side-to-side, more nervous than she cared to be. Her literary agent had spent the past hour going over various do's and don'ts while jacked up on caffeine, and the woman's zippy attitude had rubbed off so that now Rachel had the jitters, too. Apparently, five hundred people were waiting. Last night, tents had been staked in the parking lot as people waited to get her signature. So surreal. But, in a way, she was glad to have entertained so many people with her tales.

The first in her April Archer Private Eye trilogy had been filmed last winter and was now prepped for the big screen, a series she had wrapped up with a very sexy happily ever after—due to the smoking hot beast standing right beside her.

"You look super hot today." Rachel glanced at Bronco, sporting a nicely-fitted pair of black dress pants and a body-forming turquoise shirt that not only highlighted the muscles in his arms, but also the long expanse of his torso. She arched a brow and fought not to lick her lips, *'cause damn...* "I forget sometimes just how big you are."

He leaned down and kissed her cheek. "I thought I showed you that last night."

She wrapped her fingers around his neck and tugged him closer. "That you did, but how about you show me again?"

He smirked.

Instead of kissing her hard and fast like she wanted, he settled against her lips with a soft, achingly sweet kiss that melted her bones.

He pulled away, but kept her lower body pressed against his. "I'm proud of you, R.W. Hardcastle, but just remember this..." he pointed at his chest. "*I'm* your number one fan."

"Is that so?"

"It is."

"Well, number one fan." She traced a finger down his chest, locked it through his belt loop, and then nudged him with her hips. "How would you like me to autograph your big, thick—"

"Enough already." Clayton interrupted. "Are you two aware this is a public place? Aren't you past this sex-for-hours stage, yet?"

"No." Rachel glanced over her shoulder at her new partner. "As a matter of fact, I think Bronco needs to take me to the locker rooms and help me relax...work out some kinks...give me a pre-game rub—"

"Zip it, Harris." Clayton heaved a sigh with his eyes closed—a familiar expression when dealing with her. "I get the picture."

She bit back a chuckle.

"Will you please unwrap yourself from Bronco and get ready to go up on stage? I've got to check with the security guys out front because *that actress* decided to show up today."

While Rachel liked to believe most people were here for her, she had to admit the rumors Sheridan Bennett might be in attendance was likely the reason so many fans packed the house.

Sheridan was playing the lead role of April Archer, which suited her blonde bombshell body and bad-ass persona all the way. Though, when Rachel had met the actress earlier, she'd seemed really nice. Kind of quiet and reserved. Unbeknownst to her, Sheridan lived in a small suburb only an hour away. Odd, but cool.

Clayton hadn't been pleased when he'd learned last minute that the actress would be attending. She had her own bodyguard, but Clayton still grumbled over the news. He'd arrived too late to meet her, as he'd been dealing with the traffic situation outside.

They were full partners now that Clayton had left the force behind. And Rachel had to admit, she enjoyed having a partner, plus Bronco was less worried knowing his pal would keep an eye on her if, and when, she took a case. After unwrapping from Bronco, she nudged Clayton's elbow. "I saw that Hollywood beauty checking you out earlier."

"Doubtful." He shrugged.

"She's seriously hot." Rachel glanced around Clayton, hoping to catch another glimpse of the blonde. "I'd so do her."

"Now, that's something I'd pay to see." Bronco touted while waggling his brows.

Rachel elbowed his side. "Perv."

Maude glanced at Clayton. "If you and Sheridan Bennett had babies, they'd be like"—she waved her hands all over—"these tiny little angels. Beautiful people shouldn't have children together. You two procreating creates children too gorgeous for the rest of us."

Stilling, Clayton shot her a glance then simply walked away, shaking his head.

"Maude, quit matchmaking." Rachel shook out her hands. "I need a pep talk or something." She glanced back and noticed Maude now gazing at her phone. "Get off your phone. I having a diva moment."

"Who are you texting?" Bronco glanced at the screen.

"Brady." Smiling, Maude bit her bottom lip. "He's my date for Ember and Owen's wedding."

"Don't remind me." Rachel snorted. "I'm giving the maid-of-honor speech. Then, I'll probably be forced to do the same with Bronco's pop and Ms. Stone." She winked at Bronco, because she knew he was thrilled his father and nanny had finally found love.

"I know, aren't they just the cutest couple?" Maude grinned, dropping her phone in her pocket.

"You are such a sap." Rachel clasped her friend's shoulder

and took two deep breaths. In and out. In and out. "Oh, man. Why am I doing this again?"

Maude shot her a look topped with a raised brow.

Bronco wrapped them both in his arms before dropping a kiss on Rachel's temple. "You'll do great, babe."

"I'm worried about what I'll say." Rachel laughed. "I'll try very hard not to cuss."

Maude and Bronco looked at her, then at each other, and then burst into laughter.

"What?" Rachel glared and squared her shoulders. "I can go one day without cussing."

Maude held up her hand. "Pffftttt, I don't believe it."

"Time to go." Bronco clutched her elbow and pulled her closer to the stage.

Rachel took one step before turning back with a tiny squeal and leaping into his arms. "Thanks for being here today... for supporting me...for being my family." She pressed a hard kiss to his lips. "I love you."

Bronco braced his hands in her hair. "And I love you. Whether you're R.W. Hardcastle or Rachel Harris, I'll stand by your side, always. You've got this, because I've got you. Right?"

"Right." She bit her lip and then punched his arm. "Way to make me cry and ruin my mascara before I have to stand in front of a zillion people, Murray."

"No more tears." He swiped a thumb under her eye.

"Nope, 'cause I'm not alone, anymore. I've got my guard."

"You do."

"Okay." She nodded. "I'm ready." Heart full, Rachel stepped out on the platform and waved both hands over her head as her fans erupted from their seats. Her thoughts strayed to her number one fan standing along the sidelines.

Together, they'd survive any battle.

Together was the perfect place to be.

She smiled and stared at the multitude of fans and knew

exactly who she was. That being said, she grabbed the microphone. "Good afternoon, my pretties. Are you ready to start this fucking party?"

Thank you for reading *Rachel's Guard*. I hope you enjoyed Rachel and Bronco's story. If you did, please leave a review at your purchase site. Reviews are appreciated by the author.

My inspiration for Turning Pages came from Thistle Farms.
Their mission: Thistle Farms is a sanctuary for healing for women survivors of abuse, addiction, trafficking and prostitution. We are a community of survivors, advocates, employees, interns, volunteers, and friends from all across the world. We are young and old, women and men. We want to change a culture that still allows human beings to be bought and sold. We believe that in the end, love is the strongest force for change in the world.
For more information, please visit: www.thistlefarms.org

Coming Soon from Jillian Jacobs

Book #3 in The O-Line Series, *Clayton's Star* available First Quarter 2016.

Book #4 in The O-Line Series, *Maude's Score* available 2016

Erik's story and maybe even Spencer's, too.

Book #3 in The Elementals Series, *Air's Vision* available First Quarter 2016.

Available Now

Book #1 in The O-Line Series, *Ember's Center*

Book #1 in The Elementals Series, *Water's Threshold.*

Book #2 in The Elementals Series, *Fire's Field.*

Please enjoy the following excerpt from *Water's Threshold*, Book #1 in The Elementals Series.

Since arriving in Wyoming only a few months ago, Maya had experienced a strange energy pattern that interrupted her sense of peace. A consciousness never felt before, as if something attempted to anchor her in place—a pull unlike anything she had experienced since starting this new life nearly one hundred and fifteen years ago.

This internal strife was because of him—Terran Forrester. Mother had warned this would come. He was part of her purpose in being in this place at this time. Her orders were to guide him, because their destinies were entwined. Having Mother Nature set her up on a "fate date" left her feeling like a contestant on a game show. During her human life, Maya strove to control her own destiny, never handing over power. As an Elemental, she remained determined to give her all to their cause, but it chafed when Mother asked for more—to open her heart. Why now? Why was this burden of love thrust upon her with a mate she had not chosen?

Mate. What a ridiculous word.

Maya blew out a breath, causing a bevy of bubbles to dance their way to the surface. She couldn't have children so Mother using that specific word made the whole idea more ludicrous. Yet, Mother's wishes had come to fruition and that fact rankled. When spying on Terran, Maya experienced emotions surfacing she'd thought buried in a deep well long ago.

Her duties included watching him as he went about his daily human life. She enjoyed observing his frequent visits to the banks of the Snake River where he filled little glass vials. A soft hum raced through her body each time she spied him doing ordinary things, like working up a sweat at the gym or grabbing a cup of coffee at the local café. Since her last sexual adventure occurred in the free-love laced 70's, she was more than overdue for male attention. Terran would, no doubt, approach sex with the same care he did his experiments—meticulously and thoroughly.

That trickle of lust thrummed especially strong tonight at the gas station, when he'd touched her shoulder, all concerned citizen, seeking to offer assistance to an unfamiliar woman. Her waterlogged heart had pumped like a steam engine traveling uphill.

About the Author

In the spring of 2013, Jillian Jacobs changed her career path and became a romance writer. After reading for years, she figured writing a romance would be quick and easy. Nope! With the guidance of the Indiana Romance Writers of America chapter, she's learned there are many "rules" to writing a proper romance. Being re-schooled has been an interesting journey, and she hopes the best trails are yet to be traveled.

Water's Threshold, the first in Jillian's Elementals series, was a finalist in Chicago-North's 2014 Fire and Ice contest in the Women's Fiction category.

Jillian is a: Tea Guzzler, Polish Pottery Hoarder, and lover of all things Moose.

The genres she writes under are: Paranormal and Contemporary romance with suspenseful elements.

Connect with Jillian Jacobs online

Website: www.jillianjacobs.com

Twitter: https://twitter.com/GreenMooseProd

Facebook: https://www.facebook.com/pages/Jillian-Jacobs/737689872920933

Goodreads: https://www.goodreads.com/JillianJacobs

tsu: http://www.tsu.co/JillianJacobsAuthor

www.ingramcontent.com/pod-product-compliance
Lightning Source LLC
Chambersburg PA
CBHW071449170626
46811CB00007B/2514